I0774493

THE SIDEKICK

The Vinton Chronicles Book One

NIHARTA RIVER

THE VINTON CHRONICLES

THE SIDEKICK

The Vinton Chronicles Book One

JEFF MEDHURST

WICKED INK

PUBLISHING

Published by Wicked Ink Publishing Ltd.
www.wickedinkpublishing.com

Cover and book design © 2025 by Wicked Ink Publishing Ltd.
Editors: Raymond Griffiths & Adam Bamford

Illustration of Vinton © 2025 by Devon McKellar

First Edition: November 2025
Printed in Canada

Library and Archives Canada Cataloguing in Publication

Title: The sidekick / Jeff Medhurst.
Names: Medhurst, Jeff, author.
Description: Series statement: The Vinton chronicles ; book one
Identifiers: Canadiana (print) 20250259788
Canadiana (ebook) 2025026501X
ISBN 9781998278299 (softcover)
ISBN 9781998278305 (EPUB)
Subjects: LCGFT: Superhero fiction. | LCGFT: Novels.
Classification: LCC PS8626.E345 S53 2025 | DDC jC813/.6—dc23

For Tiana

For being my number one fan, my social media manager, my partner in life, and being the best mother for our children. Thank you for going on this journey with me.

THE
SIDEKICK

The Vinton Chronicles Book One

In a city that's lost its way, one sidekick must rise to
save it.

PROLOGUE

NOVEMBER 12, 1940

THE THUNDEROUS CRASH OF SONIC BOOMS ECHOED through the cities of Augusta, Boston, and Trenton. If the second jet didn't arrive in pursuit before Trenton, the first would have reached its destination in Washington. The populace didn't even see what was happening. Many fell to their knees and clutched their ears in pain at the awful sound.

It was a miracle the second pilot could even fly the jet. It was a new experimental design he had never encountered before. The British pilot flew jets throughout the war, engaging in aerial battles over Britain during Germany's siege of the city. However, he only flew a Hawker Hurricane R4118 before, and now he faced flying a jet capable of supersonic speeds.

So much of what was happening wasn't possible, or shouldn't have been possible. If they hadn't made the discovery, if they hadn't found the energy source, the war would have continued as expected. Instead, the pilot was here, defying the laws of physics he knew to be true to save the world.

His teeth rattled, and the skin on his face felt like it was going to tear off, but he needed to keep going. The pilot in the other jet was going to drop a bomb of unimaginable destructive capability. The British pilot needed to chase him out of the cities and away from the civilian populace.

Luckily, the German pilot in the other plane seemed as inexperienced as he was. When the German pilot turned, it was sudden and unpredictable, but the wings would sway with the body of the plane as the pilot tried to wrestle for control of the plane.

The German pilot also wanted to live as much as the British pilot did, performing evasive maneuvers, ensuring he avoided being lined up into a kill shot. The German pilot seemed intent on avoiding his pursuer before dropping the bomb, giving the British pilot the avenue he needed.

Before the British pilot could even think, the two were over the state of Kansas. The two were racing over farmland. They were well over 10,000 feet in the air, and it appeared like a quilt blanket below them. To the British pilot's best knowledge, there were no big populated centers around. They were far enough away from the east coast he could risk it. It was then or never.

The British pilot took a moment to recognize himself with the weapons controls while flying over the ocean. There was no way of knowing the outcome before his attempt, yet delaying further proved impossible. With the German pilot in his sights, the British pilot pulled the trigger on what he hoped was a weapon.

A machine gun erupted from the front of the plane, and a line of explosive rounds cut one of the German plane's wings off like it was paper. The German plane fell from the sky in a tailspin, and the British pilot flew past.

Checking over his shoulder, he watched the plane plummet from the sky. The British pilot breathed a sigh of relief and gazed forward, knowing the bomb would never reach its destination.

He slowed down his plane and circled to investigate, waiting to see the German hit the ground. His stomach lurched as he slowed, and it felt like the sheer act of slowing the plane gave him a concussion. He blinked into focus. He needed to know what happened to the bomb. The pilot would deal with everything else after.

A drifting parachute was visible, moving away from the plane the German pilot ejected from. The British pilot took small comfort in this, not desiring to see more lives lost. He could finally return home after everything he had been through.

Just then, there was a flash of light as the German plane plummeted and the British pilot leaned forward. Bright beams of light erupted in all directions from the plane, blinding the British pilot. He had only a second to realize his gunfire ignited the bomb.

The bomb exploded, and the sound was louder than the hum of the jet. The pilot violently rattled around in the jet as it shook from the blast, and he fought to regain control of the plane as it felt like his bones were going to pop out of his flesh.

Letting instinct guide him, the British pilot lurched forward on the throttle and tried to get out of the blast radius. However, the bomb was more powerful than the pilot imagined, and as a flash of light engulfed the plane, all its systems shut down.

The jet's engines sputtered and cracked, and the roar of the torrent deafened the pilot. He ripped his mask off his face so he could breathe, but no air entered his lungs.

The pilot felt himself being consumed by the explosion, but instead of searing heat, it was a sensation he never felt before. In the chaos and confusion of the maelstrom, he pulled the switch and ejected himself from the plane, not wanting to die in a crash.

Instead of falling, he felt like he was being carried. Like a powerful wind, it picked him up and blew him backward. Weightless, the man sensed his stomach in his throat. Then there was a strange, terrible tingling in his fingers. Next came his toes. Following that, his eyes.

The tingling spread to all parts of his body, and then it became an increasingly violent and aggressive feeling. Like nails were digging into the pores of his skin and shaking him apart. He felt himself being physically ripped to shreds.

Just when it was feeling like too much, the sensation would stop and it was like a cloth would wrap around him, stitching him back together in a warm embrace. He would be stronger, more powerful than before. Then the tearing sensation returned, digging deeper and more precisely, until again and again he was reformed.

The pilot hardly fathomed the events as they happened and blacked out in terror, in confusion, in agony. The last thing he saw before losing consciousness was a winged human reaching out to him before being torn away by the wind.

ISSUE 1

JET COMING IN FOR A LANDING

CHAPTER 1

A NEW GENERATION

A LIGHT BUZZED IN AND OUT OF EXISTENCE, illuminating the wall covered in newspaper clippings. Different articles practically wallpapered the grey metal wall. All were stuck to the wall with Scotch tape, some crudely overlapping others in ways that would be upsetting when it was time to take them down.

Many of the clippings were printouts of archival newspapers, while some were the original printings. Most were black and white, but a few could showcase the brightly coloured superheroes that dominated the wall.

Articles ranging from the 1940s to the present day provided a visual history of the rise and fall of the superhero and villain cultures across the world. While the majority focused on the events in North America, those being well-chronicled, there were a few crises happening internationally which would receive the front-page treatment.

While scattered and disjointed around the wall, a keen eye could follow key events in the world centered on the superheroes. From what the public considered the golden era of heroes shortly after World War II ended, to the ethical crisis regarding whether superheroes should take part in the Vietnam War. Then there was the rise of edgier superheroes in the fallout from the '80s to the '90s to lastly the resurgence of classic ideals and heroes in the early 2000s.

Dead in the center of the collection was one article that was specially framed. In a copy of the original newspaper printing from September 19, 1944, the headline read: *Rise of The Super Hero.*

The article documented Alpha's first press conference, considered the first superhero. Pictured was a black-and-white photo of the first superhero standing in front of a podium wearing his iconic long-sleeved white and red costume, though the color palette was grey in the old photo.

In the middle was an emblazoned A, and a large flowing cape billowed from Alpha's back. It was a prized possession among all the articles, standing out with its fine oak wood frame.

The grey steel wall displayed the dark brown frame in stark contrast. The bunker's steel walls, low roof, halls, and other rooms all shared the same design. It felt like living in a steel cage. Only a few normalities of home fixed that.

Around the rest of the small room, there was an uncomfortable-looking cot with an itchy pale tan bed sheet across from a small television set. There were DVDs in and out of their cases scattered all over the floor, and a few textbooks with a night light on a nightstand by the cot. By the door leaving the room, there was a small sink and mirror.

There was a sudden crashing noise echoing into the room, and the bedside table shuddered in response. It sounded like it came from somewhere else in this facility, like a colossal weight was thrown violently. Then the room was still, other than the buzzing of electricity whirring through the room. The generator powering the bunker was old and in need of maintenance.

However, neither of the two occupants had much in the way of electrical engineering expertise. Rather, the bunker vibrated in a sudden shock again. The hanging light flickered again and swung back and forth. Once the light calmed from its motion, there was a loud yell, and the entire room shook again, the hanging light flailing back into motion.

A third boom quickly followed the second, and then the sound of conflict continued consistently, and dust tampered down from the roof, coating the room like it did every day.

Teenager Jet Thompson slumped back against the steel wall of a large room, panting heavily. Sweat trickled down his brow, crystalizing in his brown fluffy hair. He wiped the sweat from his hazel eyes; his freckled face beat red with exhaustion. He was wearing a white tank top and sweatpants, with no socks or shoes on. In one hand he held a large greatsword practically as long as he was tall at 5'9".

Almost silver, the sword extended far out into a fine point at its tip and was just over one foot wide in width. Etched grooves provided a grip on the rounded handle, and a white gem adorned the pommel. The sword looked too large and obscene for a boy of his size to be wielding it, however, as he stood straight back up from the wall Jet twirled the sword by the handle with ease, nimbly spinning the sword in two rapid circles in the air beside him with one hand.

"Alright, that was a lucky hit," Jet said with a grin as he walked forward.

He was in a large room, meant to be a cafeteria that was transformed into a gym-like space. There were weights nestled in one corner, a running track, and cushioned mats on the ground, with a sparring circle painted on them.

It was poorly lit in the large room with only dim fluorescents illuminating them. There was a relatively constant creaking noise as the underground bunker continued to settle, and there was the smell of sweat seeping into the floors.

Standing in the middle of that circle was a tall man also wearing a tank top and track pants, his blonde hair dripping with sweat. Striking green eyes complemented his sharp, angular features. Like a Greek legend, he appeared almost unreal with his richly defined muscles across his arms, torso, and legs. A small, warm smile, radiating kindness, was on his face despite having just knocked Jet silly.

"You know as well as I do. Luck had nothing to do with it," the man replied.

Jet chuckled and pointed his sword at his mentor and responded, "Well, maybe, but this time I got you, Paladin."

Paladin was the man's code name, and Jet was never privy to his real one. Even though it was five years and Jet saw the man out of costume, he only ever knew Paladin the superhero and not the person.

While not wearing his costume, Paladin held his iconic sword in his left hand. Although smaller than Jet's, his sword measured about two and a half feet long and one foot wide, and featured gold trim. A blue line streaked down between the trim on both sides, and the sword gleamed in any light.

"Well, come on, Jet," Paladin said between pants. "We're one for one. One more to decide the victor."

Jet bit his lower lip and stood back up straight. His chest heaved from the kick he received from Paladin. He cracked his neck quickly as he glanced around the room. While at one time the large room was a cafeteria, Paladin converted the space into their gym.

Tables were pushed up against the walls, and in their place were exercise machines, weights, gymnastic equipment, and the floor mats Jet and Paladin trained on for combat. They painted a large white circle on the mats, signifying their combat ring. The light was dim from the old fluorescent bulbs in the low ceiling, every sound echoed, and there was the perpetual locker room smell of sweat hanging in the stagnant air. Regardless, it was Jet's favourite room to be in.

Spitting out a wad of blood from a punch he took, Jet said, "After this, can we skip the homeschooling stuff today? I think the beating is punishment enough."

Jet stepped forward back into the circle, twirling his sword in his hands and bringing it back into a position like he was holding a baseball bat, grasping the handle with both hands.

"No can do, Jet, we still have to go over basic algebra," Paladin responded.

Jet groaned and shook his head, but then he snapped into focus. Paladin swung his sword twice in the air and stood with his right leg slightly in front of his left with the tip of his sword pointed to the ground. While Paladin's swordplay was a mix of fencing, kendo, and Roman, Jet's fighting style was a bit more all over the place.

Jet coined his fighting style "stabby-punch" but Paladin wasn't on board with the name.

Jet grasped his sword, waiting for Paladin to make a move. If there was one thing he knew about his teacher, it was that Paladin preferred for his opponent to attack first. Paladin won every best two out of three sparring sessions the past week, and Jet wanted to try his best to take one victory.

Jet's impatience won out, and he swung down at Paladin, making Paladin sidestep backward. The teen quickly flicked his wrist to the side, sending his sword out in a small arc. Paladin's sword knocked Jet harmlessly aside, leaving Jet prone. The hero took a step in stabbing at Jet. Jet spun in the opposite direction, dodging the attack and swung up with his sword.

Paladin pivoted backward and slashed upwards. Jet reversed momentum and brought his arms down and pushed. The two swords clashed. A loud ring echoed throughout the room, bouncing off the exercise equipment. Jet forced

Paladin's sword downwards with all his weight, and Paladin grunted and heaved as he fought against Jet. Their feet slid on the rubber gym mat, squeaking.

Thinking quickly, Jet punched with his free hand. The hit connected with Paladin's cheek, and he stumbled. Jet thought he had the advantage and brought his sword up over his head and swung. Paladin blocked the attack with his sword, guiding Jet's sword down off to the side. With a jump in the air, Paladin kicked out at Jet, connecting him in the jaw.

Jet spun from the hit and shook his head in shock. Kicks to the jaw always tingled in a funny way, Jet thought to himself. He turned to receive the butt of Paladin's sword to the forehead.

A tingling jaw was better than seeing stars, Jet painfully realized. Jet continued to fumble backward, a hand on his forehead. To finish him, Paladin swept Jet's legs from underneath him.

He landed hard on his back. The foam of the gym mats only slightly cushioned the impact. Jet groaned and stared at the roof as his world desperately tried to reorient itself.

"Oww..." Jet muttered.

Paladin took a big breath of air, and his labored breathing seemed to return to normal almost instantly. It took Jet a moment and a couple of quick inhales, but then Jet felt like himself again.

The throbbing in his jaw already faded, and the blow to his forehead was a distant memory. Jet then leaped back up to his feet, standing straight up with his sword at his side. He put a hand first on his jaw and then on his forehead. Already sensing the bruises, Jet smiled despite himself. Some teenagers had chess, some had sports, some had video games. Jet had this. He loved a good fight.

"Giving up?" Paladin asked, tongue planted firmly in cheek.

"Come on, Paladin, if there's one thing you taught me, once you start something, never give up," Jet responded.

Paladin nodded in approval, and the two charged at each other again. In the moments before connecting with each other, Jet's mind flashed back to their training over the past week.

Every battle started with Jet striking the first blow and then ended with the back of his head connecting to the floor. Maybe if he tried something different, he would get a different result.

Jet moved his arm back as if he were getting ready to swing his sword, but he let go mid-swing, sending the sword hurtling forward in a fast, horizontal, spinning circle. Paladin's eyes went wide, and he deflected the incoming large projectile with his sword into the ground in front of him. Once he did, he glanced up to expect Jet's incoming attack, but Jet vanished.

Suddenly, Jet came in from up high and punched down on top of Paladin. The blow connected with the top of Paladin's head, and Paladin crumbled to one knee with a grunt of pain.

Once Jet landed, he balled his hands into one fist and slammed upwards into Paladin's chin. The attack reeled Paladin backward, and Jet spun, picking his sword back up. Adrenaline surged through Jet, carrying him into his next set of maneuvers.

Paladin recovered, shaking the daze from his eyes as Jet swung his sword in at him. Still on the defensive, Paladin blocked the attack, but the attack sent him reeling back towards the edge of the circle. Sensing victory, Jet stepped forward and thrust forward with the broadside of his sword. Jet hoped to bash Paladin out of the circle with his brute strength and end the fight quickly.

The two swords clashed with another loud clang, and Paladin held Jet at bay with a grimace. Jet grunted and pushed, trying desperately to win one. He poured all the strength he could muster into the effort. Sweat tinged Jet's brow, one drop running down his cheek. For a moment, it seemed like Paladin would slide out of the back of the circle.

Then Paladin smiled at Jet. Jet's eyes went wide. Paladin shifted his foot's position, changing the angle of his knee and rearranging his entire core into a power stance. Then, ducking low, Paladin shoved into Jet's sword and lifted using Jet's strength against him, picking Jet up off his feet. With a quick turn and spin, Paladin flipped Jet up and over on top of him, sending Jet through the air and out of the circle.

Caught by surprise, Jet wasn't able to land on his feet as he went through the air screaming and crashed into the ground. Jet landed on his back and rolled and tumbled, stopping as he collided with a rack of dumbbells. Both Jet and the dumbbells clattered to the ground, like a bowling ball scoring a strike on a set of pins.

Paladin took a moment to catch his breath and walked over to the crumpled mess that was Jet. Jet moaned and tried to stand, but he was so over the top of himself he couldn't figure out where any of his limbs were. Paladin grabbed him by the arm and helped Jet to lie on his back, who shook his head in confusion upon staring at the ceiling.

"Good try," Paladin commented. "That was smart. You anticipated my movements and tried to act accordingly. It's about time you thought that way."

Jet rubbed his eyes and didn't respond. He was so close. After all their training, Jet had almost forced Paladin out of the circle. With a sigh, Jet let his body give up, and he untensed and felt all the stress and pressure release. He then felt like a limp noodle after being boiled, lying on the ground in defeat.

"While there will always be opponents you'll need to get a measure of, eventually you'll be able to size an opponent and anticipate what they'll be able to do at a glance," Paladin continued as he walked away.

"Take a man with a gun, for example. You know they can fire at you with the gun, and that is what they'll likely do, but they can also try to bludgeon you with it or even throw it at you as a distraction. So, you need to anticipate not what the weapon will do, but what the man with the gun will do."

Paladin was toweling himself off now, wiping the sweat from his brow and then his arms.

"Erring on the side of caution is usually the smart move. A gun fired is far more dangerous than a gun thrown. But that can leave you open to an unexpected attack, like you did to me by throwing your sword. However, just because you can anticipate their next move doesn't mean you know their next move. Here, assuming you knew me inside and out, cost you the win. Never stop fighting an opponent, even if you think you've won. You assumed you had me, and that was all the edge I needed. It's a rookie mistake, and it's one you're bound to keep making."

It was common for Paladin to go on long speeches when teaching Jet. Sometimes, Jet would listen closely and soak in as much as he could.

Paladin showed his wisdom and experience many times to Jet, and Jet was eager to live up to his example and soak up as much information as he could. Other times, the blood pumping in Jet's ear after a good fight made Paladin sound like a dying trumpet to Jet.

Paladin stopped and glanced back at Jet, who had one hand over his eyes as he continued to pant heavily. Paladin glanced at the floor, seemingly about to say something, but caught himself.

"You're getting better," Paladin commented as he walked over to his towel. "I'm holding back less and less every time."

Jet forced himself to sit up, and he continued to pant.

Although he accepted the praise, Jet stared at his mentor in awe.

"How much are you still holding back?" Jet asked in disbelief.

"A lot," Paladin answered before wiping the sweat off his face with his towel.

"Man, can't you just lie a little and make me feel better about myself?" Jet questioned with a grin.

Paladin threw the towel off to the side and walked over to his student.

"I'm not letting you get a full head," Paladin replied. He extended a hand to Jet, and Jet took it and stood up.

"Confidence will get you killed out there," Paladin remarked as Jet walked over to the sword rack. "I think you can hold your own in a fight out there now, but you're not ready for the big leagues yet."

Jet placed his sword on the rack, the one place his sword could be if not in Jet's hands. It drove him crazy that he had to follow that rule, but Paladin never wanted Jet to get any ideas about taking it outside. Jet stared at it for a few moments, when suddenly what Paladin said registered.

"Wait, you think I'm ready for a fight out there?" Jet asked as he turned around with a hopeful smile.

Paladin visibly regretted his words, placing his sword on its rack and then raising two hands to calm Jet down.

"That's not what I meant," Paladin said.

"Well, what did you mean?"

"I only meant you're getting better. I just said you're not ready for the big leagues. The moment you take a step out those doors, you're in them," Paladin said.

"Well, what do you mean, big leagues?" Jet asked.

Jet was well-versed in the superhero politics of the world. He knew the prominent superheroes and supervillains not only in Vinton but also all over the world. The idea that he wasn't ready for something he was training for, that he knew inside and out, felt condescending.

"I just mean…" Paladin said, but then he caught himself. "I need you to trust me."

Paladin's eyes wouldn't meet Jet's. The two refused to look at each other for several moments.

A bit of rage stemmed to the surface, and Jet sighed angrily. He bit back his words. However, the argument his next statement would cause was repeated far too many times. Paladin watched Jet closely, and a tense silence passed between them.

"Jet, it will be soon," Paladin replied. "I promise. I will tell you when it's time."

Paladin's tone of finality hit Jet in the chest harder than any kick. Five years was a long time to be cooped up in the bunker.

Jet grabbed his towel silently and walked away. Paladin glanced at the floor and let out a little sigh, relieved to have avoided another blowout argument, but his chest was still heavy with anxiety.

"Hey," Paladin called.

Jet turned back, hopeful Paladin received a sudden, miraculous change of heart. Instead, Jet propped his hands up in time to catch a textbook aimed at his face. With a cocked eyebrow, Jet lowered the book that almost took his head off and groaned upon seeing it was his math textbook.

"Didn't think you were getting off that easy, did you?" Paladin asked with a small laugh.

Jet rolled his eyes, tossed his towel over his shoulder, and walked over to their study area. However, once he turned his back to Paladin, he smirked.

He was getting better. Paladin said so. Jet knew only two things for the last five years. He knew the walls of these bunkers, and that he was training to be a superhero. After idolizing them his entire childhood, he spent the first half of his teenage years working to become one. It made Jet more and more excited as he was getting closer.

After five long painful years in this bunker, Jet felt in his gut it would be time to leave soon. It wasn't all bad, Jet knew. He enjoyed his training and lessons with Paladin; he enjoyed the downtime the two of them would spend together playing board games or watching a movie together. Although the food always tasted weird after being cooked in the bunker's oven, and the lack of natural light gave Jet sleep problems in the first two years.

Not to mention the lack of social contact with others, gave Jet a bit of an unhealthy relationship with fictional characters in his nightly movies. However, Jet could put all of that behind him. If it all meant he could be a superhero, it would all be worth it.

Despite the darkness of the bunker, Jet's light always shone brightly. He always believed in seeing the best in things, and every step closer to becoming a superhero was a step closer to leaving the bunker, and the rest of his life would begin.

He held tight and true to the idea, refusing to let the negativity and hopelessness in. It's what his all-time favourite superhero, Alpha, the first superhero, would do. As always, he strove to be just like him.

But first, math homework.

CHAPTER 2

LESSONS IN SUPERHEROING

IN A SMALL, SECLUDED AREA OF THEIR GYM, PALADIN arranged a cafeteria table that, at one point, was an organized study area for Jet to be homeschooled in. There were a few lights hanging over the tables, making the section of the gym well lit compared to the rest.

After the first month of being in the bunker, the table had devolved into a mess of books, papers and writing utensils that would make any self-respecting teacher die of disgust. If you were to ask either of them, Jet and Paladin always found whatever they needed in the chaos that was Jet's study desk.

Jet was busy answering questions from his textbook, trying to simplify radical equations, as Paladin sat across from him. Paladin's primary job during these sessions was to help Jet when he got stuck or to keep him on task. However, it was late in the day, and Paladin was surfing his phone, doing something related to his superhero work, and Jet was finding it hard to stay motivated.

Stumped on one question, Jet tapped the end of his pencil against the table, debating his next step. His eyes went up to Paladin, and Jet could tell his mentor was less invested in Math than even he was. Paladin had a tendency not to let Jet off until he felt Jet learned something. So Jet developed a means of exploring his interests, while getting Paladin to feel accomplished in his own way.

"What happened to Super Hero City again? All these variables are making me think of the variables that led to that city's downfall," Jet asked, his voice speeding up as he became less convinced in his own lie.

Paladin smirked and let out a reluctant laugh, seeing right through Jet. Regardless, he put his phone down and folded his arms, looking at Jet. His mentor took the bait, and Jet put his pencil down, ready for whatever superhero wisdom Paladin would impart.

"Metrohaven, or Super Hero City as it is colloquially called, was founded when and where?" Paladin asked.

Jet didn't expect the question to be reversed back on him, but superheroes were his main fascination, so he could quickly dig it out of his mind.

"It was during the Vietnam War, but I don't remember any specific dates. And it was founded...somewhere off the coast of Costa Rica? On like a tiny island of some kind?" Jet responded with a slight uptick in his pitch, turning his answer into a question.

"Correct," Paladin responded. "Why was it founded?"

"Uhhhh...there were many different super people who had powers from lots of different stuff, and they wanted to avoid enlistment in the war when the USA made superheroes into soldiers. So they ended up creating a secret city that no one knew about for refugees. But like...super refugees," Jet responded.

"Very good. Sounds like you know your history, so what's your question?" Paladin asked.

Jet's eyes darted around, hoping Paladin would have freely volunteered information. His mind scrambled for a question when it suddenly came to him. Something he always wondered.

"Who was the bad guy?" Jet asked.

Paladin's eyebrows furrowed.

"What do you mean?"

"Well...I know Super Hero City fell apart because somebody revealed the city to the world, and then there was a whole like...immigrant vs refugee crisis thing..." Jet rambled.

"Immigrant vs refugee crisis thing? I'm glad the importance of the lesson stuck," Paladin jabbed with a small smile.

Jet brushed it off with a wave of his hand and kept going. "No one ever talks about who the bad guy was. Was it the USA for the superhero enlistment? The people who founded the city? Or the guy who revealed them?"

Paladin tapped his finger on the table for a few moments, considering his response.

"Well, let me ask you this: what resulted from the infamous immigrant vs refugee crisis thing?"

Jet's shoulders dropped as he frowned. Seeing his poor choice of words wouldn't get lost anytime soon. He thought back to the answer for a few moments before replying.

"That was the Super Hero Protection Act of 1992?"

"Right. And that did what?"

"Well, in all United Nations countries, it meant that anyone with superpowers or people who were superheroes were not required to register with government officials unless they caused property damage or bodily harm to bystanders," Jet responded. "Essentially, it gave people like us the right to be superheroes and not have supervillains google our secret identities."

Paladin smiled and looked down at the table, visibly happy the lesson at least sunk in.

"So a pretty good result then, right?" Paladin asked, to

which Jet nodded. "So then, why does there need to be a bad guy in this story?"

It was Jet's turn to knit his eyebrows together.

"Well, it was a big turning point, right? Weren't there some enormous battles in Super Hero City before the city got revealed? Who was the bad guy in those?" Jet asked.

Paladin leaned forward, resting his elbows on the table.

"So there was a conflict," Paladin clarified. "Does every conflict need a villain? Does every story need a bad guy?"

Jet rested back on his stool, chewing his inner lip. He wasn't a child, and didn't like that the Paladin was talking to him like one.

"No-but even then, who takes the blame? Things like this don't happen for no reason. Someone is at fault, right?" Jet questioned. "Maybe bad guys are a simple way to put it, but it feels accurate."

For a moment, Paladin seemed to have a very sad smile on his face. Jet couldn't understand Paladin's smile. Was Paladin disappointed in Jet's response, or in his own thoughts? Or if he was simply just sad about something.

"Well, Jet...maybe once you have the answer to the question, you might be a little more ready to go to the surface," Paladin quietly responded. "Then you'd be ready to face Vinton."

The statement lingered in the air for several moments, It felt like an arrow to Jet's heart. All his anticipation and excitement about returning to the surface one day was squashed in a heartbeat. What did it even mean? Why would Paladin be so cryptic about it?

"What...what do you mean?" Jet asked.

Paladin's mouth opened and closed several times, an answer seemingly on his tongue. Then he closed it and shut his eyes, shaking his head slightly as he did. Before Jet asked, Paladin glanced at the clock in the gym and his eyes widened.

"Shoot, the mentoring was longer than I thought it would be," Paladin remarked. "It looks like you'll get a pass on any more algebra tonight." Jet turned and looked at the clock, seeing it was already a quarter to 6 p.m.

"Patrol?" Jet asked.

Paladin nodded and gathered his things.

"We have leftovers from last night you can reheat. Stay in and review those notes on The Old Man and the Sea. I'll have questions for you tomorrow. Then you can relax," Paladin ordered as he picked his sword back up and walked in the opposite direction of Jet.

"I'll be back late. Go to bed at a reasonable hour or you'll regret it in the morning," Paladin said as he walked towards the door.

His annoyance temporarily diverted the sadness Jet felt at having to do more homework, but as always, it lingered in the back of his mind.

Jet sighed, and once Paladin was out of earshot he muttered, "Don't worry, I'll be here."

CHAPTER 3

MY LIFE AS A TEENAGE BUNKER DWELLER

Jet trudged down the grey halls of the bunker toward his room after having a shower in the washrooms. The washrooms somehow were even darker than the normal rooms, and the grey cold walls created dark shadows that were accompanied by a fairly consistent mildew smell.

Jet always felt uneasy showering there. The large washroom with multiple showers meant for multiple people was always empty except for him. It was much like the rest of the bunker, large and hollow, with no life spiriting it.

His discussion about good guys and bad guys from earlier rattled him a little. What did Paladin mean by, be ready for Vinton?

As far as Jet knew, Vinton was normal as cities come. Well, except for the pool of Chaos Energy in the reservoir, making Vinton a bit of a hotbed for super activity. There were several superheroes in Vinton, to Jet's knowledge, and supervillains would float in and out of the city from time to time.

However, Vinton was relatively safe, Jet thought. It was home. Even if there was something Paladin wasn't telling Jet,

Jet felt like Vinton would always be Vinton. It would always be the city he remembered it as.

Finally, Jet shrugged. Well, if Vinton wasn't how he remembered it, then he would make it that way. That was the point of being a superhero, Jet thought. To make the world a better and safer place. For the good guys.

He just needed to get out of this bunker first.

His wet slippers slapped against the ground. Jet was on autopilot. He did the same walk how many times? He could do the math, but he was worried it would only depress him more.

"Jet," he heard Paladin call as he walked towards him.

Paladin wasn't yet in his superhero outfit, but was wearing the slim black spandex he would normally wear underneath it.

"Before I forget," Paladin said.

He was holding his phone and brought it up to show Jet a video of a baseball pitcher.

"Your move in that last spar, throwing your sword at me? Really smart move to catch me off guard and leave me vulnerable. I want to give you an idea of how to improve it," Paladin explained.

Jet smiled to himself. Even though they just argued, Jet couldn't help but be grateful for Paladin. Paladin knew how much getting better meant to Jet, and it was always at the back of his mind how to better help his trainee.

"Watch how this pitcher throws the ball," Paladin instructed. "Specifically, the point of release. If you throw your sword vertically instead of horizontally, it would be trickier to time, but the velocity would increase dramatically."

After Jet struggled to adapt to more traditional sword fighting techniques, Paladin adapted by showing Jet how different athletes would perform. These little tricks Jet learned dramatically informed his 'stabby-punch' style, and he was always eager to learn.

"Yeah, yeah, okay. Next time I'm looking to get a cheap shot in, I'll try it," Jet said.

Paladin chuckled at the comment, and then a wave of regret washed over his face.

"Jet…I mean it. It will be soon. I promise," Paladin said again.

Jet's smile faded slightly, but he forced it to return.

"I know. Good luck out there tonight," Jet replied.

Jet entered his room moments later. The walls and floor were the same gunmetal colour as the rest of the bunker, but with a bright light bulb making his room significantly brighter than the rest of the bunker.

With a sigh, Jet gazed at his wall plastered with newspaper clippings of famous superhero battles and adventures, and as always, his eyes found the framed clipping of The First Superhero, Alpha. The way Jet saw it, Alpha was the real reason he was in the bunker, so he could be a superhero like him. It brought Jet a moment of peace before the angst came back.

Why couldn't he be doing his training up on the surface?

Paladin told him it was because to train Jet, Paladin needed his attention one hundred percent of the time. Then there were nights like tonight when Paladin would abandon Jet in the bunker alone, and Jet wondered what in the world was keeping him in the bunker.

Jet shook off the thought. While he was moody as a teenager could be, he didn't enjoy dwelling on it. For a moment, he considered reading over some textbooks to be ahead of Paladin's tutoring, allowing more time for combat training, but then Jet lifted his spirits with a movie.

Movies were one of the few luxuries Jet was allowed in the bunker, and he had a vast collection. Every Christmas and birthday he would get five to ten more, and while it wasn't enough to last a year, Jet liked to re-watch movies all the time.

Despite all the littered DVD cases all over the floor, Jet went to a small shelf he had in his room filled with ones that were being kept in better condition. Digging into his assorted collection, Jet searched for one he hadn't watched yet. He saw most of the action and adventure one's enough times to quote them from memory, and he watched the comedies enough times to ruin some movies, but the romance and drama section went widely ignored.

Sitting in the back corner of his collection, Jet noted one in particular that was covered in dust. Reaching in and blowing the dust off, Jet immediately recoiled upon seeing it was a romantic comedy.

"Ugh," Jet sighed.

By the looks of it, this movie was in his collection since the beginning and had yet to be watched. With a sigh, Jet stood up and turned on his television to watch what would be a snore-fest.

"Maybe I can still study some more algebra. It'll probably be better than this," Jet joked to himself, making him laugh.

As Jet opened the case, a small photo fell out unexpectedly, landing by Jet's feet. Jet stared down at it in surprise, and after putting the disc in, he reached down and picked up the photo. Walking over to his bed with it, he looked at it more closely. The photo was a little faded because of improper storage, but Jet could still make out the details.

In the photo was a picture of Jet when he was a kid. Peering at it for a long time, he tried to recall the memory. It was his fifth birthday, he realized, looking at the large chocolate frosted cake and counting the candles. He had a big goofy grin on his face, and his eyes gleamed with anticipation at the cake.

Jet chuckled and then glanced at the man next to him in the picture. Dominating most of the frame was a large man with silver curly hair and a big belly. He liked to wear tacky

Hawaiian shirts and didn't shave particularly well, but his smile was as big as Jets. It was a man Jet barely saw these past five years.

"Wow, Uncle Quinn," Jet commented.

He looked at the picture fondly for several minutes as his mind drifted back to before his time in the bunker.

A young preteen Jet awakened as the van braked to a halt, making Jet stir to life with a jolt. He rubbed his eyes and glanced at his uncle as Quinn placed his white van in park.

As Quinn switched off the van, the engine died, leaving them in darkness and silence as the van's lights dimmed. Looking out the window, Jet saw an old decrepit building dimly lit by the glow of a streetlight. There was the scent of burning rubber in the air, which stung Jet's nostrils.

It was around four o'clock in the morning, and Jet hadn't slept well after the rush of packing all his possessions the night before. He knew why he was leaving, but something seemed off about where he was.

"Where are we?" Jet asked as he looked back at his uncle.

Quinn didn't answer right away. Instead, he reached into the glove compartment and pulled out a slip of paper. Jet watched with confusion as Quinn read notes scribbled on the paper and then checked outside the window of the van. He took a long, deep breath of air and then turned to his nephew.

"Alright. We're in the Rat's Nest now, so..." Quinn said, but sirens went off in Jet's brain as those words were said.

"The Rat's Nest?!" Jet whispered, almost afraid to say the words. "Where that big massacre was..."

"Jet," Quinn said firmly, making Jet's sentence stop. "I need you to focus. Can you do that?"

Jet turned to look back out the window, and though panic

set in at the prospect of being in the Rat's Nest, he did his best to gather himself. He nodded slowly, and Quinn took another breath before continuing.

"Now we're going to have to hurry. We're going to get the bags from the trunk, and I need you to stay close behind me. I want you to grab onto my shirt and not let go," Quinn explained. "We're not far from where we need to go, but we still need to be safe."

While Quinn was such a happy-go-lucky guy, for the past few weeks he seemed on edge. This night was the worst yet. Jet peered at his uncle with apprehension, the knowledge of the awful things that happen in the Rat's Nest at the forefront of his mind.

However, Jet thought back to the framed article of The First Superhero his uncle got him as a Christmas present earlier that year. Alpha wouldn't have been scared, he thought to himself. Keeping in mind what his idol would do, Jet steeled himself and nodded again.

"Alright, let's do this," Jet said.

Quinn gave his nephew one last concerned look, but then the two both left the van and hurried to the trunk. As Quinn pulled large suitcases out of the trunk, Jet noticed a long, slender black plastic case sitting in the trunk. It was hard plastic with clips that kept it shut, and Jet couldn't tear his eyes off it.

There was a mysterious longing Jet had never experienced before in the few moments he stared at the case. Like some part of himself he never knew was inside it, something he needed to feel complete.

Quinn grabbed one of Jet's bags, and upon seeing the mysterious package was now free to grab, Jet instinctively reached for it. It was in Jet's hands before he realized it, and Jet took a moment to hold it.

For such a big case, it felt incredibly light in his hands.

There was still a clawing sensation in Jet's stomach to open the case and peer inside, to get whatever mysterious treasure he knew awaited him. He knew deep down he needed whatever was inside it.

The moment passed as Quinn slammed the trunk unexpectedly, snapping Jet out of his trance. Jet shook his head and cleared his head. He looked up at his uncle, who was holding Jet's other bags, and gave Jet an even more puzzled glance than before. Quinn's eyes went from Jet to the case back to Jet, trying to solve some mystery Jet didn't know about.

Quinn then shrugged his shoulders, muttering to himself there wasn't time. Closing the trunk, Quinn took off into an alleyway beside the decrepit building, with Jet holding onto his uncle's shirt. They dashed, and Jet found his little legs struggling to keep up with his uncle at a walking pace, having to take a couple of running steps. Jet didn't peel his eyes off the back of Quinn's shirt, but he could tell how poorly lit the streets were. He could smell the garbage roaming the streets like an infestation. Jet couldn't shake the feeling that he was being constantly watched from every dark corner.

Jet didn't have any other time to look at the alleyways as Quinn quickly maneuvered between them. He needed to trust his uncle was leading him in the right direction as they dipped in behind the buildings and Quinn led them down a back alley.

A light caught Jet's attention, and he glanced from his uncle's shirt up to the right to see a dangling light from outside a back entrance to a building. It was swinging back and forth in the small breeze in the air, making a quiet creaking noise.

Jet was more tired than he cared to admit, and the swaying light caught his attention. The breeze whistled in the air, and the burning rubber smell was more prevalent, which Jet realized was probably homeless people burning tires for warmth. It made Jet shiver in the cold of the fall.

Suddenly, Jet crashed right into his uncle's back, bumping his nose into Quinn's spine. Quinn stopped abruptly, and the impact snapped Jet back into what was happening around him. Figuring they must have reached their destination, Jet poked his head from behind Quinn's back to see they hadn't.

Standing in front of Quinn were two men with long shaggy hair and beards, in old torn-up clothing. A look at their hands showed they each had a switchblade. Jet more nervously tugged on Quinn's shirt, wanting to back away from the situation. However, he heard a chuckling noise behind him and standing there was another man with unkempt hair and tattered attire.

Jet swung his head around and saw they were trapped between two buildings, with no escape from the approaching threat. He looked up at his uncle, the big man who always took care of him and was his foundation, and saw fear clearly plastered on his face.

"Well, what have we here?" One man asked, his voice hoarse.

"Lotta bags for two guys," the other said.

"Anything valuable you wouldn't mind parting with to help the homeless?"

Quinn continued not to say anything, only staring in terror at the two men in front of him.

"It's not like he has a choice," the first man said. "Drop the bags or we'll cut you and the boy."

"Nobody's going to hear you here," the third man behind Jet and Quinn said.

Then suddenly the man behind Jet screamed in pain, and Jet's head whirled around. When once he was imposing, the man now cowered on one knee, as a mysterious figure behind him held one of the man's arms up in the air at an awkward angle while the figure's foot rested on the man's opposite shoulder.

"Walk away now," the figure commanded, his voice deep and imposing. "Walk away and no harm shall befall you."

Jet peered past Quinn at the other two men, who were much more apprehensive. Quinn blew a long sigh of relief, and Jet stared curiously at his uncle, not sure what was happening.

"Last chance," the figure said, pulling a little on the man's arm, making him groan. His voice was stern and commanding, with a deep tone, but there was a certain lightness to it. "Do it now, or you will suffer the consequences."

With his eyes fully adjusted, Jet finally saw their hero. Clad in white and silver armour with gold trim, the man seemed to wear a form-fitting iron battle suit from the dark ages. It glistened even in the darkness, and its edges were smooth. He wore a glistening white helmet that completely covered his head, obscuring his face and making his voice sound metallic.

For a moment, Jet let himself think Alpha saved him. Barring the fact that Alpha passed away years ago and his costume looked nothing like what this man was wearing, he inspired similar feelings of heroics on Jet.

"Aw, screw this," one man said in front of Quinn.

The two men yelled and ran past Quinn and Jet. Quinn grabbed Jet and instinctively tucked him in close, and Jet felt the rush of air as the two muggers dashed at their target.

The man in armour tilted his head to the side for a moment to relieve pressure on his neck. In a blur of movement, he kicked forward into his hostage's back and pulled on the arm to the cue of a loud popping noise. He let go, and the screaming man with the now dislocated shoulder crashed face-first onto the ground.

One mugger reached the man and tried to stab him in the stomach, somehow oblivious to the armour the hero was wearing. His blade bounced harmlessly off the armour, and the man grabbed the mugger by the arm. Placing his other hand on the mugger's stomach, he easily heaved the mugger off his feet and threw the man like he weighed nothing over his shoulder.

The man went soaring and hit a garbage can with a loud crash. Jet didn't realize how wide his eyes were as he watched this hero easily dispatch the grown men. Somehow, the last mugger didn't get the message and swung down with his knife at the hero.

There was a sharp ting sound and a flash of steel as the man's knife went flying out of his hand. Jet blinked and missed it, but the now unarmed man shakily took a step back, away from the hero. In the hero's hand was a long, slender broadsword.

It gleamed with a gold trim that ran down the sharp edges, and in the middle was an intricate gold and blue pattern. The hero stared coldly at the last mugger for several moments, and then, with a flourish, he sheathed his sword onto his back. The mugger stared at the hero in confusion as the hero continued to glare at him.

"I will show you mercy. But you have to walk away now," the hero said, his voice still commanding, but there was a tinge of mercy in it as he gave the mugger one last chance. His cape flowed gently behind his back in the breeze, and Jet's eyes went wide in amazement. This was a hero.

The mugger breathed rapidly through his nose in indignation, his fists trembling. In a fit of rage and cowardice, the mugger turned and ran away.

Then the hero let out a breath and removed his helmet as he glanced at Quinn and Jet, and for the first time, Jet saw his gentle features. He had light blond hair that he seemed to comb over to an extent, letting a few strands rest across his forehead. The hero had bright blue eyes, and a small, but square chin jutted out just ever so slightly.

"Quinn. I was worried you weren't going to make it," the man said.

His voice softened considerably. It was still deep, but the light tone Jet heard earlier was now the man's prominent speaking voice. Quinn grumbled in response and let go of his nephew, letting Jet take a few steps forward.

"We almost didn't. It's a miracle you showed up," Quinn responded.

"Well, I had a funny feeling that trouble would find you somehow. I hate to say I was right," the man remarked.

He then took a quick glance over his shoulder and looked back forward. He strode past the two.

"Let's speak inside. We don't want prying ears," the hero said. Quinn nodded, but Jet still stared shell-shocked at their savior.

He had never seen a real-life superhero before. At the very least, that's what Jet thought was happening. It took him another moment to realize the said superhero saved him personally. Not just some person he would read about in the paper. A superhero saved him.

"Hey," Quinn said with a pat on Jet's back. "Let's go."

Jet started walking forward awkwardly, having a difficult time maintaining his excitement. He knew it wasn't the place, but it was shaking its way out of him. Like a boy having to hold it before going to the bathroom, Jet's knees buckled together, and he nervously took his steps.

The three traveled a short distance until finally the armour-clad man opened a door into the back of a building. A single light shone overhead, and the man gestured for Quinn and Jet to enter first. Jet continued to move like a puppy on anesthetics, but he eventually made his way in. The man took two glances in either direction and then he quickly shut the door.

Jet looked around the room they were in and saw it was dimly lit with faded green walls. A torn-up couch sat across from an old TV. A dark hallway led, presumably, to a bedroom and washroom. Occupying a corner was a small kitchen unit, with pictures, newspapers, and strings decorated the opposite wall from the television.

"Well, I guess it's time for a formal introduction," the man said, making Jet turn around to face him. Jet noticed by the door they just walked through there was a set of luggage, similar to his own.

The man took a knee and outstretched a hand to Jet, saying, "I am Paladin. I have been a superhero for several years now. I will be the one taking care of you."

Jet anxiously shook Paladin's hand, feeling the firmness of Paladin's grasp.

"Oh, you're Paladin?" Jet asked, finally having a mental image in his brain of who Quinn was talking about. "You're... cooler than I expected."

Paladin released Jet's hand and chuckled while glancing up at Quinn.

"Cool, eh?" Paladin reiterated as he stood up.

"I mean it's not that I never thought you weren't cool I just didn't know if you would be because I've never seen you in the paper before or anything so I didn't know if you were cool enough to be in it or I'm going to stop talking now," Jet rambled. Paladin raised an eyebrow in curiosity, and Quinn chuckled.

"I told you. He likes superheroes," Quinn said. Paladin crossed his arms and smiled at Jet, and Jet looked at the floor as his face flushed red, thoroughly embarrassed with himself.

"Well, Jet, it's a good thing you do. Because I'm going to train you to be one," Paladin stated.

There was a moment where Jet couldn't process what was just said to him. His head slowly tilted upwards to glance at Paladin. Then, he slowly peered over his shoulder at Quinn, who seemed unfazed by this news.

Excitement rushed through his veins. The blood rushed to his head. His world spun.

That was when Jet passed out.

CHAPTER 4

PATH TO A HERO

Jet awoke later, sitting on the ground with his back propped up against the wall. Quinn and Paladin were both standing over him. Their words were hazy, and he only caught a few of them in muffled tones, difficult to figure out who was speaking.

"...are you sure he's ready? He passed out after all. Maybe this is too much too soon..."

"You and I both know...if we wait too long, then it's only a matter of time..."

"I know...I know...I'm just...maybe I'm not ready..."

"Not ready for what?" Jet grumbled as he stood up.

Both adults halted their conversation and turned to help Jet to his feet. Paladin smiled at Jet and gave him an extra little boost up.

"For you to become a superhero, of course," Paladin said.

"I...what?" Jet asked, almost passing out a second time. Quinn gave Paladin a concerned look as Jet faltered, but Paladin grabbed Jet by both shoulders and happily helped him stand. Taking a few steps, he bent down on one knee to address Jet at eye level.

"You have an incredible power, Jet, even if you do not yet realize it," Paladin continued. "That is why you are coming with me, so I can teach you to harness the power and use it for good."

Jet knew he was stronger than most kids, faster, more athletic, with no practice. He had powers? Since when?

The bewilderment was clear on his face, and Paladin couldn't help but laugh. He nodded to Quinn and pointed at the large case in Jet's hands.

"Can we show him? Or are you worried his head will pop off?" Paladin asked.

There was a long, hesitant sigh from Quinn. He stared down at Jet and finally agreed.

"Yes, it's time," Quinn answered.

Paladin knelt again and grabbed the large case from Jet. Jet's euphoria prevented him from stopping Quinn, despite the compelling nature of the case.

Paladin struggled with the weight of the case, a stark contrast to how easily Jet lifted it. Turning the case towards Jet, Paladin unlocked the clips and opened the case, and Jet's state of mind came down from the moon.

Resting on foam in the large case was a large, wide greatsword. It was like Jet was having an out-of-body experience while gazing at the sword. He felt a longing before zeroing in on the sword. Without even thinking, he grabbed it from the case, and to him, it was still light. More so, it felt like an extension of his body. Something that truly belonged in his grip.

Jet never felt incomplete before, but he suddenly felt whole. The feeling of who he was, rushed to the surface. It spoke to something absolutely primal in Jet. An enormous smile beamed onto his face. This sword was part of who he was. Jet felt like with this sword, he could do anything he wanted.

"You have had that sword since you were a baby," Quinn said. "It just...showed up one day, outside your crib. Your parents tried to get rid of it, but it somehow kept finding its way back to you. I've had it in the house as long as you've been there."

"I've had this for that long?" Jet asked in disbelief, unable to fathom that this work of art was tied to him.

"We figure it's linked to wherever your powers come from," Paladin explained as he discarded the black case. "And since I'm a sword fighter already, we decided it would make the most sense to train you to be as well."

Jet stared back at the sword in disbelief. His superpowers explained why he was so much more athletic than all the other kids while still being a string bean, why he needed less sleep than them while having so much more energy. Why he could fall from their house's roof and feel completely fine. While some kids felt invincible, Jet sometimes questioned whether he was invincible.

"Where do my powers come from?" Jet asked, glancing at Paladin and Quinn in curiosity, his appetite for the sword somewhat sated now that he held it.

Quinn and Paladin exchanged quick looks, but Paladin acknowledged Jet with a sincere look.

"We don't know," Paladin answered. Then the hero sighed and sadly looked at Quinn.

"And that's why you have to come with me," Paladin continued as his eyes returned to Jet.

Jet knew he was leaving with someone to begin homeschooling, but he expected nothing about a mysterious sword or becoming a superhero. The news was hitting him suddenly, and he wasn't sure what to make of it.

"Why? I thought Uncle Quinn knew nothing else, so you were taking over," Jet said.

"I will continue your education. While we explore what

you're capable of, we can't take the chance your superpowers will hurt anyone else," Paladin reasoned. "So because of that, you and I are leaving for a safe place where I will train you."

Paladin put a hand on Jet's shoulder and said, "When the time is right, you will be my sidekick. Then, when you're older, you will be your own man. However, right now, I need you to trust me. Can you do that?"

Jet glanced up at Paladin's eyes and saw the honesty in them. This man exuded kindness and confidence, a sincere brand of truth that Jet hadn't experienced before. When Quinn told Jet that he needed to leave to be taught by someone else, he was nervous. Seeing Paladin could beat those men in the alley and the kindness he displayed, Jet took a leap of faith and nodded.

"Yeah...yeah, I think so," Jet answered.

"Good. Then we will leave..." Paladin's sentence trailed off, and he removed his hand from Jet's shoulder.

Jet realized that standing behind him, his Uncle Quinn was sobbing. The big man's eyes were puffy and red; tears were marking his shirt. Paladin sighed and looked at the door.

"I will give you two a minute. Jet, come find me at the end of the alley when you are ready and I'll take you to where we're going," Paladin said. Paladin grabbed his luggage from beside the door and left, leaving Jet alone with his uncle.

"Uncle Quinn? Are you okay?" Jet asked cautiously.

Quinn put the luggage down on the ground and brought up a hand to his face, trying to wipe away the tears. Jet never saw his uncle like this before and did not know how to handle the situation.

"Look, Uncle Quinn, I'm sure I'll be able to come and see you every once in a while, it's not like I'll be leaving forever or anything," Jet stammered when suddenly Quinn picked his nephew up and locked him in a bear hug.

"You're just like your dad," Quinn whispered, and Jet

stared awkwardly at the roof while the air was squeezed out of him. "Just please take care of yourself. You're the only thing I have left."

Jet's eyes looked at the side of Quinn's head, feeling guilty. He never once imagined his uncle felt this way, and it suddenly made leaving much more difficult despite the promises of being a superhero. He leaned further into the hug, and he felt the gruffness of Quinn's poorly shaved chin on the top of his head. The scent of Quinn's cologne found its way into Jet's nose, and it reminded Jet of being a little kid again, playing with his uncle. Of being with the closest thing he had to a father.

"I promise, Uncle Quinn," Jet said quietly, feeling a lump in his throat forming as he thought back to his younger years.

Ever since Jet's parents died, Quinn took care of him and raised him. Some of his earliest memories were playing with his uncle, and even though Quinn got harder on him as Jet grew older, Jet treasured those memories.

Quinn released Jet from the hug and then took a deep, self-controlled breath.

"Okay," Quinn said to himself. "Okay."

Jet grabbed the luggage off the ground, awkwardly carrying one bag with his sword in the same hand. They started walking towards the door, and Quinn opened it for his nephew.

"I left you a present in the bag," Quinn commented as Jet walked out the door. Jet immediately wanted to ask what it was, but Paladin's gleaming armour caught his attention. He knew it was time.

One way down the alley lay his old life. With his uncle, and his room filled with superhero stories, everything he knew. Down the other was everything Jet ever wanted to be.

Jet hesitated for one last moment.

"See you later, Uncle Quinn," Jet said.

He turned and walked towards Paladin, leaving everything he was to become something new.

He heard his uncle say softly behind him, "Goodbye."

As the night progressed, Jet wouldn't have much memory of where they went, but a short distance away, nestled in a park, was a trapdoor that he and Paladin climbed down. It was poorly lit, and the ladder Jet climbed down was cold steel to the touch.

"Where are we?" Jet asked as he reached the bottom of the hole Paladin opened up.

Jet looked up to watch Paladin descend but needed to catch his bags as Paladin dropped them down first. With a huff, Jet caught them both, more surprised at his bags plummeting towards him than strained from the weight. His unusual strength made the bags he had to carry remarkably light, considering their contents.

"This is a Chaos Bunker," Paladin answered as he slid down the ladder. "They designed it after World War II when the Chaos Bomb was dropped in the U.S."

"To...what, protect people from Chaos Bombs?" Jet guessed as he looked around.

There was a stale smell, and dust lined the walls and floor, like no one had been down here for quite some time. Paladin reached the bottom of the ladder and flipped a switch. With the hum of electricity, lights stirred to life, and Jet saw the long tunnel reaching down for many meters in front of him. The hall was tight and constricted, and doors lined either side.

"Yes, as a matter of fact," Paladin answered. "During the Cold War, the bunkers were designed in case of an emergency involving Chaos Bombs."

"I mean, no country has ever recreated a Chaos Bomb, but these bunkers came in handy too when there was a threat of nuclear war as well," Paladin commented.

Paladin walked down the hall, leading the way for Jet. Jet

let Paladin's comment sink in for a moment, but then he raced after his new mentor.

"Chaos energy is dangerous?" Jet asked, as he scrambled to keep up. "I thought it created Alpha. And a bunch of other superheroes."

Paladin peered over his shoulder at Jet, clearly bemused by Jet's knowledge of superheroes.

"Indeed, it did. However, it's important to know, Jet, that Alpha is the only person to sustain that much Chaos Energy in his body at one time. That's what gave him his power. Other superhumans must manipulate Chaos Energy in different ways so that it's not harmful to them. Alpha is the only person ever who has harnessed the pure Chaos Energy without it killing him."

"Oh, that makes sense, I guess," Jet muttered as he followed Paladin.

"It's what makes Chaos Energy such a sought-after resource," Paladin continued, taking a left at the end of the hall. "People are always after ways to manipulate to their advantage, for good or bad."

Paladin took a right at their next intersection, and Jet was absent-mindedly following him now. The sudden history lesson was something Jet learned a bit about in his own research into superheroes, but he didn't fully understand it all.

Suddenly, Paladin stopped, making Jet stop abruptly as well.

"It's those of us who seek to use it for good that have become some of the greatest superheroes, and those who use it for bad, some of the greatest villains," Paladin said as he turned to face Jet.

"Do you guys think my powers come from Chaos Energy?" Jet asked, feeling like Paladin's last comment was directed at him.

"To be honest, Jet, we don't know where your powers

come from. It's not what matters. What matters is how you want to use them," Paladin stated.

Jet looked to the side, feeling like he already responded to this ethical dilemma once. He wanted to get to the part with the training.

Seeing the twelve-years-old's disinterest in more of this talk at the moment, Paladin opened the door next to him, revealing a small dark room. Leaning in, Paladin flicked a light switch, giving the room a bright light and revealing to Jet a small cot and a little night table.

"This will be your room until we're done with your training," Paladin commented.

Jet grimaced and poked his head inside the room. Even though his room at Quinn's house wasn't much bigger, the lack of a window made Jet feel extremely claustrophobic.

"Ummm…" Jet muttered as he looked around. "Cool?"

Jet thought he was a pretty optimistic guy, but if he had to live down here out of the sunlight for the next few years and have constant conversations about ethical rhetoric, then he would regret his decision.

"Get some rest for now," Paladin said, the apprehension in Jet's voice enough to tip off Paladin to his protégé's feelings. "We train later today."

The reminder of superhero training perked up Jet's spirits.

Five years and one decorated room later, Jet felt like much hadn't changed. While he knew how to use his powers better, he still had no idea where they came from or what to do with them. He didn't even really know why he was in the bunker.

Jet stared at the picture with apprehension. He appreciated the gesture, he truly did, and he felt bad it had taken him so long to discover it hidden away in the collection.

His Uncle Quinn must have packed it for him without his realizing. Hiding it in a romantic comedy, a movie Jet sure wasn't about to open first, meant Quinn also didn't want Jet to see it right away.

Unsure what to do with the photo, Jet looked at the framed copy of his Alpha article. His uncle Quinn bought him the frame as a birthday present. Alpha was always his favourite superhero growing up, so when they found a copy of that news article, Quinn pulled out all the stops, buying a nice wood frame for the article so it could be immortalized for Jet.

The thought sent a tinge of guilt through Jet, reminding how much Uncle Quinn cared about him. Pulling it down from the wall, Jet unclipped the back and tucked the photo in behind it, figuring that was the safest place for the picture to be so it wouldn't get stomped on. He'd have to find a better home for it later.

Securing the frame back in place, Jet hung the article back up on the wall. He stared at the article for several moments after that, at the picture of the heroic, stoic Alpha. Jet let himself get lost in a fantasy for a moment, imagining the superhero he wanted to be.

Jet sighed as it made him realize more than ever that Paladin didn't let him out into the field yet. Five long years of superhero training passed, and he still couldn't leave. He was getting to where he would never escape the bunker.

With a sigh, Jet resigned himself to watching the romantic comedy on his television. Maybe the next day he would get to leave. Jet snorted and laughed at himself. He was always too hopeful for his own good.

CHAPTER 5

THE DEMON'S ARRIVAL

Jet wasn't sure when he fell asleep, but he knew he woke up around 1 a.m. as a loud boom echoed throughout the bunker.

His head bolted upright so violently he felt the hot pain of tired muscles pushed too far. He was on his stomach, with one arm lying over the side of the bed. Jet was still in the clothes he was wearing when he started the movie, a white t-shirt dirty from night sweat, and blue striped pyjama pants with no socks on.

A fog permeated Jet's mind, unsure if he really heard anything. The DVD menu continued to repeat incessantly on his television set, and the clock on his DVD player revealed to Jet that it was after midnight. Jet glanced around the room in confusion, inspecting the scene and his clothes as he tried to register what was going on.

"Paladin must have sealed the latch too tight..." Jet yawned, and then he rolled over and lay more properly in bed. He let the television stay on, its glow comforting him.

Then there was another echoing crash throughout the bunker, rattling Jet into a seated position. Jet stared at his door as the noise continued, a loud grating noise of metal on metal like fingernails on a chalkboard. A loud thumping only drowned it out. His eyes were wide as the noise seemed to get closer and closer until it was in the hall his room was in.

"Okay, maybe not Paladin," Jet whispered to himself.

The screeching racket punctuated by booms grew closer and closer to Jet's door. Jet peered around his room and picked up the DVD case of the romantic movie he just watched and held it like a weapon. The noise came to a deafening stop outside his room.

With the dreadful grating noise gone, Jet heard what sounded like a heavy panting noise, a deep guttural wheezing. Jet unconsciously counted the breaths of whatever it was outside his door as if it would help him.

Then something grunted, and the screeching returned with loud thumps as it continued to move. Jet exhaled desperately, not even realizing he held his breath for so long. Looking at his makeshift weapon, Jet rolled his eyes at himself and placed the DVD case on his bed. Getting out of bed gingerly, walking on his toes, Jet edged closer to his door. Whatever it was, it moved further away from the door, but was still in the hall based on the way the noise was echoing, Jet figured.

Jet carefully placed his hand on the door handle, and then with a sharp inhale, he slowly opened the door. Looking through the small crack he created for himself, Jet searched for the source of his current terror.

At the end of the hall, standing eight feet tall with its head almost touching the ceiling, was what Jet could only define as a monster. It seemed to wear a kind of dark, thick overcoat reaching down to its feet. In its hand that was being dragged across the floor appeared to be a long black cleaver that was almost the size of Jet. The creature's skin was off-yellow and seemed to have scales in certain places—underneath its ears, and along its neck. Jet could only see its back and wasn't able to discern its face.

Then it stopped moving again, and its head began bobbing up and down as if it were sniffing. It then turned its head to look over its shoulder slightly. Jet could then make out the details of its face, its blood-red eyes with black slit pupils, its snake-like slits for a nose, and its large open mouth with dagger-like teeth. Quickly, Jet shut the door and backed away, praying the creature didn't see him.

GUUUUUAAAAAAAARRRRRRRRRRHHH!

A large, terrifying roar resonated through the bunker.

"Well, crap," Jet commented.

Acting on instinct, Jet locked the door to his room and backed up to his bed as the pounding and screeching noises intensified as it grew closer again. Jet searched around the room for resources, something he could use to fight this threat, but the only thing he thought that would help him was in the gymnasium where he trained. However, the monster blocked his path to the gymnasium, leaving Jet trapped in his room.

The monster grew closer and closer to his room, and as Jet felt dread setting in, he looked and saw the DVD cover of the movie he watched sitting on his bed. He stared at it longer than he should have until determination became his overriding emotion.

"I will not let a romantic comedy be the last movie I watch," Jet stated to himself.

As he continued to search, his gaze found its way to the roof, where he saw a grate he could fit through if he tried hard enough. Jet leaped from his bed and grasped the grate with one hand. Pulling up his other hand, he gripped tightly and tugged with all his upper body strength.

The grate gave way easily, much to his surprise, and Jet fell back onto his bed. He looked at the grate in his hands and the size of the screws, and while Jet knew one of his powers was strength, he didn't realize he was strong enough to tear metal.

There was a loud crash at his door, and Jet turned to see a large dent form in the large metal door. That snapped Jet back into the moment, and not hesitating anymore, Jet leaped up again to the vent, and scrambling his whole body into motion, pulling himself upwards.

It was a tight squeeze, with less than half a foot between him and the steel on either side of his shoulders. With nowhere else to go but forward, Jet wiggled his way through the vent.

Shoulder to shoulder, Jet inch-wormed his way through, as a loud bang echoed behind him. Jet peered over his shoulder for a moment back at the vent where he came from and heard the monster entering his room. He shuddered at the thought of the monster in his room. Then the monster roared again, and Jet remembered why he was fleeing in the first place.

"Man, if that monster steps on any of my favourite movies, I'll rip him a…rip him a…something," Jet remarked to himself as he continued to move forward, blanking on what exactly he wanted to rip that monster.

Reaching another grate, Jet pushed down with his hands, and the grate popped off its screws fairly easily. Jet inched forward and down the hole, turning his fall into a controlled flip. He landed on the ground softly, being mindful of the monster.

Seeing he was in the hallway, the one around the corner where the monster was originally, Jet quickly looked down either direction of the hall and entered an all-out sprint towards the gym.

In the bunker, every hallway seemed identical, the steelwork of the walls, floor, and roof not doing much to distinguish themselves from other halls. It felt like running through a hamster maze, and even with Jet's five years of experience in the bunker, the rapid sprint through the maze was a dizzying blur of grey metal. As his bare feet slapped the cold floor, Jet moved as fast as possible, relying on muscle memory to avoid becoming disoriented.

As he ran, the terrifying bellow of the monster echoed behind him, and the pace of the monster's footsteps quickened. As Jet reached a bend in the hallway, he skidded to a stop as his momentum almost carried him into the wall.

Once he maintained his balance, Jet turned to keep running, but for a moment he gazed back the way he came to see the monster at the end of the hall. There it stood, sword still on the ground, huffing and growling at Jet, its face contorted in what could only be described as an inhuman scowl.

"Um, hey big guy," Jet commented, talking over the terror lest it control and seize him. "Do you...do you want a dog treat or something?"

An awkward silence followed. The monster still huffed angrily at Jet, and Jet continued to stare in terror.

"I mean, I don't think we have any dog treats, but you're definitely not a person so I don't feel comfortable offering you real people food, I wouldn't want you forming any bad habits, you know?" Jet rambled.

Then the monster roared and broke into a run towards Jet. Jet yipped in response and his feet kicked into motion as he sprinted as fast as he could towards the gym. He didn't look back again, didn't want to deal with the reality of the moment. The loud, terrifying thumping and screeching of the monster's run chased Jet down the hall. Taking one last right at another turn, Jet ran the last short distance into the gym.

He pushed the large double doors open and then threw them shut quickly. The monster grew closer, and Jet quickly sealed the door by closing the latches at the top and bottom of the door. Just when Jet thought he gave himself a moment to breathe, the doors almost blew off their hinges as the monster rammed into it.

Jet jumped backward in surprise and horror. The doors, now dented outwards, rattled as the monster pushed on them, and Jet noticed the latches wouldn't hold. Backing away from the door, Jet ran to his sword. Right where Paladin left it, his sword called to Jet. Jet grabbed it and spun around.

Standing at the opposite end of the doors in the large gymnasium space he and Paladin were using for training, Jet glanced around the room. All the equipment, tables, and everything else they used for training were already pushed off to the side for their last skirmish. That left a lot of empty room between him and the monster. There would be a lot of room to maneuver, and he would have to take advantage of it.

Even though the lights were dim, the monster seemed to rely on a sense of smell, Jet noticed, so he wouldn't be able to use that against the monster. It was going to be as straight-up a fight as Jet ever had with Paladin. Only there wouldn't be ring outs or knockouts. This was do or die.

Bringing his sword into a fighting stance, Jet let out a cool breath as he thought about all of Paladin's training. Ready or not, it was time to put it to the test.

"Let's dance, ugly," Jet said as he watched the monster.

With a final push, the monster knocked the door off its hinges as it roared. It let out a second roar as it stormed into the room and moved towards Jet.

"Come on!" Jet yelled, and he charged at the monster.

The monster returned the charge, and for the first time, Jet saw its short, almost stubby legs pump furiously to carry its giant mass. Its enormous claws brought the sword up into a position to swing at Jet, the nature of the attack easily telegraphed. Jet held his sword vertically, his hands high in the air and his blade pointed down, and blocked the attack as the monster swung in with a wide arc.

The block protected Jet from being cut in half, but the strength of the monster sent Jet reeling backward as his arms flailed. His bones rattled and his teeth clattered, but Jet shook off the blow with a full-body wiggle as he landed on the edge of the training mat.

Jet quickly chastised himself, realizing he shouldn't have tried to block an attack from an opponent obviously stronger than himself. Then Jet quickly looked back at the monster and saw it was already upon him. The monster raised its sword high and swung down.

Jet rolled forward out of the way, landing in a crouched position. A loud, thunderous bang echoed as the monster's sword hit the floor. Not lifting the sword again, the monster dragged it across the floor as it swung at Jet again.

Seeing the sword come in low, Jet sucked in a breath and sprung forward towards the sword from his kneeling position. Just as the monster raised the sword to swipe at Jet, Jet leaped and planted one foot on the flat side of the monster's sword as it swung in.

Using it as a springboard, Jet jumped higher in the air and pushed the monster's sword back down. The monster's strength and momentum forced it into the ground. It was defenseless for a moment as Jet jumped high in the air in front of the monster. For a moment he felt weightless, but then Jet seized control of his body and its momentum.

Twisting, Jet spun in the air and kicked at the monster. His foot impacted the side of the monster's head with a hard *THWACK*, making the monster recoil for a moment.

As Jet landed from his jump, he brought his sword close to his body and then he spun again and slashed at the monster's side with his sword. Jet could feel his sword slice through the monster like a thick stick of butter as a hissing noise gushed out from the wound. The monster howled and shuddered.

As the monster turned with its massive sword heading in

towards him, Jet flipped backward. He cleared the sword as the monster swung it. When Jet landed, he quickly dashed forward, seeing an opening the monster just left.

Jet ran past the monster, slashing at its torso with his sword and leaving a large gash and cutting off a chunk of the monster's overcoat. Adrenaline was kicking in. Jet was feeling amazing as he landed blow after blow.

As Jet turned, he expected the monster's next attack to be as predictable as the last few. However, the monster powered through the last hit it received from Jet and was already on the offensive faster than Jet expected.

The monster spun its body, letting go of its sword in a massive throw. Jet just brought his sword up in time to avoid becoming a skewer as a loud *CLANG* echoed when the monster's sword collided with his.

The impact sent Jet off his feet and backwards off the training mat entirely, his sword being knocked out of his grasp from the force of the blow. Jet crashed onto his back, and his whole body felt numb, every bone in his body reverberating.

Before he could get up, the monster was on top of him. Its claws grabbed his whole torso in one grasp, fingers going over his shoulders and around his legs. Jet had a moment to wrestle against the strength of this monster as it lifted him up. Then it slammed him hard onto the steel ground.

Jet's back collided with the ground with such force he saw white for a moment. The adrenaline carried him through, and Jet snapped back to reality as he was lifted again.

Before he crashed into the ground again, Jet braced his head, knowing the hit couldn't have been good for him. The impact still made his ribs and spine scream in agony, but at least he could still think clearly.

As the monster prepared to slam him again, Jet wrapped his arms and legs around the monster's claw and forearm. The monster slammed him again, and again, each hit booming throughout the gym and hurting more than the last. But Jet was working furiously, his entire body straining against the monsters' strength.

Before one last slam, Jet leaned to the side with all the strength in his body. A sickening *SNAP* echoed as the monster's contorted arm twisted the opposite way, releasing Jet. Jet fell to the ground on his back, and he quickly rolled over onto his hands and knees, knowing he needed to keep moving.

The monster was stumbling backward in shock and pain, but Jet couldn't take advantage of the moment because as soon as he tried to stand, he coughed and wheezed in pain.

His ribs were likely broken or at least cracked. Jet desperately scrambled to get back to his sword. Just as he got his hands off the ground to run, he received a kick in the stomach from the monster. Its long, claw-like feet left long, deep gashes across his chest, and he felt his ribs further crunch from the kick.

Jet let out a cry of pain as the force of the hit sent Jet hurtling across the room, and he crashed into a roll just before the wall of the gym.

Jet stopped on his back, his head lolling to his side. He looked to the monster, who huffed angrily at Jet, then turned and walked towards its sword. Jet craned his neck to look at his sword.

With a few deep inhales and exhales, Jet tried to stand, but he fell onto his back, unable to move. The monster grew closer to its sword, and Jet tried and failed again to stand.

"No...not like this," Jet muttered to himself with a grunt.

He kept trying, but his body wouldn't obey him like he wanted as the monster picked up its sword and walked towards him. Jet refused to quit, refused to give up. He was going to find a way out of it. He just needed to move.

As the monster, one hand brandishing the sword while the

other hung limply, walked over to Jet, the teen realized he was running out of time.

"Come on...come on..." Jet said, and after inhaling deeply, his lungs in agony as they pushed against his broken ribs, he rolled onto his stomach.

Using all the strength he could muster, he pushed himself up and ran to his sword. His momentum almost carried him past it, but Jet grabbed the hilt of his sword as he tripped over the blade. Rolling forward, Jet spun and held his sword out in front of him while in a seated position.

The monster snorted and continued to walk towards him. Sweat rolled down his brow and stung his eyes. Jet's breathing was raspy and heavy, and he watched as the monster approached.

His adrenaline was fading, and the crash was hitting him as his energy faded. It took almost all the energy he had to get up and get his sword, so he wasn't sure how he was going to fight the monster.

All Jet knew was he was going to try.

"Hey!"

Jet and the monster both turned to the double doors the monster had destroyed. Standing there, with his sword in hand and helmet on, was Paladin.

"Step away from my sidekick," Paladin instructed.

The monster grunted and turned towards Paladin, leaving Jet to stare at his mentor. Never had Paladin appeared so regal, or majestic, then he did at that moment. Standing up to the monster, the knight in shining armour, it brought back feelings of the first night Jet met Paladin. He was no longer a person; he was the hero, Paladin.

With a roar, the monster charged at Paladin. Paladin leaped forward, and his feet never seemed to touch the ground as he closed the gap between him and the monster, meeting it in the same circle he and Jet sparred in every day.

The monster swung in, and Paladin returned the attack, batting at the monster's sword with his own. As the two swords connected, there was a loud *RING,* and the monster lurched backward in surprise.

Paladin had not only matched the monster's strength, but overcome it and pushed it back.

Paladin didn't waste any opportunity, bringing his sword down low and stabbing it into the monster's side. The monster roared and tried to swing its massive blade down. Paladin extracted his sword and spun. With his spin, he slashed his sword, tearing into the monster, a black dust spurting out from the exit wound.

Coming out the other end of his spin, Paladin ducked down low, dodging a follow-up horizontal swing from the monster, who was trying desperately to hit Paladin. As the monster's sword cleared over top of him, Paladin stabbed his sword in the monster's other side and leaped into the air, trailing a large, deep incision up the monster's side.

His leap trailed him up and over the monster's shoulder, and Paladin slashed his entire way through. The monster's already broken, limp arm crashed to the ground, amputated from the rest of the body. Jet stared wide-eyed at the spectacle, his eyes fixed on the severed limb.

The arm then dissolved, and Jet watched in wonderment as black flakes seemed to float off it, and the rest melted into dark ash onto the training mat. In a matter of moments, the arm was nothing more than a black stain.

Not for the first time that night, Jet wondered if he was still dreaming. Another gigantic crash caught his attention, and he looked up to see the action continuing to unfold. Having blocked an attack from the monster, Paladin kept his feet planted on the ground, but he skidded backward.

The monster roared and stomped in, almost more terrifying with one arm missing. It swung downwards at

Paladin, and Paladin leaped to the side, dodging the attack. Jumping backward, Paladin threw his sword at the monster and, like a rocket, it connected and stabbed in the monster's side.

Paladin gave the monster no time to rest as he jumped up in the air. The monster glanced down at the sword and pulled it up, but then its head darted upwards as Paladin descended upon him. Rearing back a fist, Paladin punched down at the monster as he descended. The monster had time for one last guttural roar.

In a flash, Paladin descended through the monster, punching through its whole being. It exploded into flakes and ash, like its amputated arm before it.

Paladin landed on the ground fist first, the fluff and material from the training mat exploding upwards, and he was covered in the ash as the black flakes descended slowly to the ground. Paladin's sword clanged to the ground, its support now literally disintegrating.

After a moment's pause, Paladin stood up with a sigh. He turned to look at Jet, who was still only watching in disbelief. Paladin walked over to his seated apprentice, and Jet shakily tried to stand.

"Are you okay?" Paladin asked.

Jet went to respond, but as he put weight on his feet, his ribs screamed at him. In a flash of pain, Jet saw white and black flashes before he fell to the ground.

He swore that somewhere in the distance he heard Paladin shouting his name, but it faded into silence.

CHAPTER 6

THE SECRET OF THE BUNKER

Jet awoke in his bed, his world slowly coming into focus. Confusion overrode all sense, and he sat upright in a daze. He scanned his room, bewildered by how someone moved him from the gym to his room so quickly. His television was off; the overhead light no longer glowed. Time passed. Putting a hand to his forehead, Jet tried to remember what happened.

The memory of collapsing onto the floor from his injuries sank in, and Jet raised an eyebrow in confusion. Putting a hand to his stomach, he didn't feel any soreness in his ribs. Perhaps a bit too recklessly, Jet began patting down his entire torso, and there were no shocks or jabs of pain. Jet let his hands rest at his sides.

"Huh," Jet muttered to himself.

For a moment, Jet thought everything that happened the night before was a dream. Then Jet looked at what used to be his door and saw it was completely gone. The monster must have blown it off its hinges, leaving an empty door frame where Jet's sense of privacy used to sit. The lack of a noise barrier was gone, however, and Jet heard two people talking down the hall. One Jet easily recognized being Paladin, and the other was familiar, but Jet couldn't pin down from where.

Jet scratched the back of his head in uncertainty. After what happened, what was Jet supposed to do? There wasn't really a protocol for surviving a monster attack. Deciding it was best to find Paladin, Jet started pulling the white covers off himself.

Standing up from his bed, Jet tiptoed towards the conversation. He wasn't entirely sure why he was on his toes, but he felt like he was listening to something he shouldn't have. As he exited his room and realized the voices were coming from around the hall, he continued following the noise as the events of the night ran through his head.

He had gone from angry, too terrified, to even more terrified, to...happy? Jet wasn't sure why, but as he thought about the battle against the monster, he couldn't help but smile. Unsure if it was an adrenaline rush caused by sheer panic or if he found it fun, Jet reflected on the battle fondly, much to his confusion. Confusion, but also delight.

"I almost died," Jet said quietly to himself, so as not to be heard for fear of sounding insane. "I almost died, and I had a *blast.*"

Rounding the corner back through to the cafeteria, Jet saw the doorway had exploded forward, hinges shattered, and the frame dented into the room. So used to seeing the doors closed in front of him for the past five years, the moment took Jet aback. But then he realized he recognized the other voice.

"Uncle Quinn?" Jet asked as he started jogging forward.

The voices stopped talking, and as Jet came into view of the two, Paladin and Uncle Quinn were sitting on two stools that were used before for when the gymnasium was a cafeteria. Paladin was still in his armour, but with his helmet sitting on the floor next to them.

Quinn looked like he walked out of one of Jet's old

photos of him, a tacky red Hawaiian shirt with khaki shorts on. His hair was still silver and fluffy, and he still broke a taboo by wearing sandals with socks. They both were looking in his direction and had mixed reactions. Quinn, who was in a somber mood at first, smiled warmly at seeing Jet. His eyes seemed to light up in a way they likely hadn't in a long time. Paladin seemed somber and glanced away with a small sigh.

"Hey there, kiddo," Uncle Quinn said.

"I...uh...hey, hey Uncle Quinn," Jet said, putting a hand behind his head.

He stared at the two adults for a moment.

"What's going on?" Jet asked.

Quinn's smile diminished and turned to Paladin, who looked back to Jet. There was a brief pause, where everything was silent.

"We need to talk about last night," Paladin said.

"Well, duh," Jet immediately followed up.

Paladin scowled.

"I...right, sorry," Jet stammered.

"And about the last five years," Quinn added.

The red in Jet's face flushed away at the comment. Confusion overrode embarrassment for Jet.

"What do you mean?" Jet asked as he stepped forward.

Paladin let out a long sigh through his nose and then rubbed his face. Quinn took a cursory glance at Paladin and then turned on his stool to fully face Jet.

"Last night, the Construct attacking you is a problem not just because of the danger you were in, but because of what it means," Quinn explained.

Jet raised an eyebrow, not following.

"The Chaos bunker, which shielded people from chaos energy, was also meant to protect them from radiation. Create a chaos energy dead zone," Paladin explained, breaking his silence. "We hoped that here, Constructs wouldn't be able to find you. They wouldn't be able to detect this space."

Jet tilted his head, trying to process what was just been said.

"Wait...Constructs? Find me? This space? What?" Jet asked.

Too many of the words and concepts said to him were unfamiliar, and Jet found himself suddenly lost in the details of his own life.

"We should start at the beginning," Quinn remarked, noting Jet's visible confusion.

Paladin nodded and then motioned for Jet to pull up a stool. Jet absentmindedly dragged it over while still trying to sort out the ideas in his brain.

"When you were very young and showed signs of being super-powered, your sword materializing, your enhanced physical skills, shattering your cradle leg with a kick," Quinn recalled, a slightly nostalgic smile on his face. "Around that time, you seemed to attract these mysterious creatures that I never saw before."

"The first few times I called animal control or the police, and they would usually deal with it. Chase it away or catch it, but eventually, they started getting bigger and bigger," Quinn explained. "Until...well, do you remember my old house?"

"Your old house?" Jet asked.

He put a finger to his chin and thought about it, and like a lightbulb went off, he snapped his fingers.

"Oh yeah! We moved when I was five, right? To the place you have now?"

"Do you remember why we moved?" Quinn questioned, and as he said it, he nodded to the door frame. Jet glanced at it and then looked back at Quinn and Paladin.

"You mean a monster like that attacked us?" Jet asked in disbelief.

"It wasn't even as big as that one," Paladin chipped in. "But it was enough to total your house. It was lucky for you two that I was around."

Eyes wide, Jet stared at the two for a moment.

"I...I don't remember any of this. You've been around since I was five?" Jet asked.

Paladin nodded in response.

"How come I didn't meet you until I was ten, then?" Jet demanded to know.

"Well, when Paladin fought the monster, he killed it, and that was when we realized it was a Construct," Quinn explained. "Knowing that we could set up an alarm system around the house. Every time it went off, Paladin would hurry over and destroy it."

Jet put a hand to his forehead as the pieces of the puzzle lined up.

"Okay, so wait, back up the bus. What's a Construct?"

Paladin furrowed his brow and stared hard at Jet, making him involuntarily gulp.

"We've been over Constructs before. I've explained them to you in our sessions," Paladin grumbled.

Jet scratched the back of his head, not sure how to respond.

"I mean, I'm fifteen, not, like, fifty like you. You expect me to remember stuff?"

"You think I'm fifty?" Paladin asked incredulously, in a rare moment of broken composure. Jet felt his lips twitch upwards as he shrugged his shoulders, the jab intentional.

"Let's stay focused," Quinn said to the two of them, even though he had a hint of amusement on his face as well.

With a hopeless smile, Paladin continued, "Constructs are beings, creatures, made up of Chaos energy. They are chaos energy taken solid form and tasked with a single purpose."

"So the thing I fought last night...was pure chaos energy?" Jet questioned.

"Yes, Constructs are primitive and single-minded, great henchmen for supervillains," Paladin continued. "However, for whatever reason, a select few have deviated from their missions to hunt...you."

Jet's brain raced as he recalled all the facts Paladin taught him about Constructs, and all the things he promptly forgot. He knew they popped up from time to time in historical superhero versus villain battles, and that Constructs were part of a large crisis in the nineteen-sixties. However, they had always seemed like a problem far removed from Jet's world.

Yet here they were. They were always in Jet's world.

"I...huh," Jet remarked, leaning back on his stool. "I don't know what to think."

Quinn and Paladin shared another look and then turned back to Jet.

"That was part of the reason Paladin brought you here," Quinn explained. "So you could be trained somewhere where you would be safe from Construct attacks."

"Why did you guys not tell me this?" Jet asked.

Quinn and Paladin exchanged glances. Paladin let out a small breath and then turned to face Jet.

"I had...concerns," Paladin said.

"Concerns?" Jet repeated back. "What concerns?"

"Concerns. Jet. My concerns. Not yours," Paladin said sharply.

Quinn's eyebrows raised as Jet's narrowed. This was a tone Jet recognized. A 'it's time to stop asking questions, Jet' tone. He heard it whenever Jet pried into things he shouldn't. Paladin's personal life. When he could go topside. Things Paladin wasn't ready to discuss yet, and made Jet well aware he wasn't ready.

Jet wanted to circle back around to it, but there was still

lots he was learning. Jet leaned back heavily on his stool, many parts of his life coming into focus. But then, like it hit him in the back of the head, a sinking thought came to Jet.

"Wait...so I'm not here to become a superhero?" Jet asked, bending forward abruptly. His stool rattled on the ground in response to the abrupt movement. "To...to be your sidekick?"

Paladin looked at Jet with his confident, warm smile. Jet felt a sense of ease wash over him.

"You are here to learn both of those things. Keeping you safe is why we are doing that here, and either until we find out why these Constructs are hunting you..." Paladin said, but Jet stood up from his stool.

"Well then, we should be out there!" Jet proclaimed. "We should be out there trying to find out why Constructs are hunting me, and busting heads and stopping crime, and doing those things superheroes do while we're at it. Why keep me safe when we can do things that also help other people? Use these powers for something good?"

That was the moment, Jet realized, that he was waiting for. While he knew he was going to start an argument that he and Paladin had countless times, he finally had some new information. He knew what his obstacle to leaving the bunker was, and with that knowledge, he fought back against it.

Jet pointed from himself to the door out of the cafeteria. He took a long, deep breath, watched Paladin and Quinn intently, waiting for their reaction. Quinn glanced from Jet to Paladin and then rubbed the back of his neck.

"Listen, Jet," Quinn said. "While I'd like to have you out of here too, there are a lot of factors that are in play here."

Jet shrugged his shoulders and let his arms hit his sides dramatically. He was so ready to tackle the issue from the moral high ground, but as Quinn refuted him, a wave of sudden anger bubbled up.

"Yeah, I guess like Paladin's *'concerns?'* I guess there are a lot of factors I don't know. I just found out I've been half-lied to for the past five years!"

"It's more than Constructs Jet. The world out there is not safe," Paladin quietly said.

The reserved tone with which Paladin caught Jet off guard. He almost sounded afraid, Jet thought. Catching his anger, Jet walked over to Paladin.

"Paladin, all I want is to be out in the world and do the great things other heroes do. I want to help," Jet said softly, trying to go in a lighter direction with the conversation. "I...I want to be a superhero."

He sensed his stomach lurching with the rollercoaster of emotions he was going through. Jet was confused, angry and excited, and he rotated through them like a revolving door.

"Being a superhero isn't all it's cracked up to be, Jet. You don't know what the world out there is like," Paladin said dismissively, and then he stood up and walked away from Jet.

"You read news articles, you watch movies, and it gives you this fantasized version of what the world out there looks like, but it's just that, a fantasy. And nowhere else is that more true than in Vinton," Paladin continued, turning around to face Jet and letting himself lean against some workout material.

"Vinton is a brutal, dangerous place and will eat up your idealism and spit it back out at you," Paladin finished.

Quinn's eyes widened as his eyebrows narrowed, and he looked hard at Paladin. However, Paladin's sad, defeated expression silenced any rebuttal. It was clear Paladin didn't want to believe what he was saying, but a lifetime of frustrations embittered him to this moment, to this stance. Quinn softened and looked away.

Jet felt his heart sink into his stomach, and his face tingled as the blood left it. Never had he heard Paladin sound so hopeless. His icon, his hero, seemed so defeated, and the words coming out of his mouth ran opposite to everything Jet thought he knew about Paladin.

"I'm sorry, Jet," Paladin said, rubbing his eyes. "I know how badly you want this. I'm just...I'm tired. It's a war on multiple fronts up there, and there are nights like last night that make the world seem hopeless. I've never told you this, but...I'm Vinton's last superhero."

Jet's eyes shot wide open.

"I haven't wanted to tell you because I didn't want to embolden you further and rush your training. I don't want you out there until we're sure you're ready. But I'm your mentor, and I should try harder. Sorry."

Jet looked at the ground.

"Do you not like being a superhero?"

Paladin didn't remove his gaze from the ground.

"Not all the time, Jet."

It made Jet feel defeated, and like his mentor in front of him, Jet felt hopeless. Like he would never be a superhero, as if there was no point in trying.

However, deep down in Jet, something stirred. Faced with despair, a spark of light seemed to ignite in Jet. His convictions pushed back, bubbling to the surface and overtaking Jet in a moment of sheer truth.

"The world is what we make it be," Jet responded. "However bad, or rough it can be, we can always make it a better one. That's why I want to do this."

There was no quiver or stutter in his voice. Jet said it with such certainty that the room seemed to freeze around him. Paladin stared at his apprentice, no expression marking his face. The two locked eyes for several moments. Jet knew, deep in his soul, that this was the person he was.

Quinn, who had remained silent for a while, slapped his knees and stood up, breaking the silence.

"Well, Paladin, I think he has you there," Quinn stated.

Both Jet and Paladin looked over to Quinn as Quinn walked over to Jet. Standing behind Jet, Quinn put a hand on his nephew's shoulder. Jet glanced up at Quinn and saw a small smile on his face as Quinn looked at Paladin.

"I'm going to take Jet out of the bunker, because I think it's time for him to experience the world out there, not through what we tell him, not through what he reads and watches, but with his own two eyes," Quinn said.

Jet did a double-take to see Paladin's reaction back to his uncle in surprise so quickly he put a crick in his neck.

"Really?!" Jet gasped.

Quinn nodded, and Jet's mouth went agape in the largest smile he ever experienced. He would have smiled even bigger if his head would have let him.

"Whether you want to help him in this transition or not and keep mentoring him is up to you," Quinn said to Paladin.

Paladin sighed and rubbed his forehead. He took a few moments to collect his thoughts, and then his honest smile returned. The person Jet knew to be his mentor returned at that moment, and relief washed over Jet.

"You're right, both of you. I apologize again," Paladin said. "It has been a long few nights, and I let it drag me down deeper than I should have."

Paladin walked over to the two with his hands on his hips.

"I still think the city might be too dangerous for Jet, with the Constructs and the gangs. But you're right...it's time he sees it for himself. And of course, I'll continue mentoring him," Paladin said. "Jet has a bright future ahead of him, and I want to do anything I can to help him get there."

Jet beamed at Paladin, and Quinn patted Jet on the back.

"Go pack your things," Quinn said. "It's time to go home."

ISSUE 1 EPILOGUE

JET NEVER MOVED FASTER IN HIS ENTIRE LIFE. AFTER sprinting back to his room, haphazardly packing his things, and then re-packed his things again because he caused such a mess the first time, to finally taking his time and doing it properly the third time, Jet was ready to leave in less than twenty minutes.

The only thing he was truly delicate with was the framed copy of the Alpha article, cushioning it with lots of clothes.

Wheeling out all his worldly possessions in the same suitcase he wheeled it all in with, Jet headed towards the exit of the vault with a spring in his step. Quinn was already there waiting for him, Paladin standing next to him. The two were having some kind of discussion, but Jet barreled his way through it, rushing towards them.

"Okay, ready to go!" Jet proclaimed.

Quinn and Paladin stopped what they were talking about and both turned to Jet. Then Paladin turned back to Quinn.

"You sure you're ready to say goodbye to the peace and quiet?" Paladin asked.

"I'm not sure, but I bet you're looking forward to

grabbing some actual sleep again," Quinn joked. Paladin chuckled and then looked down at Jet.

"This isn't the end of your training, but the next step. Stay safe during the day, and only go out on patrol when I come to meet you. Your uncle is going to show you where to meet me on your drive home," Paladin instructed.

Jet nodded in understanding, his mind brushing off the part about only being on patrol when with him. Paladin smiled and reached behind himself. Jet realized there was a small box wrapped in coloured paper with a small bow on it sitting behind Paladin's leg.

"I had this made for when it was time to leave. I guess the time is now," Paladin said as he picked up the box and passed it to Jet.

Jet stared, confused, at the present for a few moments, grabbing it from Paladin. Jet glanced from Paladin to the box, to Paladin, back to the box.

"Don't open it until you get home, but you'll need it tomorrow when you meet me for patrol," Paladin said with a small smirk.

Jet continued to look from the present to Paladin until he realized. His mouth went agape, and his eyes were the size of dinner plates.

"Is this my superhero costume?!" Jet exclaimed and asked in one rapid breath.

Paladin nodded, and Jet jumped up and down on the spot. It took Paladin and Quinn a few moments to calm him down, but eventually Jet was grinning as he stared at them. Extending a hand towards Jet, Paladin matched Jet's smile.

"Jet, it has been a pleasure having you here these last five years. I know you've been eager to leave, but it has been a joy watching you grow, and I'm excited to keep working with you," Paladin said.

Jet blushed a little, and then eagerly grasped Paladin's hand.

"I literally can't wait," Jet agreed.

Jet let go of Paladin's hand, and Uncle Quinn patted him on the back.

"Alright, time to go," Quinn stated, grabbing some of Jet's things as he made his way up the ladder.

Jet grabbed his suitcase and followed, but he caught himself. Surprising himself, he turned around and peered back down the hall of the bunker. It was five long years since he first arrived, but he still remembered the moment he came down that ladder so vividly.

Five years of memories flooded through Jet. Being tutored by Paladin in academic subjects, discussing the morals and ethics of being a hero, and lots and lots of combat training. There were also quieter moments, the moments when Jet and Paladin would watch a movie together, or when Jet would doodle ideas for his superhero costume.

He hated the bunker, but despite himself, there was a tinge of sadness as he left.

The bunker had been home.

With a small sigh, he heaved his suitcase over his shoulder. Jet climbed up the ladder.

He forgot what the sun felt like. Jet's world immediately became way too bright, like a photo with too much exposure. Stumbling, Jet tried to orient himself, and he reached out to grab something to support himself. His hand immediately prickled as he grabbed something rough and pointy.

"Yowch," Jet exclaimed, the sharp pain unexpected.

As his world refocused, he looked at his hands and saw them covered in pine needles.

A small laugh escaped his lips. He almost forgot about pine trees. He stared up and saw a brilliant blue sky. The sun was warm, the last few days of August bathing him in the heat.

It was so long since he felt natural heat. So long since he had been out of the poorly lit bunker.

He turned to see Quinn looking at him with an amused grin. The two were in a small alcove of a forested area, surrounded by pine trees.

"How does it feel?" Quinn asked.

Jet took a few moments, unable to formulate words. He was finally free. Finally, back in the world. It was hard for him to describe, but by rejoining the world, he felt like a person again. No longer a bunker dweller, who lived underground and trained all day long. He could be a real person again, who was more than the walls that confined him defined as. Jet could be whomever he wanted.

"Amazing," Jet replied, and then he gazed up towards the sky, unable to believe there was no roof above him.

ISSUE 2

THE BLADE BOY COMETH

CHAPTER 7

WELCOME TO VINTON

A FEW BRIEF MINUTES AFTER LEAVING THE BUNKER, Jet was riding in Uncle Quinn's van as they drove through suburbia. They were just in the same park that Jed had submerged into the bunker from all those years ago, which was in one of the safer neighbourhoods of Vinton. Jet's head was out the window like an excited dog as he watched the houses, streets, and sights of the neighbourhood fly past him.

Eventually, Quinn got tired of the rushing air and closed the window as he turned on the air conditioning, and Jet kept his face glued to the window, continuing to watch. The bright green leaves on trees, the faded colour on the sidings of houses. Other people, actually other people, were out mowing the lawn or raking the leaves.

Their drive took them through one of Vinton's urban centers, Wernsworth. Jet observed as suburbia temporarily became a trendy street lined with cafes, pubs, and little boutique shops. The aroma of bakeries and the sounds of people wafted into the van. Jet pressed his face as hard as he could against the window. People were walking their dogs, riding their bikes, and drinking coffee together. The city buzzed with energy.

The van came to a stop as they hit a red light. Jet took the moment to take in as much as he could when his eyes found their way to the corner. A relatively nondescript boy, likely around Jet's age, stood alone, staring at his phone. He had dirty blonde hair and gentle features, his leather jacket pressed tightly against himself as the autumn cool wind arrived early. Jet thought nothing more of it until he noticed three older men approaching him.

All the activity in the area seemed too quiet. Everyone who had the sense to walk to the other side of the street did, as everyone but this boy realized he was being approached by the three men. It would all have been harmless. If the men didn't wear dystopian-future clothing.

Wearing black jackets rolled up at the sleeves, they wore dark sunglasses that were rectangular. Their hair colours varied, including green, purple and blue, and their styles were a mismatch of a mohawk, a crop top, and shoulder length. They all seemed way too serious, and for a moment Jet thought it was the happening style. What did he know? He was in a bunker for five years.

But then one of them reached into their jacket, pushing it aside. At that moment, Jet saw what was hiding underneath, holstered to the man's side. It was a gun, and along the shaft it seemed to crackle with blue energy. It curved back slickly, with a flat trigger that compressed into the handle.

They approached the boy and turned him around harshly. His eyes went wide, and the men all pushed their jackets back, revealing more of the futuristic sidearm.

"Uncle Quinn," Jet said.

"I know," Quinn replied curtly.

Jet glanced at his uncle, who appeared to struggle to avoid looking at Jet or out the window.

"We've got to do something!" Jet exclaimed.

"Jet, wait…" Quinn's sentence was cut short as Jet unlocked his car door and threw it open. Practically leaping across the street, Jet dashed towards the group. The boy was reaching into his pockets when he saw Jet approaching.

The man angrily shoved the boy as he felt ignored, sending the boy to the ground. He turned to see what had his victim's attention, only to receive a fist to the jaw. The man reeled back with a grunt, crashing into the light post on the corner of the street with a loud *GONG* noise.

Jet maneuvered himself to be between the men and the boy. He brought up his fists as the men drew their sidearms, making Jet realize his sword was still in the car's trunk.

"Now who do you think you are?!" one man shouted at Jet. "Some kind of junior hero?"

Jet gritted his teeth, readying himself to fight, when a funny thought crossed his mind. A grin formed in his grimace's place.

"I'm someone who's going to kick the crap out of you if you don't back down," Jet said. "I'll turn you into sidewalk street art titled 'Stupid People Make Stupid Decisions.'"

Jet chuckled to himself, and the boy behind him stepped forward.

"Dude, what are you doing? You'll get us both killed," the boy whispered.

Jet shook his head and braced himself.

"Nah, you'll see. Someone will call the cops. I just gotta buy some time," Jet replied.

As he said this, his conviction sank midway through the sentence. Surveying the street showed it was empty. No one was watching the events unfold. People took cover and hid. Jet took a further look, and even Quinn was trying to take cover in his van, but he at least kept his eyes on Jet.

Jet put his hand to his head as he locked eyes with his uncle, making the 'phone call' gesture with his thumb and pinky, trying to get his uncle to contact the authorities. At this, one man laughed out loud. Jet turned to glance up at him as the man he punched rejoined the others.

"What, you think the cops will come to save you? Do you know what this gun fires?" the man asked.

Jet looked at the man's sidearm and shrugged.

"Water? Is it a Super Soaker? Are those still popular?"

"This gun will rip you and your buddy here faster than the blink of an eye and still has enough force to create a crater the size of your head on the sidewalk," the man boasted. "No cop wants to go up against tech like this."

Jet put on an impressed expression and stood up straight, dropping his fists.

"Wow, really?"

"Really."

Jet turned to face the boy. With a small smile, he shrugged again.

"Well then. No one can blame me for doing this then."

Jet spun and jumped in the air, kicking at the man to the furthest right of him, aiming for his hand with the gun. The man lurched, making the other two men jump back as he suddenly pointed his gun at them. Jet dashed forward and grabbed the man's hands that were clasped firmly around the gun. Jet aimed before firing the man's gun while he held it.

The recoil was intense, and the force of it tossed Jet backward, causing him to release the man. The gun blast shattered the other two men's guns with a loud *KA-CRACK*, knocking them from their hands and sparking electricity as it irreparably damaged them.

As the two men recoiled, Jet rolled forward and then leaped up with both his fists, punching both of them in the chin. They both fell backward, and Jet looked back at the man who was recovering in the street.

The man was trying to stand back up, and Jet dashed forward towards him. Grabbing the man by the collar, Jet picked him up and punched him in the face, sending him back to the ground.

With their one man with a functioning gun unconscious and their guns destroyed, the two who Jet uppercut stood up and ran back the way they came. Jet left the one thug in the street as he shook his hand, trying to ease the numb feeling punching the one man caused. He walked back towards the boy, who stood there slack-jawed.

"You okay?" Jet asked.

It took the boy a few moments to respond, but eventually, he shook his head.

"I, yeah, I'm fine," he responded.

"What's your name?" Jet asked.

"Alan," he replied, still staring at Jet in awe.

Jet nodded and then stood there awkwardly. He never saved someone before and wasn't sure what the exit procedure should be.

"Okay, well, bye," Alan said finally, waving at Jet.

"Uh, yeah, bye," Jet said, but then he caught himself as Alan walked away. "Ooh! Could you call the police? So these goons here get arrested?"

Alan turned around and looked at the unconscious man in the street and then at Jet. The look he gave Jet unnerved Jet for a moment, as it was a level of hopelessness he never seen before. However, Alan nodded and pulled out his phone as he walked away.

Jet stared after him for a few seconds, but then a car honked to his left. He turned to see Quinn, and snapping back into reality, he hurried over to the van. Sitting back down in the passenger seat, he closed the door and fastened the seat belt.

Jet went to ask Quinn why he didn't act, but the long, hard look Quinn gave Jet spoke volumes. With a sigh, Quinn put the van into drive, and they began rolling forward. Jet glanced at his uncle in confusion for a few moments, and then he slumped in his seat. He continued to gaze out the window in tense silence for a few minutes until Quinn finally broke it.

"They were Brigands," Quinn said.

Jet peered up at Quinn, who didn't take his eyes off the road.

"The Brigand is the most powerful gang in the city, and they have the police in their pocket. There are stories of them tracking 911 calls back to the caller on their guys. They don't end well," Quinn explained.

"Isn't that super illegal? Shouldn't someone get The Guardians or the VGB involved or something?" Jet asked.

Quinn sighed again.

"The VGB is also in their pocket."

Jet looked to his feet. He instantly felt guilt about Alan, asking Alan to take that chance. He wasn't sure why at that moment, but as he gazed out the window again, Vinton lost its luster.

***

Back in his own bed, Jet couldn't sleep. He unpacked his clothes and put them away, but didn't even begin hanging the news articles. It was odd being in his old bedroom after all this time. The off-white coloured walls shone with the streetlight peering in through his bedroom window like it used to when he was a kid.

He knew being back wasn't why he couldn't sleep,

however. Sitting up, he wore no shirt and was just in his pyjama pants. The bedroom window was above him on the wall next to his bed, and Jet rolled up the blinds. The moon shone into the room, casting a light over Jet's slender but built form.

His toned abs and muscles he developed over five years of training should have been at rest, but he found they were tense. He stared at the night sky for a few moments, gazing out the window. In assessing his ability to fit, Jet emitted a helpless laugh.

"Yeah, screw this," Jet said to trying to sleep.

Throwing on a quick shirt and sneaking out the window, Jet let himself fall onto the lawn. The sensation of grass prickled and tickled his feet as Jet realized he didn't even bother attempting to put on shoes. Too many thoughts flooded his head, however, and Jet broke out into a run.

Leaping from his point, he grabbed onto a neighbour's tree by one of its thick branches and he used it to vault himself onto the roof of a house. He landed with a gentle, catlike thud, careful not to make too much noise and alert anyone in the house. From there, he ran across the roof and leaped from roof to roof.

He ran as silently as he could, and he easily acclimated his running to accommodate the slope of the roofs as he ran. The shingles of the roofs felt funny on his feet, but helped Jet maintain his grip. He ran to the end of the block, jumped off the roof, and rolled onto the lawn next to the house at the end. He sprinted across the street and vaulted his way up to the top of the houses again, and continued his run.

Jet knew he was running away from something; he just didn't know what it was. Five blocks later and he reached the end of the community. The community sat on top of one of the large hills in Vinton, and at the end of the street was a large blue fence. Peering down from the hill was one of the ring roads in Vinton, and even at this time of night, cars still busily drove up and down it. From his rooftop position, he enjoyed a clear view of the moving lights, so Jet sat and observed the vehicles for a time.

The cool autumn air felt good in his hair. As he rested his arms on his knees, he sat and took in the night. He didn't spend five years in the bunker to remain cooped up at night, Jet figured. However, the longer he sat and stared, the more he realized being outside wasn't making him feel any better.

The events in Wernsworth stuck with him in a way he didn't expect. He beat up some bad guys, saved people, and even met another teen. So why did it all leave a bad taste in his mouth? Was it because no one called the cops? Or because no one else even stepped up to help?

Jet was aware he couldn't expect people without superpowers or some kind of training to do anything. He took a risk even doing anything in civilian clothes. Paladin told him superheroes did their thing in costumes so that way they could protect their identities and loved ones from fallback after stopping crime.

Something seemed amiss, though. An innocent person was in trouble, and no one did anything. No one shouted to watch out; no one tried to intervene. Everyone around Alan was okay with watching him be mugged or hurt. Whether they would put themselves in harm's way or not, it felt wrong to Jet. Shouldn't people be better than that?

Jet sighed and glanced up towards the stars. Maybe today was an anomaly, and people are normally better than that. Maybe people were just bad. He didn't know. He understood what Paladin told him, and what he saw in movies. But he thought back to all the heroes he had read about growing up, and Jet knew people needed to be good to make the choice to be heroes.

Standing up, it dawned on Jet what was required of him. He would be as good as he could be. So in those moments when people weren't what he wanted to be, he could try to live by example. Try to create what he wanted and hoped to see in the world.

If everything failed, he was going to be someone who protected people who couldn't protect themselves. Deep down, Jet already knew he would become a superhero.

CHAPTER 8
THE FIRST DAY

As the sun beamed into Jet's room, lightly showering the dust that collected in his absence, the unexpected light stirred Jet awake. At first, Jet groaned and rolled over. Then he realized he was feeling the sun on his face in the morning for the first time in five years. A smile that went from ear to ear crept across his face.

Throwing his blankets off himself in a crazed cacophony of coloured covers, he bolted upright and ran to the shower. After dealing with the temperamental water temperature of the bunker, a hot shower at home was the single greatest sensation Jet ever experienced.

Quickly tossing on some clothes with little thought to fashion, Jet ran down the stairs to the first floor. He jumped up on his way down the stairs and ran his feet along the wall. He hit the floor with a loud thump and dashed to the kitchen.

Operating on muscle memory, Jet knew exactly where to find Quinn's cereal and milk. Pouring himself a bowl, Jet devoured it. The sooner he was done with all his morning routines, the sooner he could go out and be a superhero, he figured. The moment he was done, he stood upright, his chair screeching along the floor behind it as he shoved it back. He glanced at the oven clock to check the time, and all the momentum drained from his body.

It was six in the morning.

Jet stood there blinking for a few moments and dragged his chair in close and sat back down. He wasn't sure what to do. Paladin didn't assign him any more homework. He had no place to train. No movies to watch. Jet sat and contemplated for a few moments.

Roughly an hour later, Quinn emerged from his room and saw Jet's face planted on the table, snoring loudly. Quinn chuckled to himself and walked over to his nephew. He gently placed a hand on his nephew's back as it rose and lowered with his breathing. For a few short but sweet seconds, Quinn enjoyed having his nephew home again.

Then Jet woke with a start, bolting upright in place and nearly scaring Quinn to death. Quinn backpedaled and crashed into the back counter as Jet's momentum knocked the chair backward, sending him sprawling backward onto the floor.

"IS IT TIME TO PUT MY COSTUME ON?!" Jet yelled as he tumbled.

His eyes came back into focus as he took in his surroundings, and judging by Quinn's housecoat, it was not yet that time.

"Wait...is it still morning?" Jet asked.

Quinn panted heavily with one hand over his chest as he tried to mitigate the shock Jet had caused him.

"It's 7 a.m.," Quinn answered.

Jet let out a whining noise and covered his face with his hand.

"It's time to get ready for school," Quinn said.

Jet separated his fingers to peek at Uncle Quinn with one eye.

"What?"

Quinn's smile returned, and he stood up straight, regaining his composure.

"You're going back to school today," Quinn said.

Jet glanced up at the roof in confusion. Then his eye practically exploded as he rolled upwards. He jumped to a standing position and looked at his uncle.

"I get to be an actual superhero, and I'm going back to school!?" Jet exclaimed.

Quinn looked from side to side and nodded in confusion. Jet spread his arms out wide and stared around the room, almost as if his world was shaking.

"Best. Day. Ever!" Jet shouted as he ran back up to his room to prepare a backpack.

Quinn was left standing in the kitchen by himself. He listened to Jet running around upstairs with excitement, his feet pounding against the floor with the energy of a hyper puppy.

"I didn't think teenagers were excited about school," Quinn mused to himself.

***

A short drive later, Jet and Quinn pulled up to Brian Pichelli High School, a large building with an exterior composed primarily of brown bricks. Thin, tall windows dotted the outer wall, and a few outdoor spaces lined the outside. Jet gazed at it wide-eyed, unable to believe could finally go back to school.

"You know," Uncle Quinn said as he pulled them into a parking spot. "I don't remember you being so excited about school when you were little."

Jet thought back to his childhood and remembered being yelled at for not sitting in his seat, having a hard time following instructions, and the most common complaint directed at him as he had a hard time focussing. From what Jet remembered, he felt about school like most kids did. You didn't want to go.

"Well, I don't know if it's the school stuff I'm so excited about. I mean, Paladin was teaching me stuff in the bunker. But I'm so excited to meet other kids again. It's been me and Paladin for years. I can't wait to make some new friends!" Jet proclaimed.

Jet unbuckled his seat belt and opened the car door to jump out. Quinn smiled and shook his head.

"Ever the optimist," Quinn remarked.

The two walked in through the enormous front doors of the school and through the foyer towards the school's office. A large open room sprawled out into multiple different hallways. Beneath him, Jet noticed the school's coat of arms painted on the floor. He looked around and saw a couple of students noticing him, while others seemed too preoccupied with what they were doing to give him any mind at all.

It all felt a little different from what Jet remembered. There was no smell of packed lunches in the hallways, or kids wearing snow pants. He realized that the last time he was in school, he was still in primary school.

This was high school, and the smell of textbooks, cologne, and perfume drifted through the hallways instead. There was no visible eagerness to be at school. Instead, it all looked like indifference. It was a jarring shift for Jet, but he did his best to recall several John Hughes movies he watched while in the bunker. With that knowledge of high school in tow, Jet did his best to reset his expectations.

After a brief meeting with a counselor whose name Jet didn't catch, a staff member showed Jet around the school. He promptly forgot where all his rooms were as he walked back into the foyer with his Uncle Quinn.

"Alright, I'll pick you up at the end of the day," Quinn

said. "Maybe after that you can walk to school. It's not a long walk, maybe half an hour."

"Yeah, sure!" Jet said, eager to meet some of his classmates. Then he felt slightly uneasy, and Jet looked around nervously.

"Is this too soon?" Jet asked, though he wasn't sure why he did. He was so excited to be back in a social setting. But he couldn't stop talking. "I mean, I got out of the bunker yesterday. Like maybe I need some more time to get used to being outside and stuff."

Quinn put a hand on his shoulder, stopping him short.

"Jet, you are the most talented, thoughtful, and determined person I have ever met. If anyone can survive high school, it's you," Quinn said.

Jet let out a nervous sigh and nodded.

"Thanks, Uncle Quinn, I'll see you after school," Jet said.

Just as he said that, the school bell rang, and the school burst into motion. Jet blinked, and Uncle Quinn was gone. He looked at the schedule in his hands and realized truly how quickly he forgot where to go.

Jet spent the next five minutes frantically searching the school for his classroom. After asking a few students he bumped into which way to go, Jet arrived in his English Language Arts room a few moments after the second bell went.

The desks were arranged in rows and columns, with Shakespeare posters adorning the walls. The teacher, a short, portly man, stopped talking as Jet walked in. Jet stood awkwardly at the doorway and looked at the classroom, filled with students who all turned to look at him.

"Um, sorry," Jet said. "I got lost."

The teacher peered at Jet for a moment and then nodded.

"Right, right, you're the new student. Grab any free seat," he instructed.

Jet eyed the classroom and noticed the only free desk was

one directly in front of the teacher. Clearing his throat, Jet worked his way towards the desk and felt loud as he pulled out the chair.

The class proceeded as normal as Jet figured it did, with the teacher discussing Shakespeare. A few times, Jet thought he would get to participate in the discussion but didn't feel confident at the last minute as he hadn't read Macbeth yet.

The class seemed to last an eternity and be over in an instant. The bell rang, and Jet needed to get up to find his next classroom. As he scrambled to find his next room, he realized he had never even learned anyone's names in the room.

Jet walked into his next room, this time under the wire of the bell. This room was almost identical to the last white brick walls, with only minimal windows to allow in outside lighting. If it weren't for those windows, it would have shockingly felt like being back in the bunker again.

The only actual difference between this room and his English room was that instead of Shakespeare posters, there were posters of Math equations and Math related memes adorning the wall.

To Jet's surprise, there was a familiar face in the room. Sitting in the middle of the room, taking the break between classes to look at his phone, was Alan.

"Hey!" Jet proclaimed upon seeing him.

Alan didn't immediately acknowledge Jet, and Jet hurried over to the seat next to Alan. Only then did Alan finally glance up from his phone, and his eyes widened.

"Hey..." Alan responded in confusion.

Jet was all smiles as he sat down next to Alan. There was a brief pause as Alan stared at Jet in confusion, and Jet glared at Alan happily.

"I didn't realize you went to school here..." Alan commented quietly, seemingly nervous.

"Today is my first day!" Jet exclaimed.

"Really…" Alan muttered to himself. He rubbed the back of his neck and glanced around the classroom for a few moments.

"Look, I'd really appreciate it if you didn't tell anyone about, uh, yesterday, I guess," Alan said quietly to Jet.

Jet shrugged his shoulders and nodded.

"Okay, sure. I mean, I don't want people to know I'm a superhero, right?" Jet said.

"Yeah, sure," Alan agreed half-heartedly. "Can't let people know."

Jet missed the audio clues in Alan's tone and leaned in closer to whisper to him.

"Actually, I'm going to be heading out soon with my costume, so next time people won't recognize me!" Jet said excitedly but quietly.

Alan nodded and raised his eyebrows with an uncertain smile. Jet leaned back in his own seat to let a student pass, and by the time he did, Alan was opening his binder and preparing his math notes. Jet looked forward and saw the teacher preparing for class, and Jet did the same.

For the rest of the class, Jet didn't talk to Alan, as the class was filled with Jet attempting to scribble down the notes the teacher was leaving on the whiteboard. When the class was over, Jet felt exhausted and didn't even think about talking to Alan as Alan hurried out of the room for lunch.

With his lunch in tow, Jet walked into the cafeteria to find more people than he had ever seen milling about. He glanced from table to table, trying to pick a seat, but found they were almost all full. Seeing an occasional free seat, he would ask to sit there but be told they were holding it for someone else. Feeling slightly dejected each time, Jet eventually gave up on eating in the cafeteria and walked into the foyer.

Sighing quietly, Jet sat on a bench in the foyer and ate his lunch alone.

His only solace during this time was Paladin sending him a video of a baseball player hitting a home-run. Paladin sent a text saying:

> Try this with the broadside of your sword…
> could be a good way to launch a projectile.

A small smile found its way to Jet's face. He was out of the bunker, but Paladin still thought of him.

After lunch ended, Jet's next class was chemistry, which Jet really didn't understand. He spent the entire class scrambling to write notes and trying to figure out what was happening.

The day ended with gym, which should have been perfect for Jet to meet some new faces and show off his athletic ability, but the classroom was writing a test as part of the fitness unit they finished, leaving Jet to sit around awkwardly and collect his gym strip to finish his day.

When his Uncle Quinn came to pick him up, Jet was feeling a little hollow. Quinn saw right away Jet was feeling off, and he reached into his center console. Pulling out a CD, Quinn gave it to Jet to put in his car's stereo. Jet read the cover of the CD and saw it was a band called *The Mighty Mighty Bosstones*, with the CD title reading *Devil's Night Out*.

"What's this?" Jet asked as he took out the disc.

"They're a hardcore band, or more technically, I guess a ska-core band from the 90s," Quinn said. "I was big in the ska scene when it first started but fell off the bandwagon when the genre fell apart as well."

Jet eyed the CD with some apprehension. He could see it was well-loved, but before Jet could ask more questions, Quinn kept talking.

"Through it all, though, I've always enjoyed the *Mighty Mighty Bosstones*. Whenever I feel down, or happy, or somewhere in between, the Bosstones have a song for my mood," Quinn finished. "Now put it in and listen to the second track."

Jet shrugged his shoulders, not knowing Quinn was passionate enough about anything to be passionate about this one band. Jet put the CD in and skipped to the second track. It was a bizarre blend of horns and classic rock mentality that Jet wasn't sure what to think of it.

It seemed to be pure noise, especially when the coarse singer sang, and Jet was a little put off. But as the song went on and it talked about what life used to be like and what it was at that moment, Jet connected to it.

Glancing at the back of the CD, he read the title of track two, *Howhyz, howhym*. Jet nodded and continued to listen to the song as he thought about the turns his life was on.

The day did not go as expected, and felt like it lasted over a hundred hours, but Jet wasn't sure if he was unhappy or not. Deep down, something told him not to be-that this was one thing he wanted. So then why did it not feel like it was anymore? Jet wasn't able to sort through his feelings about it.

With a resigned sigh, Jet slumped in his seat and gazed out the window. Maybe he was tired. Tomorrow would be better, Jet thought to himself. There was always tomorrow.

CHAPTER 9

ENTER BLADE BOY

JET LAY ON THE COUCH WITH HIS NOSE IN A BOOK AS Quinn worked in the kitchen preparing dinner. Quinn's main floor was an open concept. There was no wall separating the living space from the kitchen. The front-yard wall, which had a large window, was painted a dark red accent colour, and the rest of the walls were light brown.

Quinn's house was always a strange combination of smells-while Jet didn't know what Quinn did for a living and never thought to ask. He was always cooking. Trying out different recipes for his own invention and often with unique ingredients, seeming to live in his kitchen.

Jet was on a black leather couch, which had its back directly to the kitchen, and across from him was Quinn's large television set flickering with colour. There were two other chairs in the room. One was a recliner next to a small table with a lamp for reading, while the other was a smaller bucket chair sitting next to the couch, pointed at the television. The news was on, but Jet was letting the nightly update drown out into noise as he tried to make heads and tails of Shakespeare.

However, the news caught his attention, and he turned to regard the television to watch.

"City Council today was alarmed to receive yet another threat from the supervillain known as Xanor," the anchorwoman reported.

The feed cut to footage from a city council meeting, where the police force and Guardian agents stood behind the mayor. The mayor then read the note out loud.

"To the weak-willed city council, this is the last warning I will deliver. Submit to my demands, outlaw these superheroes once and for all from Vinton, or I will unleash a wave of Constructs unlike any the world has seen."

The footage cut back to the anchor, who continued to talk about how the logistics of Xanor's demands couldn't be met because of the Super Hero Protection Act of 1992, but Jet tuned her out as he sat up on the couch. In his hands was his copy of Macbeth, whose pages were scribbled over by students from past years. Jet was gathering the concept of the tragedy, of something terrible happening to good people, or at least people who used to be good.

"Hey, Uncle Quinn?" Jet asked over his shoulder.

Uncle Quinn continued to work away in the kitchen, asking over his own shoulder, "Yeah?"

"Who's this Xanor guy? Guy is threatening the city council," Jet asked, his eyes still on the television.

Quinn continued to work for several moments, stirring away at something in his wok bowl. Jet lowered the volume of the television using the remote and turned to face Quinn. After another moment, Quinn put down the wooden spoon he was working with and turned as he grabbed a rag to wipe his hands.

"A supervillain who's been in Vinton for a while, shortly after you went into the bunker, so you probably never heard of him," Quinn stated. "He was pretty effective at reigning in the gangs and kicking out the other supervillains and most of the superheroes."

Jet stared at his uncle in confusion.

"Why would he be concerned with kicking out the other super villains? Or keeping the gangs 'in check?' I thought they were pretty much already running this city," Jet questioned.

Quinn nodded his head in understanding. As he reached into the pantry and pulled out two bowls, he continued to explain.

"Well, they do, really. The Brigand and the Shinogi really are the true powers of the city, but under Xanor, they don't go to war with each other. Speculation on the internet is that he likes them existing in this state of cold war because they don't get more power, and then threaten him," Quin answered as he continued to set the table. "As for the other supervillains, well, I guess Xanor enjoys being a top dog. He doesn't want anyone else to get any bright ideas that they can take him down."

Jet put a hand to his chin and contemplated it. While it was normal for there to be at least one or two 'big bads' in a city, it was strange for there not to be more. If Xanor came on the scene after Jet went underground, then it meant this was probably the case for at least five years. The status quo for that long was the most unusual part to Jet.

"So, why is Xanor so powerful that no one can take him down? Like, haven't a team of superheroes or, heck, a team of supervillains tried?" Jet asked.

Quinn chuckled as he dished up the teriyaki stir-fry he prepared into the bowls on the table.

"I forgot how much you enjoyed talking about this stuff," Quinn commented.

Jet draped his arms over the couch in dramatic fashion, and with a big smile, he responded, "I'm all behind on my current events!"

Quinn smiled, but then the smile diminished ever so

slightly. Jet's big grin subsided a bit as he noticed an emotion he only saw once before in his uncle nearly overtake him again. Quinn shook his head, and the fear passed.

"Well, no. While from what I can understand that yes, Xanor is apparently powerful and would be a handful for the most capable of superheroes, or teams even, it's not necessarily him alone keeping the superheroes away," Quinn responded.

Jet tilted his head to the side.

"What then?"

Quinn stood up straight and looked at his nephew. Undoing his apron, Quinn turned away from Jet and dropped the subject entirely.

"I don't honestly know. Now let's eat dinner. Paladin will be here soon to pick you up for your first night," Quinn said.

The thought of hitting the street to be a superhero picked Jet up ever so slightly. However, the conversation sat in his mind for several moments. Jet glanced back at the television and looked at the news ticker. It read 'Super-Villain Xanor continues to threaten Vinton' in big bold letters.

He didn't push Paladin about how he became the only superhero, because it felt like the first time Paladin was honest with him in a long time and he didn't want to spoil the moment. Now Jet felt like he had only more questions. If it wasn't Xanor, what was it?

Jet rejected a part of that concept so internally. How could heroes, people who swore to uphold public safety, be scared away from a city that needed it?

They were supposed to be the ones who put everything on the line to protect others. For the briefest moment, Jet sensed a tinge of disgust. The heroes he idolized would never do such a thing-Alpha or Paladin, especially. Why weren't more heroes like them? Jet glanced back at his uncle.

Jet narrowed his eyes, thinking Quinn knew more than he let on. There was something, someone out there, that was frightening enough to keep away superheroes in Vinton. Jet would not let it stop him. Whatever it was.

After finishing dinner, leaving only crumbs and some extra sauce on his plate, Jet heard a knock on the door. Quinn put his fork down and stood up, leaving Jet confused for a moment. As Quinn opened the door, Paladin walked through. It all came rushing back to Jet.

"Well, come on, Jet, it's time to go on your first patrol," Paladin said with a knowing smile.

Jet leaped out of his chair so fast it went sprawling across the floor. His feet practically never touched the floor as he rushed upstairs to his room, scrambling to the box he pushed into his closet the night before. His hands operated faster than his brain could follow, and in his excitement, Jet tore the box open with such force his costume practically exploded outwards.

It sprawled out all over his bedroom floor, and Jet froze and stared in wide-eyed amazement. While he wasn't sure exactly what it was going to look like when on, he saw the blue with hints of brown covering his costume. The texture seemed to be a mix of leather and spandex. As he placed a hand on it, he could feel lightweight armoured padding.

"This is the coolest thing I've ever seen," Jet whispered to himself.

Once the costume was on, Jet's feelings changed slightly.

Jet's costume wore like an all-body motorcycle suit, with tighter spandex pieces around his joints. The base layer was dark blue, and the armour padding provided a second layer over his elbows, knees, chest, back and his knuckles. He was wearing combat boots that went up past his ankles, which were also primarily blue with brown highlights.

While it felt amazing to have his own costume custom-made for him, something about actually being in the costume made Jet feel incredibly silly. He sat on his bed and looked at himself in the mirror for several moments.

In his open palms was a large green bandana, with two eyeholes. Jet assumed it concealed his identity, but Jet's hair and most of his face would still be visible. He didn't see how it was going to hide who he was from anyone who knew him. Jet shrugged and put the bandana over his face, tying it behind his head. A bit of the end trailed off backward, and as Jet glanced back at himself in the mirror and saw the costume completed, he still felt very ridiculous.

It wasn't how he imagined the moment being for the first time. Jet always thought the first time he would put on the costume, he would feel heroic. Jet always imagined it as the moment he would have 'arrived,' as it were. However, dressed in his costume and sitting on his bed, Jet felt himself wanting.

Jet let out an inaudible sigh and stood up. Maybe once he was out in the field, fighting crime, taking names and saving lives, it would feel different, Jet figured. Once he was doing superhero work in his superhero costume, it would all click together. Hopefully, Jet thought to himself.

Much more slowly than he went up the stairs, Jet came back down the stairs. Paladin still stood at the doorway, and Quinn sat on a chair in the living room and was talking to him from there. As Jet walked into view, their conversation stopped as they both took in Jet's new look.

Paladin's expression was one of excitement upon seeing Jet in the costume. Jet did his best to put on a smile, for Paladin's sake, seeing how excited he was. A glance at Quinn, however, mirrored much more of how Jet was feeling about the costume.

"Hey! It turned out even better than I thought!" Paladin stated. He looked at Quinn and pointed to Jet.

"Right?" Paladin asked for confirmation.

Quinn nodded his head and disguised his incredulous expression with one of amazement.

"Yeah, absolutely," Quinn agreed.

Jet stifled a laugh, not thinking Quinn did a good job of hiding his true intention. Paladin either didn't notice the poor effort or didn't care to acknowledge it, as he turned back to Jet.

"Well, Jet, it's time for you officially to become my sidekick," Paladin said. He gestured to Jet to walk over to him.

As the thought of having his superhero name sunk in, Jet sensed his excitement spike once more. Standing tall, Jet strode over to Paladin, pride swelling in his heart. It was long at last time. Jet saw this as the moment he would finally 'arrive' as a superhero. Paladin put one hand on Jet's shoulder and looked him in the eyes.

"From this moment on, when we are out in the field together, your code name, your superhero name, will be…" Paladin waited for a brief pause, creating a dramatic effect.

Jet felt his heart racing with adrenaline. This was the moment. He could feel it.

"…Blade Boy."

It wasn't the moment. Jet felt a little blue.

"B…blade Boy?" Jet asked.

Paladin nodded in confirmation. Jet stared up at Paladin, his smile as forced as could be.

"Awesome," Jet said with as much conviction as he could muster. "Blade Boy. Super, super awesome."

Somehow, against all odds, Paladin didn't seem to notice Jet's lack of enthusiasm. Jet was doing his best not to ruin this for Paladin, but it was a struggle.

"Yes, Paladin and Blade Boy. Together, it's up to us now to help save this city," Paladin said.

He released Jet from his grip and turned back to the door. Jet stood there, slightly stunned. Was Paladin monologuing?

Jet couldn't believe his ears. In all the years Jet knew Paladin, he never figured Paladin to have this, for lack of a better term, dorky side to him. That was the only way Jet described him. It was like Paladin walked out of one of his news articles from the 60s, or even the 40s. He was stoic, but so silly. Was this how Paladin acted when in full superhero mode?

"Come, Blade Boy, it's time to go dispense justice!" Paladin said as he opened the door.

Yep, this was how he acted.

Jet paused for several moments, unsure what to think. He turned back to Quinn, who at this point had his hands over his mouth as he was stopping himself from uncontrollably laughing. Jet raised an eyebrow in confusion.

"I've waited for this moment for a long time," Quinn said between high-pitched, stifled chuckles.

Jet hung his head for several moments. Clearly, Quinn had experience with this side of Paladin.

"I'll be home later tonight," Jet said with a resigned smile.

As Jet closed the door, it took all his effort not to join Quinn's infectious laughter as it exploded outwards from the house.

Standing on the edge of a roof in downtown Vinton, Paladin posed with his hands on his hips. His cape blew out behind him as he gazed down over the city. Paladin was wearing his helmet that night, a rare thing for Jet to see. Jet wasn't sure what caused it, but in the slits where Paladin's eyes would be visible, a small yellowish glow emanated instead.

While Paladin's behavior and stature felt a little out of the era in terms of how superheroes acted, Jet admitted his mentor looked cool posing in the night like that. He seemed to radiate power and awe. While Jet might have thought that of him back when he first met Paladin, it was a long time since Jet saw Paladin this way. A true superhero.

Jet walked up behind his mentor and examined his pose. Ensuring he was a few steps back from Paladin, Jet then similarly raised his leg up to pose on the edge of the building. He glanced apprehensively at his mentor one more time, examining the body language. With a bit more confidence, Jet put his hands on his hips and jutted his chin upwards slightly.

Paladin glanced back at his newly minted sidekick for a moment. Jet couldn't see it, but under the helmet, Paladin had an enormous grin on his face. He stepped away from the edge of the building and towards Jet, making Jet abandon his pose and look up at Paladin.

"Alright, rule number one of your first night on patrol. I will only address you by your super alter ego while in the field. Understand, Blade Boy?" Paladin asked.

For whatever reason, punctuating the instruction with the actual name was like rubbing salt in the wound for Jet.

"Yep, you got it," Jet answered.

"Second, if it is a school night like tonight, we don't push this past ten, eleven p.m. at the latest. Your education is still the most important thing, and you won't learn anything if you're asleep in class," Paladin said.

Jet rolled his eyes but nodded, understanding what Paladin meant.

Paladin nodded and then gestured for Jet to gaze out over the city.

"Third, you are only to patrol with me until I clear you for patrol by yourself. I know in the past you have felt I have restricted your actions too heavily, so I want you to understand I say this not to dangle an impossible to reach carrot before your eyes, but to give you a goal to reach," Paladin continued.

Jet's look of confusion said a thousand words, so Paladin continued, "It means that if you follow my instructions well enough, act with discretion, handle yourself in a crowd, and show good moral judgment, then I will allow you to patrol on your own."

It seemed like Jet was eleven years old again when he was first being lectured in the bunker about rules. But Jet was no longer the little boy-he felt like-yearned to be-something more now. Jet brought up a fist and began recounting Paladin's points with a raised finger for each one.

"Listen to you good, don't be dumb, don't get my crap kicked, and be a good person. Did I get it all?"

Paladin's body language shifted slightly, and Jet saw the disappointment.

"Jet. You need to take this seriously. Do you understand this?" Paladin asked.

Jet shifted away for a moment. With a slight sigh, Jet nodded.

"Sorry. Yes, I understand," Jet said.

Paladin readjusted himself back to his heroic form. He then walked Jet back over to the edge of the city and knelt. Jet crouched down beside him.

"Good. So, while you're doing this with me, there will be a few different things we'll do. Whatever I choose for us to do on a select night, I never want to hear any complaining or whining, got it?" Paladin asked.

Jet let out another breath of air. He knew he was a little flippant with Paladin, but it was no reason to go back to treating him like a kid.

"Got it," Jet answered.

"Good. Now, on a normal night, we'd patrol and search for trouble. Sometimes we might take more deliberate action depending on whether I find something during the day, some supervillain makes a threat to the city or anything else we might have to react to. Tonight we'll be looking into something I chanced upon earlier today. It'll be an excellent test of your ability to handle a crowd, and it might help us find some leads on why Constructs are targeting you," Paladin explained.

Jet blinked twice.

"Wait, wait, wait," Jet said. He rubbed his temple for a moment and waited for Paladin to look his way. "You lost me a little after deliberate action. These guys might have a lead on that giant monster attacking me in the bunker?"

Paladin nodded.

"What do you know about Xanor?"

Jet thought back to the conversation he had with his uncle before dinner.

"That he's a psycho supervillain who liked to threaten the city with an army of Constructs. Oh, and also he has control issues," Jet said.

That caught Paladin a little off guard as he laughed out loud.

"Not bad. Xanor has a unique power over Chaos Energy, the substance we discussed, which makes up Constructs. They are his means of enforcing his rule over the city. I'm not entirely sure how his power works, but from what I've deduced, he can only create so many Constructs at one time before he needs to rest and make more. So in those cases, he likes to store them in warehouses," Paladin explained.

Paladin pointed his finger at the warehouse directly across the road from him.

"A warehouse like that one," Paladin finished.

Jet leaned forward and examined the nondescript warehouse. White walls were on the outside, large enough to cover several city blocks and an empty parking lot.

"So you think he's got the army of Constructs he wants to unleash on downtown in there?" Jet asked.

"Maybe not all the army, but I know there's a large gathering of Constructs," Paladin answered. "There's a gigantic mass of unmoving Chaos Energy my readings picked up earlier today coming from that warehouse. Basically identical to the reading of a typical Construct, just amplified by a lot."

"Any guesses what we're going to do?" Paladin asked Jet, peering at his sidekick. There was a bit of mischievousness in his voice Jet picked up on, making him smile.

"We going to go in and knock his army down a few pegs?" Jet guessed.

"Exactly. And we'll see if we can find any evidence to see if it's Xanor who's been targeting you for years," Paladin acknowledged.

Jet nodded and then looked back at the warehouse. He wasn't sure what they were going to find there. The anticipation had his stomach in knots, but he couldn't quell his excitement.

The warehouse's lights lazily flickered to life. The fluorescents were old and barely illuminated the concrete floors and moldy wooden beams.

Paladin, with one foot back in the doorway, flicked the light switch, eyed the area carefully, and motioned for Jet to follow. Their boots clomped along the floor, echoing loudly in the large, empty room. Jet pushed his way in as Paladin stepped out of the way. The aggressively stale scent stung Jet's nostrils.

"Are all supervillain hideouts this...smelly?" Jet asked, as his eyes watered.

"Only the particularly evil ones," Paladin responded.

With a shake of his head, Jet did his best to clear his mind of what he was smelling and examined his surroundings. They were in what must have been a front waiting room that had never finished construction. A low wooden roof with the lights attached by flimsy-looking wires nestled above.

Across from the door they entered was a sheet of drywall with a cropped-out segment clearly meant for a door, and darkness awaited beyond it.

Nestled to it was a half-constructed closed-in reception desk. The wooden frame was built, but a tabletop was missing to create a flat surface. Where it appeared the room would have closed off into a small square, was just wooden beams from the floor to the roof. On the other side was a larger empty room where the sheet of drywall in front of Jet extended all the way through to the far wall of the warehouse.

Jet's gaze fixed on the darkness beyond the drywall. An ominous sense lingered. He gazed for a moment until Paladin put a hand on his shoulder, making Jet jump a little in surprise. He looked over his shoulder to see Paladin also glaring at the dark room ahead of them.

"You can sense it too?" Paladin asked.

Jet's mind raced for several seconds. What did he sense? Evil? Constructs? Xanor? Monsters? What could Paladin sense he assumed Jet also saw?

"Danger," Paladin said with confidence.

Oh. Jet's shoulders slumped slightly.

"Yeah, totally," Jet said in agreement. He was having a tough time dealing with Paladin's surprising hokiness.

"Stay close," Paladin instructed, and then he moved past Jet deeper into the warehouse.

There was a sharp sound of steel as Paladin unsheathed his sword and advanced. Jet steeled himself and followed in behind Paladin, similarly equipping his sword.

Paladin walked deep into the pitch-dark room, out of Jet's view. Jet stopped at the entranceway to the room, watching Paladin walk into the darkness. It seemed like he blinked and Paladin was gone, making Jet hesitant to continue.

The warehouse opened into a large empty room with nothing to be seen. The walls of the warehouse seemed to be the boundaries of the room, and the roof opened to a presumably second story. He took a quick glance around the room. To his right, there seemed to be an incomplete staircase, which must have led up to a second-story office. Then, to his left, was a convenient light switch.

"Hey Paladin," Jet commented as he flicked the switch. "I found the lights."

A dim, hazy light slowly illuminated the room. Jet walked with more confidence than before, strolling up beside Paladin. Paladin stopped walking, and Jet assumed Paladin was waiting for him.

"Isn't this easier?" Jet asked.

Paladin didn't respond. He peered over his shoulder past Jet, making the teen stop in his tracks for a few moments. He turned and looked past him as the light continued to etch away at more and more of the darkness. Then Paladin looked in the other direction, before glancing up.

"Easier? Yes," Paladin said.

With one hand, he made Jet walk closer to him, which Jet slowly did. Paladin's eyes remained fixed on the ceiling.

"However, you'll have to keep your cool. You accidentally set the stage for a scene from one of those horror movies you hate."

Jet truly hated horror movies. The big reason was their nihilistic approach to humanity, a far cry from the superheroes he grew up admiring. He appreciated the ideas and complex themes of some, but his problem was jump scares. Not jump scares themselves necessarily, but the tension and build-up to a jump scare set him on edge and made them so much worse.

As this thought ran through his head, he followed Paladin's gaze up to the roof. Once he saw what was up there, he instinctively went back to back with Paladin and lifted his sword into a fighting position. Nestled on the high roof of the warehouse, furled up like bats, were strange brown masses. They slowly shook one by one.

They dropped to the floor, surrounding Jet and Paladin. As they hit the floor, they opened to reveal themselves in their full forms, and they proceeded towards the duo.

"Hey, Paladin?" Jet asked.

"Yes?"

"These are Constructs, right? Not horror movie monsters?"

"Sometimes, Jet, it's hard to tell the difference."

CHAPTER 10

A WARRIOR AWAKENS

Jet and Paladin stood back to back as the Constructs closed in on them. Gripping the hilt of his sword tightly, Jet sensed fear trickling as the Constructs resembled Tim Burton's creations on steroids.

Their skin was sickly pale yellow and grey, and they stood at roughly five feet tall in a humanoid shape. But their arms were long, thick blades dragging along the ground as they slowly walked towards them. What creeped out Jet the most was where their necks should have been. It formed more of a bulbous-like head, with no nose or mouth.

There were black slits with red glows emanating from them that appeared to be their eyes, and even though there was nothing relatable about them, the eyes seemed to stare into Jet's soul. When Jet gazed back into them, he saw nothing in return.

Bumping into Paladin's back returned Jet to reality, and he shook away the fear. This was what he spent five years training for. Five long years in a bunker for a moment, like this. Jet let out a long, cool breath and readied himself.

"Get ready, Jet," Paladin instructed, almost reading Jet's

mind. "They're Constructs, so typical rules of engagement are different. Go for the kill."

Jet nodded and stared at the Constructs. They weren't human. They weren't even alive. Jet reminded himself that they were like machines. Machines possessing long sword arms and scary red eyes, Jet thought to himself. He shook the thought out of his mind.

It was time.

Paladin charged at the horde of Constructs closing in on him. The sudden movement and erupting sounds of chaos spurred the Constructs in front of Jet to dash in at him. Jet stopped hesitating and ran at the Construct nearest him.

With one arm, the Construct swung down at Jet, who blocked the attack by raising his sword. The Construct bounced away as Jet continued running and brought his sword back down and tried to slash at another Construct. Jet's sword bounced off the Construct with a *DING* as its arms were crossed defensively.

Unprepared for the parry, Jet recoiled and then leaped backward as two Constructs swung at him. A hard smack on the back interrupted Jet's consideration of his next strategy. Not painful, but it was enough to make Jet lose his balance.

It launched Jet forward off his feet, and he landed on his stomach. He turned to see it was a Construct who hit him with the broad side of its arm. Jet glanced forward and quickly rolled off to the side to avoid being cut in half. Rolling backward, Jet jumped to his feet. He tried to think about what to do next as the Constructs closed in.

Realizing he was about to be boxed in, Jet thought it would be best to create some space between him and the Constructs. Without looking, he swung his sword around behind him, trying to get the Constructs to back away.

However, his sword sharply bounced back with a *CLANG* as it was deflected by a Construct. His momentum thrown off,

Jet staggered as the Constructs closed in. Jet turned, spinning on one foot, and barely leaned back in time to avoid his head being cut off.

Jet stood back up, and two swords came in at him. Jet leaped up into the air and split-kicked out his legs to avoid them being cut off. He felt the impact against the Constructs as his feet connected, like kicking tough leather.

As Jet landed, he sensed the sweat rolling down his face. He saw a brief opening where he could run to get back to Paladin's side, who was cleaving through the Constructs like nothing.

He needed to get back to Paladin. Paladin would know what to do. There were too many things happening, too many enemies. He couldn't process everything he learned and apply it at the same time. It was too much.

Just as Jet tried to run, a Construct tackled him and knocked Jet over. Jet landed on his back and looked up to see Constructs closing in all over him. Five blades from five different Constructs all swung in on Jet all at once.

Jet panicked and lifted his sword to block the incoming blades. There was a hard *CLANG* of steel as he kept all the blades from splitting him into a five-piece pie.

He strained against the force of five different Constructs. Jet tried to think and remember all the strategies Paladin taught him. He could sweep the legs of the Constructs, but it would leave him vulnerable to at least two of the blades. If he pushed up and rolled backward, he would just have to flip again quickly to avoid more blades.

Right as the last thought crossed his head, one Construct pushed down hard enough that its blade scratched Jet's cheek. The cut immediately began to burn and feel hot. Jet perceived a drop of blood trickle down his face. He winced and instinctively pushed back in anger. He pushed back harder than he thought and all the Constructs briefly recoiled up and then slashed back down upon Jet's blade again with another loud *DING*.

Jet felt its weight come down upon him, but he was even more distracted. How was he strong enough to push that many Constructs off him? How strong was he?

As Jet pushed back against the swords, he shut his eyes and let out a long breath. He was overthinking everything. If Paladin taught him all these things, then he knew how to do them. More importantly, his body knew how to do them. It was time he trusted it.

Jet let out one more long, cool breath.

Then with all the strength he could muster, he slashed upwards, sending all five Constructs recoiling. Jet leaped to his feet and slashed in a wide circle, his sword whistling as it cut through the air.

The five Constructs dissolved to ash as he split them in the middle. Jet didn't even feel them as he cut through them. They just fell away.

More Constructs filled in the newly created gap to attack, but Jet stopped considering what to do next and just started acting. He sprinted to his right, ducking low underneath one Construct blade as he slashed upwards.

A Construct split in the middle, crumpled into ash, and Jet slashed down hard to his right and sent a Construct's blade coming in towards the ground. Jet then stepped his foot down on the blade and pivoted as he turned to square his body with the Construct.

He sensed his muscles ripple as he punched the Construct in the torso.

THWOMP.

It felt like connecting with a punching bag, but one that gave way with incredible ease. He sent the Construct flying backward. It crashed into several other Constructs and knocked them all over.

His hair prickled on the back of his neck, and Jet hoisted his sword behind his back over his shoulder and deflected an incoming attack. The Construct blade bounced off, and Jet let out a gleeful laugh.

Amazed, he stopped the attack without seeing it. He then spun around and kicked the Construct with a spinning jump kick.

KATHWACK.

It went spinning away, and Jet lunged forward with his sword leading the way.

SHUNK.

He impaled it through the spinning Construct and continued to dash forward, carrying the Construct forward on his blade. He stuck his sword through several more Constructs creating a three Construct kabob.

His adrenaline was channeling into pure focus, and Jet realized he was in full control of his body. After filling up his sword, Jet swung out wide with a yell, sending the three Constructs out across the room in an arc.

Paladin, who dispatched a Construct, leaned back sharply to avoid an airborne Construct as it crashed into the wall behind him. Confused, he turned to see Jet tearing through Constructs. The youth jumped up in the air and slashed down into a Construct and cut it in half.

For a moment, Paladin thought of calling out to Jet, thinking he almost went feral. But then, as Jet turned and blocked an incoming attack, Paladin noticed how Jet was moving. The fluidity. A small smile crept onto Paladin's face. Confident in his pupil, Paladin resumed battling Constructs on his own.

Jet held a Construct at bay with his sword and then he pushed hard and violently sent the Construct's blade arm back through itself. As its body dissolved to ash from the point of the slash, Jet reached forward and grabbed the edge of the

Construct's sword arm and ripped it from the Construct's body.

Jet pivoted and threw the blade arm like a javelin through three other Constructs, closing in, the sword dissolving to ash along with all the pierced Constructs.

He turned and parried another attack as it came in, and Jet truly felt unstoppable as he let out a devastating punch at the staggered Construct. The Construct dissolved around his fist, and Jet then stepped forward and slashed down at a Construct. He stabbed forward through another Construct and cut upwards through it.

Jet spun around on his back foot, putting his back to an incoming Construct who leaped up and was descending upon him. Jet thrust his sword behind his back, and it skewered the Construct in the air.

As Jet extracted his sword and turned around to face the Constructs again, Paladin's shouting distracted Jet for a moment.

"Jet! Find the generator!"

Jet turned to face Paladin, who was being swarmed by Constructs. They were crawling all over each other to get him as he slashed away endlessly at them.

"Generator?!" Jet called back in between cutting down Constructs.

"They keep coming, which means there must be a source! Something that's generating them!" Paladin shouted. "Find it and break it!"

Jet took a quick, searching glance around the room. He couldn't immediately see what Paladin might have meant. All he saw was the writhing mass of Constructs as they approached from all sides. The large warehouse seemed full of them. He glanced back and saw the second-floor office room from earlier.

"Okay, uh, cover me?" Jet requested as he tried to cut a

path to the office.

Jet quickly jumped up and planted his foot down on a Construct's head. He launched himself off, sending the Construct into the ground. With his next step down, he again bounded off a Construct.

Leapfrogging his way across the room, Jet used the Constructs to keep himself above them. An occasional sword from a Construct would swing up and try to cut him off at the knees, but Jet either moved too fast or would parry the blades with his own.

Once Jet reached the far wall, he saw the large windows that looked into the office. With all the strength he could muster, Jet leaped up high and covered his face by crossing his arms. He burst into the office, the sound of glass shattering echoing through the warehouse. Jet landed with one knee on the floor and one hand placed on the ground.

There was a hum of electricity, and Jet glanced to his left to see something he never seen before. In the mostly open room, there was a large, five-foot-tall cylindrical device glowing with green energy.

Three large triangular stands were affixed to the floor around the cylinder. Blue electricity crackled around the device, and connected by several cords to it was a waist-high control panel. The whole machine seemed to create a minor wind which blew through the room, but as soon as Jet took in as many details as he could, he noticed he wasn't alone.

Standing in front of the device was a tall man wearing a trench coat. His coat seemed to sway with the wind, and he took a few small steps around to face Jet. He shaved the hair on the sides of his head, leaving a small, black, loose mohawk blowing in the wind. His facial hair was untidy, scraggly, and shaved with a minor goatee around his mouth. One of his eyes was deep blue, while the other was pale white and glassy.

Upon seeing Jet, the man smiled slightly.

"Ah, I see," the man commented. "Another teenage pain in my side. And one trained by Paladin."

Jet stood up and stared at the man. He wasn't sure what to say to the stranger.

"Well, I'm not ready for a fight today, so I'll take my leave," the man said.

He turned back the device and outstretched his hands. There was a moment's pause, and then suddenly the green energy and blue electricity drained from the device and drifted towards the man.

Jet's eyes widened as the man inhaled sharply as the energy seemed to enter him until the machine's hum and the wind died down entirely. It sat there lifeless, and the machine's iron rusted rapidly before Jet's eyes.

The man walked to a window facing the outside of the warehouse, seemingly not giving Jet another moment's thought. Jet glanced from the man back to the warehouse, and he saw the Constructs all began dissolving into ash. Jet saw Paladin catching his breath, and then Jet turned back to the man.

"Wait!" Jet yelled at the man.

Paladin would want to know who this was, Jet figured. Even though this person outclassed him, Jet tried to stop him. The man didn't falter in his step, and seeing his words had no effect, Jet charged at the man from behind.

The man reached the outer window, but he turned to Jet, advancing. He grinned and then pointed a finger at Jet. From his finger, the green energy with blue electricity shot forth like a straight beam.

ZAZAP.

Jet brought up his sword in time and blocked the beam, but the force of it sent him flying backward. His back crashed into the window facing the warehouse.

It rattled Jet, and he slumped over a bit upon the impact.

He did his best to go back to a full standing position and look up at the man. The man waved his hand, and the outer window he was facing shattered into nothingness. The same energy that almost laid Jet flat glowed from the man's back, and suddenly two large, grey bat wings spanning the length of a tall person formed from nothing on his back.

Jet watched in awe, perplexed by what he was seeing. It totally knocked the wind out of him, but he still tried to ask.

"Are you Xanor?!" Jet shouted at the man.

The man peered over his shoulder at Jet for a moment. Then he turned to stare more properly at Jet, and his smile said it all.

"I am," he said. "But if you continue to get in the way, it won't be me you deal with next. Tread carefully."

The man pointed a finger again at Jet. Jet's eyes widened.

CRASH!

The window behind Jet blew backward into the warehouse as another attack launched Jet through it. He fell down from the second story and hit the base floor with a hard thud. His whole back ached with pain, and Jet coughed a couple of times involuntarily.

"Jet!" Paladin called.

Paladin rushed over to Jet's side, and Jet rolled over and pushed himself up. As much as it hurt, Jet felt it probably should have hurt more. Jet was up on his knees as Paladin reached him. His mentor knelt at Jet's level and took off his helmet.

"Are you alright?" Paladin asked.

Jet coughed and nodded, and he glanced back up at the warehouse. Xanor's words were so cryptic, he wasn't sure what to think.

"What happened up there?" Paladin asked.

With a short explanation later, Jet and Paladin were walking back out of the warehouse.

"I see, so he took the energy back out from the machine then," Paladin said.

"Is that what he does? He has machines that make Constructs. He has to put energy into them?" Jet asked.

"In a way. Chaos Energy on a good day is just unstable. He uses these machines to focus his Chaos Energy. Without it, he doesn't have proper control and can't maintain anything." Paladin answered. "At least after all my investigating, I believe that's how it works."

"Hence why you wanted me to destroy it," Jet said.

"Yes, it's why I try to get to where he builds them before he can take the energy back," Paladin said. "If I can destroy enough machines, his energy will be wasted. Slowly but surely, I can weaken him to a point where we can bring him to justice."

Jet stopped walking for a moment, making Paladin stop to look back at him.

"Why do you think he's sending the Constructs after me?" Jet asked. "Was there anything in here that would tell us why?"

Paladin shook his head and turned to face Jet more fully.

"No...nothing here would indicate why. In fact...all the Constructs seemed to target us equally. So, for whatever reason, he's programming individual Constructs to target you. That...or Xanor has nothing to do with it and there's a third player we don't know about."

Jet nodded in understanding, but then something else crossed his mind.

"What do you think he meant when he said to tread carefully? What would it mean?"

As soon as Jet asked, he saw a moment of concern in Paladin he never seen before. Paladin shook it off quickly though and walked back towards Jet.

"It'll be nothing you have to concern yourself with. More importantly, how do you feel?" Paladin questioned.

What did that mean? Nothing to concern himself with? Why wasn't Paladin answering the question?

When Jet failed to answer, Paladin elaborated, "The bad guy might have gotten away, and we might not have accomplished as much as we'd like, but you handled yourself well out here. You seemed to really understand your power and your skills. So after all that, how do you feel?"

The question distracted Jet from his earlier thoughts, so he pondered it for a few seconds. The fight was terrifying at first, but as soon as he reevaluated how to fight and began to truly battle, it felt amazing. He felt more alive than ever.

Analyzing his opponent's fighting tactics, using strengths and his opponents against them, and winning? It was the most fun he ever had. It was the moment he was waiting for all night.

"Honestly, like I've arrived," Jet said with a smile.

ISSUE 2 EPILOGUE

Paladin walked down the streetlamp-lit streets of Vinton suburbia. It was well after 11 p.m. by the time he returned Jet home, and the neighbourhood was asleep, paying no mind to the armoured figure walking in the middle of the road.

It was quiet and cold outside, with a nighttime breeze rustling his hair. His pace was a far cry from the heroic gaunt he aimed for before, when he was looking to inspire Jet. This was a slower, meandering walk, the walk of a man contemplating his decisions.

Was it too soon? Jet held himself remarkably well in combat, but his critical misunderstandings of what life was like in Vinton, besides his general impatience, made Paladin anxious. Could he keep Jet from getting in over his head? Should he?

There was no manual on how to train a sidekick.

However, Jet had such a heart in him. Such courage and goodwill. Such optimism. How could Paladin hold him back? Was he just being selfish if he did, preserving Jet's innocence? Or did Jet need to see the world for what it was, and either persevere and become stronger for it, or risk ruining the light in the boy?

It was why he so desperately dodged Jet's questions. No matter how much he knew Jet needed the truth, he couldn't bring himself to do it. Not if the truth about Vinton would destroy him.

Paladin heaved an enormous sigh, taking his helmet off. He rested it under his arm and glanced up at the night sky. What should he do?

The weight of being Vinton's last real superhero weighed on him in ways he never expected, but the weight of being this boy's leader threatened to sink him.

"You were never one for taking risks, Paladin."

Paladin recognized the voice instantly. Perturbed that he was snuck up on, Paladin didn't give any more ground by turning to face the man.

"I've always told you that you're taking the biggest risk of them all, Xanor."

Xanor stifled a laugh and shoved his hands into the pockets of his trench coat.

"What's your endgame for the boy? Make him a superhero? Have him bring down the gangs? You and I both know how this is going to go," Xanor said, his tone accusing.

Paladin knew what Xanor meant. They both saw so much death during the time they were active in Vinton. Whatever their disagreements, Xanor had always made sure no one directly died by his hands. Xanor was angry Paladin brought a teenager, a child, into this lifestyle. Then Paladin remembered the Constructs he spent years fighting.

"I could ask you the same thing," Paladin said. "All these years and you've been hunting him with Constructs. Why?"

Xanor's eyebrows crossed, but not in anger. In confusion.

"What are you talking about?"

"That boy has been hunted by Constructs since he was a

toddler. I've only just removed him from a Chaos Bunker where I kept him safe from your Constructs, and only because one finally found him. What's your game, Xanor?"

Xanor's eyes darted to the corners, visibly thinking. This made Paladin just as confused. Xanor was not one to lie either, and if he was confused, then something was seriously wrong.

"I have never sent a Construct after the boy. I didn't know he existed until tonight," Xanor finally answered. "Maybe it was someone else...I can look into it. But there have been a few times I've...lost Constructs."

"Lost them?"

"You know I have a psychic connection with my Constructs. But they are still simple beings. I merely point them at something," Xanor responded.

"Like me," Paladin shot back. Despite himself, a small smile came onto his face. For a moment, one marked Xanor's face as well.

"However, destroying the Constructs and returning the Chaos Energy to me severs that psychic connection. Unless something else happens, like something severs my connection or someone else takes control of them. I don't fully know how else to explain it," Xanor finished.

"So you're suggesting someone else has seized control of your Constructs and sent them after my sidekick?" Paladin asked, skeptical.

"Or someone else is making Constructs," Xanor replied. "Either way, I'm not the one trying to kill him. You are bringing him into this fight."

Paladin couldn't help but let out a sad laugh. All of his doubts and insecurities from moments before lay bare in front of him. As he thought of Jet, there was a small surge of confidence. A small light that his sidekick, his friend, lit in his chest.

"I think you'll discover he was going to enter this fight

with or without me. That's just who he is. All I'm trying to do is point him," Paladin remarked.

With that, Xanor let out a small scoffing laugh and turned away.

"Well, make sure he's aimed at me. Don't let the gangs get to him first," Xanor commented as he started walking away.

Paladin watched him go for several moments, a dull ache in his chest. He badly wanted to call out to Xanor, to remind him of who he used to be. But he could only muster a question.

"You know I will bring you down one day, right?" Paladin called after him.

Xanor paused, only for a moment.

"I know. And you and I both know what a mistake that will be."

ISSUE 3

FINDING HIS WAY

CHAPTER 11
FITTING IN

"Is this a dagger that I see before me, this handle toward my hand? Come, let me clutch thee. I have thee not, and yet I see thee still. Art thou not, fatal vision, sensible to feeling as to sight? Or art thou but a dagger of the mind, a false creation, proceeding from the heat-oppressed brain?"

Jet's English teacher, a shorter man who wore a suit jacket both days since Jet was in school for, read Shakespeare in front of the room. He was reading from his copy of the play, which was littered with sticky notes emerging from different pages. He closed the book and waited for several seconds as he looked out over the room.

"So? What do we think? We know this takes place just after Macbeth has murdered the king. We watched the stage performance a couple of days ago. For those who weren't here, he was hallucinating a dagger of some kind. What do we think this means?"

The room was silent. The dull hum of fluorescent lights reminded Jet of his tutoring in the bunker, and if it weren't for the thin windows, he might have thought he was back there.

Jet glanced around at his classmates. Some were heads

down on their desks, looking up at their teacher with half-closed eyes, while others were looking at their phones tucked into their laps. A select few seemed to reread the passage again, trying to look for clues.

With some hesitation, Jet put up his hand.

"Yes?" the teacher prompted while gesturing towards Jet.

"Well, it means he's feeling guilty, right? He feels guilty for having killed the king," Jet said.

The teacher smiled warmly at Jet and nodded.

"Yeah, absolutely he would be feeling guilty. Duncan, not a few scenes earlier said Macbeth was like a son to him, and so for Macbeth to do that for the promise of power, while at this point in the play when he's still feeling remorse, would absolutely weigh on him," the teacher agreed.

The teacher continued to talk, and Jet sat with the thought for a moment. He tapped his fingers against his desk for a few seconds before raising his hand.

"Yes?" the teacher asked, stopping his pace.

"Well, I know I just started the book yesterday, but I'm a little confused about something," Jet stated.

"By all means," the teacher prompted, sitting down on an empty desk and looking at Jet intently.

Jet swallowed, unsure why he was nervous.

"If this Macbeth guy is our main character why is, well why is he murdering the king? That's not very heroic of him."

There were a couple of awkward chuckles, some students thinking Jet was joking at first. Then they realized he was serious, and a few of them shifted in their seats uncomfortably. The teacher narrowed his eyes slightly at Jet and then stood up.

"Have you encountered the concept of tragedy before?" the teacher asked.

Jet scratched the back of his head and thought back to some movies he watched over the past few years.

"It's where something bad happens to good people, right?" Jet answered.

The teacher nodded and went to continue, but Jet interrupted him. "And then it works out in the end somehow, right? Bad people get their comeuppance of some kind."

The teacher unexpectedly laughed at this, making a few of the other kids laugh.

"Well, not to spoil the ending of a play that's hundreds of years old, but the bad guy will get his comeuppance in Macbeth," the teacher replied. "But, in most classic Shakespearean tragedies, what we witness is good people having bad things happen to them, or those good people doing bad things, and most result in them becoming tragic figures."

A blank stare met the teacher, who responded with a smile, raising one hand while lowering the other.

"With Macbeth, we witness Macbeth's star, which at the start of the play is high," the teacher continued. "And throughout, we watch his star fall farther and farther."

As he lowered the raised hand to emphasize his point, he lifted his other hand as he continued to talk.

"Meanwhile, we witness MacDuff's star rise throughout the play, to truly showcase how far Macbeth falls."

Jet sat back in his seat and folded his arms. The teacher saw something was still on Jet's mind, so he waited for Jet to process his next question.

"So essentially, the good guys become bad guys. That's what makes them tragic figures?" Jet asked. "That doesn't seem realistic."

A few in the class laughed, while others let out an awkward breath. The line of questioning was dragging out the lesson, and a few wished Jet would stop talking. Even though Jet didn't seem embarrassed, others seemed to suffer it secondhand.

"It's more realistic than you think, Jet," the teacher remarked. "You might be tempted to segregate people as good or bad, but Shakespeare shows us that the truth is seldom that simple. These tragedies, watching characters transform, serve as cautionary tales for the rest of us. In some, like Macbeth, it shows the dangers of ambition. Romeo and Juliet shows us the potential follies of lust. Othello is all about jealousy."

Jet's eyes went to his desk.

"Ultimately, we read these because, despite the tough language, Shakespeare shows us that our perceived lines between good and bad are just that. They are only real in the beholder's eye. And if we can acknowledge that, we can try to navigate murky waters and grow as people," the teacher concluded.

The class was silent for a few moments. A couple of students looked from Jet to the teacher and back again.

"Does that make sense?" the teacher asked.

Scratching the back of his head, Jet replied, "Kind of. You used a lot of figures of speech there, but I guess I'll put it together as I go. I'm down to learn more about this."

The teacher smiled and nodded in response.

"Good answer. That's what I like to hear," the teacher said.

The teacher then carried on with his original point, and Jet smiled. It wasn't the answer he was looking for, but he felt encouraged at the prospect of learning more about Macbeth. He wasn't sure what answers awaited him for the questions Macbeth was positing, but he was excited to find out.

It was a good thing Jet was back in school because he realized he quite liked it.

Jet walked into the cafeteria, ready for round two of trying to sit with students his age. The cafeteria was still wall to wall people, with the noise of various conversations carrying over the room.

Although smaller than the bunker's cafeteria, the number of tables, chairs, and people made the room feel bigger. There were distinct smells of warmed meals, fresh, and leftovers. Jet spied around the large room, trying to spot a free seat.

Finally, he noticed a free seat right next to Alan, who was quietly listening to a conversation between two other students. There was a girl on the other side of it who was chatting with some of her friends, but seeing an opportunity to make some new friends, Jet decided to just focus on Alan.

With an eager smile, Jet hurried over to the seat beside Alan. The circular seat remained open the entire walk over, making Jet feel very hopeful for a much better lunch than the day before. As he neared, Jet slowed down and swallowed any trepidation he had left.

"Hey man, is it cool if I sit here?" Jet asked.

Alan glanced over his shoulder to see Jet. For a moment, his eyes widened in panic, but then he caught himself and seemed thoughtful. After a moment's pause, Alan nodded and gestured for him to sit down. Jet grinned and moved to sit when suddenly a pair of girls' hands blocked the seat.

"Uh, actually I'm saving this for a friend," the girl on the other side said.

Jet stopped and stared at her. She had long black hair and blue eyes, but she was looking more at Alan than at Jet. It took Jet a moment, but he recognized her from his English classroom. Alan leaned back and peered down the row at her friends sitting next to her, which made Jet do the same. They were all mid-giggle, trying to catch themselves.

"Jen," Alan said, sounding skeptical. "I see all of your

friends sitting right next to you. Who are you saving the seat for?"

Jen shook her head slightly and rolled her eyes.

"It's a new friend. You haven't met her yet," Jen argued.

"Really," Alan said rhetorically, not believing her.

"Really, Alan," Jen said back firmly.

By this point, Jet took the hint.

"It's okay, Alan," Jet said dejectedly. "I'll catch you around."

Jet turned and walked away. His heart felt like it shrank in his chest. As he sauntered away, he overheard the girls talking about him.

"Is that the weird one from English who asked so many questions?" one girl asked.

"Yeah, oh my god, it was so annoying. Macbeth is bad enough, don't drag it out," Jen said back, attempting to sound quiet. Her voice carried more than she likely thought it did. Whether it was intentional, it still stung.

"Hey, wait," Alan said.

Jet turned to see that Alan was following him.

"Screw them. Let me grab my lunch, and I'll come to eat with you," Alan stated.

The idea warmed Jet quite a bit, but then he looked at the table behind Alan. All the girls and Alan's friends were now looking at Alan with raised eyebrows and apprehension. It gave Jet the impression they all thought Alan was crazy right for talking to him. The last thing Jet wanted was to bring the one person who was nice to him down with him.

"Nah, it's okay," Jet said. "I got a sweet eating spot, so it's all good."

Jet turned and walked away, one hand holding his bag lunch and his other in a pocket.

A few minutes later, Jet sat in front of his locker. He ate his lunch alone again, chomping away at the wrap his uncle made him. The wrap contained lettuce, salami, and cheese. But he didn't taste much of it. Even though the hallways were noisy and crowded as people walked by and socialized, Jet's world seemed quiet.

He glanced up from his lunch and sighed. It wasn't how he thought returning to high school was going to go.

CHAPTER 12

THE YOUTH OF VINTON

"You seem distracted," Paladin commented.

Jet shook his head. They perched atop a building overlooking the market district in Vinton. There were jewelry stores, high-class restaurants, and small fashion boutiques lining the street below them.

The glow of the streetlights and stores gave the district an almost ethereal feeling. It was relatively quiet, with not much street noise below them, leaving Jet trapped more in his thoughts than he realized.

"Ah, I'm fine," Jet replied.

He scratched the back of his head and peered up at Paladin. While Paladin was wearing the helmet, Jet sensed Paladin's gaze piercing into him. Jet shuffled uncomfortably as if to escape Paladin's eyeline. After being unsuccessful, Jet stood up straight.

"I'm just thinking about Macbeth. We've been learning about it in school," Jet lied.

Paladin nodded and looked back over the city. Whether he believed Jet, Jet couldn't tell. It prompted Jet to continue babbling in case Paladin didn't.

"Our teacher was talking today about how tragedies are all about the rising and falling of a character's stars, which didn't quite make sense to me, but about good guys can become bad guys and I had a hard time wrapping my head around it. Like that doesn't really happen, does it?" Jet asked.

This seemed to grab Paladin's attention more closely. He shuffled in his armour for a moment and then peered more intently at Jet. Jet looked apprehensively at Paladin, unsure of what Paladin was thinking.

"Jet...this is why I said..." Paladin said, but he caught himself. "It happens. It happens more than we like to admit."

Paladin stared at Jet for a few moments, and Jet's confused expression met Paladin's stone one like a wave of water over a rock.

"Xanor used to be a hero," Paladin said while turning his head back to the city. "A great one, actually."

"Really?"

"Yes."

Jet's eyes averted downwards, and his body slumped. It almost felt like a defeat at the moment, like Jet lost something. He couldn't place what it was, but it rattled him.

"What happened?"

"I'm not sure," Paladin said with a sigh. "He went by a different name before, Delta Man, I believe. And he even showcased a unique power set before, too. He would fly, possessed super strength and endurance. Classic superhero type."

Jet listened to Paladin talk wistfully about Delta Man, and couldn't help but think it sounded awfully familiar to Alpha's power set. He didn't have time to linger on it though, however, as Paladin continued to talk.

"But there are several rumors about why he changed his name and became a villain. Honestly, most of us wouldn't know it was the same man unless we saw him unmasked before. He never told us his identity, but we had a few maskless meetings with other heroes," Paladin continued. "The biggest rumor is he had a child and needed the money. He mentioned his wife was pregnant. But others think he snapped and wanted power."

Jet pondered the thought for a moment.

"I mean, however powerful he was, it sounds like there was more than just you back then. Why couldn't you guys have stopped him from controlling the city?" Jet asked.

There was an unsettling quiet, and then Paladin answered.

"For a while, he didn't. He just did the usual bank robberies and such. But then...well, he and the gangs struck a deal of some kind. Then Marath..." Paladin answered.

An uncanny chill ran up Jet's spine. The name struck a chord Jet couldn't have expected. A dark cloud entered Jet's mind. A boogeyman that existed in the shadows of Jet's conscience, something he didn't know was there before.

Before Jet asked, an alarm nearby went off. Both Jet and Paladin involuntarily jumped and turned their attention to the sound.

"It's time to be heroes!" Paladin declared, any sense of trepidation or fear in his voice gone. Back was the over the top bravado that still shocked Jet.

Paladin leapt from the rooftop, using perches and mounts on the wall of the building to scale down, using a lamppost as his final stepping stone to the ground. Jet chuckled to himself for a moment, still laughing at Paladin's hero persona. He then followed Paladin's lead, using the same ledges and the lamppost to reach the ground.

The alarm was coming from a jewelry store nearby, a block down the road from their location. Paladin and Jet dashed to the location, Paladin several feet ahead of Jet.

The jewelry store had a large lit sign hanging above its front entrance, which was covered with large front-facing windows and a glass door. The lights inside the building seemed to be dimmed; otherwise, the store would be a beacon on the side of the street.

As Paladin neared the shop, he skidded to a stop and peered more intently inside. He paused and waited for Jet to catch up, who much more ungracefully slowed to a stop, nearly tripping over his own two feet upon arriving. Jet glanced at Paladin and then into the shop, and back to Paladin.

"Jet, I want you to go in first," Paladin instructed.

Jet's widened in excitement and confusion.

"You sure?" Jet asked.

Paladin glanced down at Jet and placed a hand on his shoulder.

"If you want to be a superhero, you need the opportunity to make heroic entrances, and this will be a perfect chance to practice yours. There aren't too many in there; you'll be okay. I'll follow up if you need help," Paladin said.

Jet swallowed and eagerly dashed forward. It meant the world to him. Paladin trusted him enough to do something like this, to take on real bad guys without his help. It was a chance for him to test himself and to be the hero he always wanted to be.

With a tenacity that was building for years, Jet propelled himself forward. Not really thinking things through, Jet crashed through one window of the shop. He landed in a roll, trying carefully not to cut himself on the glass he broke on his way in. His mind raced, trying to think of the perfect quip, the perfect one line to say as he encountered the villains he was about to fight.

Name's Blade Boy, let me introduce you to my fist! Don't you dorks know that crime doesn't pay? For trying to rob jewels, I'm going to kick you in the jewels!

The last one made Jet laugh the most, so as he sprung upwards from his roll, he smiled and prepared to say it.

However, the words only got half out as he saw who was in the room.

The jewelry shop had a large glass display case running the perimeter of the room, with some space for sales associates to stand on the other side. In the middle was a smaller square-shaped glass display case with space for an attendant to stand and serve people.

Jewelry like necklaces, rings, watches and others all glistened brilliantly from the cases, and there was a pleasant, sanitary smell. On one side of the room there were three Brigand-appearing goons. They were wearing large shoulder pads with exposed circuitry, wires of various colours protruding out of the front, and the top of them. In their hands were obscenely large rifles of some kind, at least three feet long and thick as a tree log.

Across from them, standing between the jewelry and the wall, were two men clad entirely in tight black linen with katanas drawn. They were being standoffish, and the Eastern vibe they gave off made Jet realize they were Shinogi.

Standing between them in the middle display case with hands outstretched to both groups, was a figure clad from the top of its head to its very toes in a smooth, metallic-looking armour. They shone with a black matte covering most of their body, and they had a purple outline glowing outwards in a thick line along with the frames of the armour.

The form was lean and lithe, with a very circular head. They were shorter than Jet, and Jet got the impression based on their general build that they might have been a teenager. Their backs were to Jet, and upon Jet's crashing entrance, they swiveled their heads back to look at him. They had large, slanted green eyes illuminating outwards. Upon seeing Jet, the eyes narrowed slightly, and then their head glanced back to the two goons.

Jet didn't know what to say. Was there another superhero in there, in front of him?

After learning they were all gone, Jet couldn't fathom that one was in front of him. Mixtures of excitement, awe, and anxiety coursed through him. As usual, when those emotions swirled through Jet, he ran his mouth.

"Um, sorry, I didn't know this robbery was already spoken for," Jet commented.

"Don't worry," the figure said back. "It looks like there are plenty of bad guys to go around."

The voice sounded slightly hollow, like it was coming through a speaker, but Jet picked up that it was light and had a bit of a bounciness to it. It wasn't readily obvious from the armour, but this was a girl.

One of the Brigand thugs, who was bald with several nose, ear, and lip piercings, turned to another who was also bald but wearing skull face paint.

"Rex, what is this? I thought we were here to teach some Shinogi a lesson, not a bunch of brat kids," the one with piercings said.

"I don't know Ibsen. Maybe if someone didn't set off the alarm when we found the Shinogi, then we wouldn't have attracted the attention of super brats," Rex responded.

The two Brigands then looked to their third, who, for whatever reason, was wearing a gas mask. He looked from the Shinogi to the superheroes, to his comrades.

"What?" he asked, his voice sounding muffled by the gas mask.

"Stupid Flax," both Rex and Ibsen muttered as they readied their guns.

Jet stood up more properly than before, drawing the aim of the Brigand thugs and causing the Shinogi to angle their swords at him.

"Did...did you guys miss the memo? It's not the eighties anymore, your punk rock thug look is old, and actually is kind of offensive to honest, hard-working punk rockers everywhere," Jet commented while walking forward apprehensively.

Jet knew if he got them talking, he would better position himself to be an asset in the fight to come. Fortunately, it seemed like the girl had the same idea.

"Yeah, and nobody has thought about the Three Stooges in like a decade, so this whole routine is wildly outdated," the girl chipped in.

That drew forth an honest laugh from Jet as the three Brigand thugs all glanced at each other in a mix of confusion and a bit of insecurity.

"Ha! Nice. What's your name?" Jet asked as he continued to inch forward.

"Sting. You?"

"I'm Blade B...uh, you know what, just call me Blade for now," Jet responded, his name feeling awkward as it almost left his lips.

Jet was almost beside Sting, trying to position himself between her and the Shinogi as shuffled to the inner square of that display case. He didn't know what Sting was capable of, but the look of her armour gave Jet the impression she would be more capable of taking whatever those giant guns were packing. She even shuffled slightly to let Jet on that side, telling Jet he had the right idea.

"Enough talk!" one of the Shinogi yelled. His voice had a definite accent, however, unlike in some movies Jet watched with ninjas in it, his accent wasn't stereotypical enough for Jet to pick up.

"Do you really think the Shinogi were foolish enough to fall for your trap, Brigand?! We came knowing we would kill you and destroy your shield pads and rifles to send a message to your leaders. Bringing young heroes into the mix will not help your cause," the Shinogi shouted.

"Wow, monologuing now," Jet said quietly to Sting. "This is just an unfortunate day for stereotypes everywhere."

Jet made sure he said it loud enough for the Shinogi to also hear, once again drawing their attention.

"It'll take more than two teenagers to stop..." The Shinogi's words were cut short as the wall behind him exploded inwards into the shop.

The Shinogi leaped forward to avoid the rubble of the wall crumbling on top of him. There was the sound of cracking glass as stone and brick landed hard on the display cases, but nothing had broken yet.

Everyone in the room stared at the new hole in the wall—a remarkable feat, given its reinforced brick construction. As the dust cleared, standing in the hole was an unfamiliar figure.

Standing taller than Jet and covered in more medieval-looking armour was an imposing figure. Their armour was a dark shade of green, and it had gold trim running along the armour's edges and grooves.

The armour covered from the base of the neck down to below the waist, and it appeared heavy and stiff. There were thigh and shin guards, which led into grieves that had the same color scheme as the rest of the armour, but they were wearing a pair of light tan slacks underneath. They were wearing a helmet with a round top, but it didn't fully cover the face as a slit came just to cover the nose, leaving the rest exposed. In their hands was a giant, large silver hammer, with its handles almost the length of the wielder's body. The head of the hammer was the size of a watermelon and was circular; the front end was flat and the back end protruded into a spike.

They lowered their hammer toward the ground after swinging it downwards. With legs crouched, the figure stood tall to face the room. While they did that, they started talking.

"You criminals are done flaming this war in my city. Run back to your masters and tell them this is Siege's city now," the figure was saying, but it trailed off upon seeing Jet and Sting.

His voice was deep, but despite the tall and muscular stature, there was almost a nasally aspect to the voice. Jet finally got a good look at its face and saw that, much like his voice, its features were masculine but still developing. He was also a teenager.

Two superheroes? What was happening? Jet wondered to himself. Also, another who was likely his age.

"Siege, was it? Welcome to the party, nice entrance, very bravado-esque," Jet mentioned.

The face under the helmet scowled, a cross between annoyance and embarrassment.

"Never trying that again," he mumbled to himself.

The Shinogi backed up slightly, looking more apprehensive at the room. Even the Brigands got nervous as they swiveled the points of their guns between all the opponents in the room. Rex turned to Ibsen and made a head motion to back up. Ibsen stared at him in confusion, so Rex more vigorously tilted his head towards the shop's back entrance.

"What? You kidding me? We kill all these punks and will be made lieutenants for sure," Ibsen argued.

Before Rex could argue, a voice cut him off.

"Yeah, that's not gonna happen."

There was a clicking sound behind Ibsen's head, and he turned to see someone new standing behind him. Standing under six feet tall, this young black man was wearing a pin-striped suit with a fedora. He was wearing a blue scarf and a domino mask over his eyes. In each of his hands was a handgun, pointed at Ibsen and Rex.

It felt like Jet was in a fever dream. Four superheroes in one place, all around the same age, and all on the same side?

This was like a story he read from the 1960s about superheroes, when team-ups were common but also random. A deep-rooted joy sprouted within Jet. His superhero fantasies were coming true.

In the room there was a quiet pause, broken only when Jet spoke.

"Did anyone see him come in? Or am I the only one who didn't see him come in?"

The young man smiled, not taking his aim off Rex and Ibsen.

"I was going to watch and record for evidence, but since that's all shot to hell with the broken wall, windows, display cases, and presumably soon to be faces, I figured I would have some fun," he explained. He tilted his head back to reveal some of his features. "Since we're sharing codenames, I'm Hunter."

It was one of the quietest, most surreal moments of Jet's life. In less than a few minutes, the standoff between Brigands and Shinogi escalated to involve some kind of cybernetic armour girl, a medieval-looking knight, a noir-style detective, and him. Nobody moved; it felt like nobody breathed, lest a new combatant enter the room. When nothing happened, that was when everything else did.

Jet swore in the quiet moment before all hell broke loose. He watched a blood vessel pop in Ibsen's forehead.

Ibsen roared and spun around in a circle, firing his rifle at Hunter. Bright yellow and pink blasts launched from the rifle. Hunter dove out of the way while firing his own guns back at Ibsen.

For a moment, Jet was worried Hunter was going for the kill, but as the bullets hit Ibsen, a blue translucent field materialized, taking all the impact from the bullets. Ibsen seemed unfazed as the bullets fell to the ground.

On the other side of the room, one of the Shinogi jumped

into the display case and slashed at Siege. Siege blocked the attack with the handle of his hammer. The Shinogi tried a follow-up kick, but his foot hit the armour with a loud *CLANG!*

Siege grabbed the foot of the Shinogi and picked him up, swinging the man like a club into the display case, shattering glass and showcasing his awesome strength with a loud *KA-CRASH.*

The Shinogi recovered from the impact with a panting grunt and barely rolled backward out of the way as Siege swung his hammer down in what would have been a fatal blow. The attack missed, shattering the remains of the jewelry stand.

Surprised by the teenager who nearly killed him, the Shinogi grimaced behind his mask. It was all revealed to be feint, however, as in the chaos of broken glass and jewelry, Siege jerked the end of his hammer forward, slamming it upwards into the Shinogi's chin.

The Shinogi recoiled back, and dropping his hammer, Siege reached forward and grabbed the Shinogi by the sides of the head. To finish him, Siege slammed the Shinogi's head into his knee, knocking the assassin out cold.

"Some ninja," Siege commented.

As Ibsen fired at Hunter, he suddenly felt his gun pull away from his target. It flew out of his hands towards Sting, who had one hand outstretched towards the gun.

As it neared her in the air, she lowered her hand, and it dropped towards the ground, its momentum gone. Before she did anything else, Rex opened fire on Sting. Leaning backward, Sting dropped to the floor and dodged the blasts as she took cover behind the display case.

Planting her hands on the ground, she sprung forward feet first, clearing the display case and soaring across the room and kicking at Rex.

Sting's kick impacted Rex's force field with a *BWOM*.

She turned the recoil into a graceful flip, landing in a crouched low position. Rex took aim and tried to fire a blast from his rifle at point-blank range. Sting raised a hand in return, and as Rex fired, a bolt of green energy shot from Sting's hand with a crackling *BAZAP* sound into the blast from Rex's gun.

The two created a mini-explosion in the air, stunning Rex. As Rex tried to recover, he felt his armour being lifted off his shoulders. Rex yelled, but the armour spun in the air and landed back on his head.

WHUMP!

The weight knocked him out, and he collapsed to the ground. Sting lowered her hand, again having made that happen with her own movements.

Hunter landed from his dive and continued to fire at Ibsen.

BANG! BANG! BANG!

Ibsen spun back around to face Hunter, and with a growl, he closed in to attack him. As Ibsen neared, Hunter sheathed one gun and reached into his coat pocket. While he was doing so, Ibsen roughly picked up Hunter by his collar, lifting Hunter to his feet. Ibsen reeled back a fist to punch out the teen while he held him in place, but Hunter quickly slapped one of his hands over Ibsen's wrist, holding him in place.

"Gah, what the hell?" Ibsen demanded to know, and he let go of Hunter to inspect his wrist.

There was a small square device digging into his skin right where Hunter slapped him.

"One of my dad's inventions. A small, low-powered taser," Hunter explained.

Ibsen's eyes widened, and then suddenly a surge of electricity shot through him and seized his muscles. It was short but painful, and Ibsen panted.

"It's high enough to short-circuit electricity like force fields, though," Hunter mentioned, sheathing his other gun.

Ibsen's eyes narrowed as he thought about it, and then they widened again.

"Oh."

Hunter kicked Ibsen in the leg, dropping him to one knee. Ibsen tried to punch up at Hunter, but Hunter grabbed Ibsen's punch by the wrist and pushed it aside. With one hand still on Ibsen's wrist, Hunter pushed in on Ibsen's elbow and dislocated it with a disgusting *CRACK*, making Ibsen yell in pain.

Ibsen slumped over and looked up just in time to receive a brutal punch in the face from Hunter, knocking him out cold.

Jet, meanwhile, dashed forward as a Shinogi charged Sting while she somehow stole Ibsen's gun. He attempted to slash at her, but Jet interposed with his sword and blocked the attack.

The katana bounced off Jet's larger sword. Jet attacked with his sword, attempting to push the Shinogi off-balance, but the Shinogi spun around the slash. He stabbed at Jet, and Jet brought his sword in front of himself vertically and deflected the blow, just diverting the attack off Jet's cheek. Air burst past his face as the sword narrowly missed.

Jet swung upwards wildly, making the Shinogi jump back to avoid the long-reaching sword. Landing on his feet, the Shinogi was shocked to see Jet drop his sword and lunge forward with a fist.

BOOMF!

The punch hit the Shinogi hard, sending him through the glass of the display case with a crash and hitting the back wall of the store.

The Shinogi slumped against the back wall, and Jet closed in to make sure he was unconscious. As he neared, the Shinogi sprang forward with a slash aimed at Jet's neck.

Jet barely leaned back in time to avoid the slash, but it left him vulnerable as the Shinogi reversed his grip and stabbed his sword forward. For a moment, Jet thought it was all over when there was a sound of cracking bones and the Shinogi stopped mid-lunge, dropping his sword.

Siege stood there, his hammer lodged up in the Shinogi's torso.

"That's all your ribs broken," Siege stated to the Shinogi. "You'll live."

The Shinogi fell off to the side of Siege's hammer, and Siege shot a look at Jet. It reeked of disapproval for a moment, but then Siege's attention, like everyone else's, went to the last one standing.

Flax, who didn't move since the first shot, apprehensively stared at the four teenage heroes. With a bit of a cry, he tried to run away but didn't look where he was turning and crashed into the wall. The force field shot up, and he bounced backward, falling onto his back like a turtle.

"He's not going anywhere," Hunter commented while peering down at Flax.

There were a few quiet moments, and then Jet eagerly proclaimed, "That was awesome!"

Siege lifted a finger for Jet to be quiet and glanced at the other three heroes.

"Not here. There's a rooftop three blocks down, on top of a pizza place. Meet there," Siege instructed.

As the police rolled up, all they found were four unconscious criminals and one squirming on the floor, trying to wrestle with force field pads.

CHAPTER 13
MAKING FRIENDS

FIVE MINUTES LATER, JET VAULTED UP THE SIDE OF Michaelangelo's Pizza, unsure of what exactly he was going to find. He debated not going up, not meeting with these three strangers.

His experience with other teens earlier in the day already went poorly, and he feared isolating himself more. After trying and failing to find Paladin, Jet worked up the courage to meet the heroes he fought alongside.

Pulling himself up the neon red pizza sign, Jet cleared the side of the building with a graceful leap. The wind picked up, and the night was cloudy, causing a bit of a red hue to fall on the city from the light pollution. He landed and crouched down to brace his legs.

As he stood, he saw Siege, Hunter, and Sting standing in a half-circle, waiting for him. Jet scratched the back of his head awkwardly and approached the group. Siege stood with his arms crossed, while Hunter had his hands in his pockets. Sting stood with one hand placed on her hip, and she leaned her weight on that side.

"Sorry if I kept you guys waiting...I was looking for Paladin," Jet said.

"Paladin?" Hunter asked. There was recognition in his voice, but confusion as well.

"Yeah, I'm his...his, uh, his sidekick," Jet explained.

This drew mixed reactions from the group. Hunter's eyes widened a little, and he nodded. Sting stifled a laugh, while Siege stared at him incredulously.

"You're his sidekick?" Siege asked. "Do people still have sidekicks anymore?"

Jet felt his face flush red and regretted his choice to find the group. However, Hunter pointed a finger at Siege and chirped him back.

"I mean, is this legally 'Siege's city', or are you in the process of applying for a mortgage?" Hunter replied.

Sting couldn't stifle a laugh anymore and burst out laughing. Siege glanced at Hunter and Sting, and his whole body lurched slightly. A small smile found its way to Jet's face, feeling like someone had his back for the first time since leaving the bunker. With a sigh, Siege took off his helmet. Hunter and Jet both straightened in surprise while Sting fought to regain control of herself.

With his helmet off, Jet got a full view of Siege's face. He was definitely around Jet's age, maybe a little older. However, his head was shaved, leaving the thinnest trace of hair on his head. Siege rubbed his head, and Jet and Hunter exchanged looks.

"Look sorry man, you don't have to show us your identity," Hunter said. Siege waved a hand dismissively at him.

"It's fine. That whole, my city 'shtick' wasn't really me," Siege said. "I wear the stupid helmet only so they can't make out enough of my features."

Siege's eyes wouldn't meet the groups for a moment.

"It just kind of felt like what you were supposed to say, right?" Jet asked.

Siege glanced at Jet and then sniffed and looked away.

"Yeah, I guess so. At any rate, just stick with Siege. You don't need to know any more than that," Siege finished.

Jet nodded and then looked at Hunter and Sting.

"Actually, I think the only code name we don't know is yours," Sting pointed out, peering at Jet.

For a moment, Jet forgot he was even given a code name. As he remembered it, he rued sharing it.

"It's uh...uh...Blade Boy..." Jet mumbled.

"What?" Sting asked. "Say that again."

With a resounding sigh, Jet said more loudly, "...Blade Boy."

There was a brief pause before everyone laughed.

"Can't help you this time, man," Hunter said between laughs.

While Jet felt embarrassed, something about this laugh felt good. He was the butt of the joke, but he didn't feel like he was being made fun of.

"Well, I mean, I got an enormous blade. I'm a boy, so Paladin thought Blade Boy fit!" Jet argued, a small smile on his face. As the laughter continued, Jet pushed, "It's not like I had a choice in it! Or in this costume!"

That got a few more laughs, making Jet's smile grow. As the group got control back, Jet pointed at Sting.

"You're awfully content to just sit and laugh at us, but what's your story? Were you using telekinesis in there?" Jet asked, trying to shift the conversation away.

Sting let out the last laugh before settling herself back down. When she was calm, she outstretched her hand.

"Not exactly," she replied.

The three boys watched as the armour covering Sting's hand lifted into the air in small pieces. It revealed her brown skin, and as she rotated her hand, the pieces of her armour floated further upwards, some swirling in the air around her hand. She rested her hand back down, and the armour settled back on her hand, each piece shuffling back into place to reassemble the gauntlet.

"I don't fully know how to explain it, but this suit, this armour, they're like little robots and I'm their hive mind," Sting explained. "They help me manipulate magnetic fields, so if I'm close enough, I can move metal around. I can also glide, kind of, if I can find the right fields."

Jet, Siege, and Hunter stared wide-eyed at Sting. She looked at them, and even though they couldn't see her face past the large glowing purple eyes, Jet was pretty sure she was grinning at their dumbfounded expressions.

"What...how is that all powered?" Hunter asked. "That's some advanced tech to just have."

"Well, I don't just have it," Sting replied. "From what I can tell, it's powered by kinetic energy. So the more I move, the longer I can use it."

She glanced to the side. She extended a hand towards the edge of the building, and then suddenly a blast of green energy shot forth.

BAZAP!

It hit the edge of the building and blasted away a chunk of the railing, making Jet jump back slightly.

"Or, if I really feel like it, I can burn some of that energy to do that," Sting commented.

Jet didn't realize he was cowering slightly, his arms tucked into his stomach. Not really thinking about it, Jet raised a hand to ask a question. Realizing he wasn't in school after a moment, Jet shook his head and spoke up.

"So what happens if you run out of energy? And where do you get it?"

Sting shrugged her shoulders.

"I've been too afraid to find out, honestly. It's part of the reason I did this, to make sure I move around enough that I don't," Sting answered. She let out a sigh, and with her voice tired, she said, "I haven't really slept since...anyway, as for how I got it, I don't know you guys well enough to share that."

Although disappointed, Jet nodded in understanding. Sting then pointed at Siege.

"Okay, your turn," Sting commented.

Siege raised an eyebrow.

"What?"

"I just spilled my guts about what I do. What about you?" Sting motioned to Siege's armour and hammer. "I mean, you're a big-looking guy, but it takes more than what you're packing to bust through a wall like you did."

Siege gripped his hammer tightly and stared at it.

"We really doing this right now?" Siege asked.

"Doing what?" Jet asked in confusion.

"If we're going to be sharing this stuff, I think we need to set up some ground rules," Siege said. "First, we shouldn't share any personal information like names. We're safer if we don't know. Second, we should only contact each other or see each other for things related to...well, this kind of stuff."

Hunter crossed his arms.

"Contact each other?" Hunter asked.

Siege glanced at Hunter and then took a step forward. He grumbled a bit and rubbed his head.

"I don't know about the rest of you, but I know I stand a better chance against the hell this city can throw at me with backup. Now I'm not saying every time I go out here I want you guys tailing me, but if we know something is coming up, then, well, that just makes sense to me," Siege explained.

Jet's jaw dropped in excitement, and pumped his fists in the air.

"Do you mean like a team-up?!" Jet exclaimed.

Hunter smirked and hid a chuckle as Sting laughed outright again. Siege pointed a finger at Jet but refused to make eye contact.

"No, not like a team-up, just us working together occasionally. Emphasis on occasionally," Siege retorted.

Jet brought his arms down but looked at Hunter and Sting with a glowing red face.

"Guys, that sounds like a team-up to me," Jet commented.

"You're going to make me regret this, aren't you?" Siege asked, twisting his head slightly to glance at Jet.

Jet beamed at him, too excited at the possibility of being part of a mini team like this. Siege sighed and stood up straight. He held out his hammer far in front of him, displaying it to the group.

"Anyway, Sting there was correct, I am more than just muscles," Siege explained. "An order of knights trained me. They picked me up under the pretense of a boarding school when I was a kid. They gave me this armour and this hammer, claiming it was magically enchanted. The armour gives me super strength, and it's bonded to the hammer, which makes it easier for me to lift when I'm wearing it."

Siege retracted his hammer back into himself and rested it on the ground.

After scowling for a moment, he said, "But don't think I couldn't take any of you without the armour. I'm pretty fit underneath it."

Sting scoffed a little, drawing Siege's ire.

"Sorry, it was a very macho moment," Sting said. "Tell us more about how you're jacked."

Siege's glare softened a bit as he smiled, Sting's sarcasm well placed.

"Sorry, toxic masculinity is something I got from the order of knights. I'm still working on it," Siege replied.

There was a quiet moment where no one could tell if Siege

was joking or not, his tone not quite right for the statement he made.

"Toxic masculinity from something that was based in the 1500s? Nah, I don't believe you," Sting followed up with.

Siege nodded a head towards Hunter.

"What's your deal?" Siege asked.

Hunter let out a breath of air and reached into his jacket. He pulled out his two pistols and spun them in his hands with a quick flourish before letting them rest in his open palms.

"My dad was a policeman and then a detective here in Vinton, and he taught me everything I know," Hunter said. "The gangs had him killed a few years ago, but he left all his files and stuff to me, so I've been trying to pick up the pieces, see if I can bring down the gangs through the legal system."

He shrugged and placed his pistols back in his jacket.

"When it looks like I can't, I've got those. I've never used them lethally, but I know how to if I have to," Hunter said, his voice sullen.

There was a quiet moment where no one said anything.

"So, you don't have any powers?" Sting asked.

Hunter shook his head.

"I do what I can with what I've got," Hunter replied.

Jet was looking at Hunter's costume for several minutes, trying to discern why it bordered on familiarity. He knew he had never seen Hunter before, but there was something about Hunter's clothes Jet recognized. Finally, it clicked, and Jet snapped his fingers.

"You're basing your costume on The Spirit, right?" Jet asked.

Hunter turned to Jet, his eyes wide in surprise. Siege and Sting looked in confusion from Jet to Hunter, not sure what Jet meant.

"*The Spirit!* The old pulp comic by Will Eisner. I used to

read that in the bunker. I loved those comics! That's what you're going for, right?" Jet pushed.

Hunter laughed and went to respond, but the words were stuck in his throat for a moment.

"Yeah, actually," Hunter said awkwardly. "I didn't really think anyone else was into old Eisner comics."

Jet smiled and shrugged his shoulders.

"I read whatever I could get my hands on down there," Jet replied.

"First sidekick now, bunker?" Hunter prodded. "What's your story, Jet?"

Jet stopped and pondered the thought for several moments. With a smile, he put a hand on his hips.

"I guess mine is just getting started."

The four teens exchanged phone numbers, promising Siege they would only contact each other if they needed something superhero related. They then went their separate ways, Jet going back the way he came from, climbing up to the roof he and Paladin were perched on earlier. As he did, he found Paladin with his helmet off, scrolling through his phone.

"Hey!" Jet called as he saw him. "What happened to you?"

Paladin glanced up from his phone with a smile.

"Did you catch up with them afterward?" Paladin asked.

Jet nodded and walked towards his teacher.

"Yeah, we exchanged contact info and power sets," Jet replied. "In case any of us need help with something."

Paladin nodded and stood up.

"I saw that one in the black tech suit, and thought it'd be best to let you stumble into it," Paladin said. "I wanted to let you navigate the situation on your own."

Jet scratched the back of his head.

"Well, I did, I guess. I thought you said there were no other superheroes in Vinton, though. That you were the last one."

Paladin scratched the back of his head with a nod of acknowledgement.

"I should have been clearer…I'm the last I knew of. And the last adult one," Paladin explained. "I have heard rumors of some teenage superheroes, but I haven't had the time to track them down yet. It's lucky we ran into some of them, if not all of them, tonight."

Jet pursed his lips and looked out over the city skyline. Were there more kids like him out there? Others with powers who wanted to do good? How many were there and afraid to step up?

"Will you be cool with letting me patrol with them occasionally?"

Paladin appeared contemplative at that moment. With a sigh, he rested a hand on Jet's shoulder.

"I'm glad it looks like you have some friends now in the superhero scene, but let's say maybe for now," Paladin said. "I haven't seen quite enough yet to be okay with that."

Jet nodded in understanding, expecting that answer. Paladin turned and picked up his helmet and placed it back on his head. He headed back towards the city center, and Jet followed but lingered for a moment.

It was frustrating Paladin didn't trust him enough, but he was feeling a sense of elation about something else Paladin said. He had friends in the city. He didn't have them for long, and he wasn't totally sure they were his friends yet. But the possibility was there, and it filled Jet's heart more than he expected.

CHAPTER 14

LIFE CHOICES

Jet paced around the living room of his house, murmuring lines from Macbeth to himself while holding the book a few inches from his nose. He was trying to wrap his head around the language, but without the help of the notes on the sides of the page that helped translate it.

"Here's a farmer that hanged himself on the expectation of plenty? What does that even mean?" Jet commented to himself.

He was interrupted mid-stride as he crashed into an immovable force. He shoved the book into his nose by accident and took a step back. Quinn took the book from his hands and turned it over.

"Oh, sorry," Jet said sheepishly. "I guess I should watch where I'm going."

Quinn didn't respond right away. He simply started reading the passage Jet read out loud.

"It's Porter talking to himself. He's speculating if whoever is knocking is a farmer who killed himself, thinking that he was going to get more profit from his harvest that year," Quinn explained.

"Oh, that's dark," Jet replied.

Quinn passed Jet the book and walked into the kitchen. Jet watched Quinn and saw there was a chicken burger waiting for him on the table. Jet tossed the book onto the couch and followed his uncle.

"A lot of Shakespeare is," Quinn commented. "Except for his comedic plays, but even those have dark elements."

Jet scratched the back of his head and sat down at the kitchen table, not really sure what to think. All he knew was there was a chicken burger with lettuce, onions, and ketchup for toppings, and it had his name on it. Jet snatched it up in both hands and took a big bite.

"You know, there's something to be said about expectations," Quinn commented. "How have the first few nights of super-heroing been?"

Jet paused mid-chew, a piece of onion falling out of his mouth. He stared wide-eyed at his uncle, trying to gather his thoughts. With a hard swallow, Jet stared off to the side and considered his answer.

"It's been good, really good. I've been getting into some pretty sweet superhero brawls and stuff. Met some other teens last night who were cool and had neat powers and stuff," Jet responded.

There was a quiet pause, and Jet continued to eat his burger. Quinn smiled a little and then ate his burger. A few bites in, he paused again.

"Has it been what you expected?"

Jet slowly stopped eating. He placed his burger on the plate in front of him and crossed his arms. With a sigh, he glared at his uncle.

"No, it hasn't been," Jet replied.

"Is that a bad thing?"

"I don't think so. Meeting those other kids last night was fun, and I enjoy the fighting part of it, but I guess...I don't feel like I've saved anyone yet, you know? Like I'm fighting other people's battles," Jet answered. "I guess being a superhero would involve actually saving people."

Quinn nodded. He put his burger down and looked at his nephew.

"Yeah, that makes sense to me," Quinn answered. "But this city... it's all wheels within wheels. There's so much going on below the surface all the time that it's hard to make an impact that has a surface-level impact."

Jet and Quinn looked each other in the eyes, and Jet saw the fear in Quinn's eyes again. However, Jet understood it better, having seen more of the city. He could empathize with it, but it still upset him.

"It shouldn't be that hard, though," Jet remarked. "People should be able to see what's right and want to do the same. That's why people become superheroes, right? To set that example."

"Everyone has their truth, Jet," Quinn said.

There was an unsettling silence following as Jet contemplated what Uncle Quinn said, and why he said it. Was Uncle Quinn that scared of the city? So frightened by it he couldn't even stand up to it in the safety of his home?

It made Jet wonder, and he was ashamed to, but he wondered if his uncle was a coward, or was the city that bad? Was it saveable?

"So...Jet. What subjects are you enjoying in school so far?" Quinn asked unexpectedly.

Slightly rattled by the change in topic, Jet scooched around in his seat for a moment. One terrible squeak later, Jet took a bite of his burger and contemplated.

"Well, math and chemistry are fine. They're just boring. Gym is kind of tough because I have to hold back or risk giving away my superpowers...but I kinda like English," Jet responded.

"Yeah? Why's that?" Quinn continued to prod.

"I like the stories, I guess. Reminds me of reading all the news articles about superheroes and stuff, except they're different. But there are also similarities?" Jet rambled. "I don't know-it just gets me thinking about stuff."

Quinn smiled warmly at this and took a chomp out of his meal.

"So, do you think you would want to do something with English if..." Quinn's voice trailed off, visibly hesitating. Jet raised an eyebrow in confusion, and then Quinn let out a sigh and finished, "If the superhero thing doesn't work out?"

Jet rattled his head around on his neck.

"What do you mean? How would being a superhero not work out?" Jet asked, an assault on all of Jet's preconceived beliefs.

"I mean...it's good to have a fallback, another dream to fall back on if the first isn't what you thought it would be," Quinn responded, his eyes refusing to meet Jet.

When Jet noticed this, his eyebrows narrowed. While Jet was not the most observant, Quinn was hardly the most subtle.

"You don't want me to be a superhero?" Jet asked.

"It's...it's not that, Jet, it's more that..." Quinn tried to explain.

"I spent five years in a bunker, not here, to train to be a superhero, and you want me to throw it all away?" Jet asked angrily as he stood up at the table.

"Jet...no, just wait a moment..." Quinn tried to interrupt.

"Being a superhero is all I've ever wanted! It's what I've always dreamed of! And now that I'm almost there, you're telling me you don't want me to be one? How is that fair, Uncle Quinn?" Jet yelled at his uncle.

"Because I don't want to lose you too!" Quinn snapped.

Discomfort nestled on both their shoulders like a heavy

blanket. Jet's mouth was agape, staring at his uncle. Quinn still refused to gaze him in the eye.

"I'm sorry. I don't want to keep you from your dreams. I would never do that. But how am I not supposed to be worried about you? How am I not supposed to be scared I would lose my last living family?" Quinn quietly asked.

With this, Jet's eyes went to the table. Quinn was his dad's brother and took Jet in after his parents died. It was always just the two of them until Paladin came along. Jet didn't always stop to think about what his departure meant for Quinn.

But giving up, of trying a different path, still burrowed deep into Jet's skin. He couldn't give his uncle what he wanted. Not after that.

"I'm sorry too, Quinn," was all Jet could say.

Jet grabbed his plate, cleaned it off in the sink, and went upstairs to prepare for patrol with Paladin. All without saying another word. Quinn sat at the table motionless for several minutes until wiping away a tear.

CHAPTER 15

LEGIONS OF XANOR

QUINN'S WORDS RANG IN JET'S EARS AS HE PERCHED on another nearby rooftop. Jet and Paladin typically started their nights perched heroically on rooftops. While Jet admitted it felt very cool, it also bled into his thoughts on the matter. Why did they spend so much time doing this?

There was so much more he felt like he could be doing.

That night they were in the Rat's Nest, an incredible run-down part of downtown. The wind was stronger than usual—the first signs of autumn truly nestling in. The Rat's Nest was even quieter than other parts of Vinton because of its general lack of population, but the smell of garbage was far more present. Jet remembered the smell of burning tires the first night he was in the Rat's Nest, the poignant stench stinging his nostrils. It made him think of how many things changed since then.

"Jet!" Paladin practically shouted.

Jet shook himself out of his trance and glanced at Paladin. Paladin was staring at him, and even though the helmet was on, Jet sensed the intensity.

"Did you hear a single word I said?" Paladin asked, his tone curt.

Jet looked back with wide eyes, and then his facial expression quickly turned to one of shame.

"No, I'm sorry, Paladin. I was distracted," Jet replied.

"I've noticed," Paladin replied. "I'm worried about your focus. If I can't trust you to be focused out here, then I'm not sure if we…"

"No, no, I'm good, I promise," Jet responded, cutting off Paladin. "It's just been a lot with…school and stuff. Lots of new stuff to take in."

Paladin eyed Jet for a few moments, but then let it go.

"Alright…well, what I was saying is I finally have a lead on Xanor's base of operations. However, we need to act fast or he will move it," Paladin explained. "It's five blocks from here, and when we near it, we have to act fast to destroy his Chaos Energy containers. This could be our one chance to destroy them and his energy for good."

"Oh wow," Jet commented. "No wonder you were upset that I was spaced out. This could be huge."

"Exactly," Paladin responded.

He walked towards the edge of the building and pointed.

"We're going to head in that direction. It's an old water treatment site," Paladin said. "We'll need to move fast and be silent. As soon as he knows we're on the way, he'll store up his energy and leave again."

Paladin turned to Jet.

"This might be the most important thing we do. If we can stop Xanor's power source, that'll get the Constructs off of you, and let us tackle some of the other issues the city has been having," Paladin explained.

"Like the gangs?" Jet asked.

Paladin paused and took his time answering.

"Maybe, we'll see," Paladin answered.

He said nothing more, and before Jet asked, Paladin leaped from his perch.

"Come on!" Paladin shouted.

Jet shook himself and hurried to keep after Paladin. The two leaped from rooftop to rooftop, speeding along the night sky like a set of blurs. Jet could just see the water treatment plant in question. It was a block away when a scream caught Jet's attention. Jet screeched to a stop and turned in the direction he heard it coming from, just behind him.

He heard the scream again, and Jet hesitated for a moment. Paladin was already almost at the water treatment site, and Jet wouldn't be able to get his attention without a lot of noise. The scream he heard was one of terror, and Jet couldn't ignore it. Someone may be injured or threatened.

Paladin could handle Xanor, Jet figured. He would save whoever was screaming. Jet dashed back toward the source of the sound.

The scream faded, and Jet couldn't quite pinpoint anymore where it came from as Jet descended onto a lower rooftop. He focused on his hearing and heard a burst of small laughter coming from a nearby alleyway. It sounded mischievous, and Jet had a feeling in his gut that was where he needed to go. Jet hurried to the alley and peered down to see a woman on the ground and three men who were approaching her.

Jet didn't hesitate for a second. There would be no time for banter, no time for a pre-fight quip. He didn't know if she was already injured, but he refused to risk causing her more harm. Jet descended from the roof, vaulting off a fire escape to slow his descent, and kicked down hard.

WHAM!

Jet easily toppled one thug.

The other two quickly turned to see Jet, but Jet sent one sprawling with a left hook, and kicked the other in the torso. The thug went flying backward and landed in a pile of trash, the sound of garbage clanging, punctuating the impact. Jet quickly assessed the situation. Jet looked at the three thugs and saw that they resembled Brigand gang members, though they lacked some of the tech Jet was used to seeing.

He turned to the woman, who had long blonde hair and was wearing, peculiarly, a red dress. Maybe she was going for a night out? Jet thought to himself. Jet walked over to her and extended a hand as he crouched down.

"It's okay, you're safe now," Jet said to her.

Her long blonde hair covered her face, but she turned slightly towards Jet. She lithely reached for his hand, hers covered with a long red glove reaching to just below her elbow. Jet helped her to her feet but still couldn't quite see her face.

"Are you okay?" Jet asked.

She nodded slightly enough for Jet to see, and then Jet turned back to the goons. The one he descended upon was writhing on the ground, feeling for his head. Jet grimaced slightly and then walked towards him.

"Sorry, that's probably a concussion. I mean, that's probably not as bad as what you were about to do to this lady," Jet commented. "So I'm not really that sorry. I should work on my entrances, though. I could have caused a lot more damage if I wasn't careful."

Jet glanced up at the alley and saw a homeless person across the street who was staring at him. The nagging thought about the woman's dress returned. Why was she dressed as if she were going to the opera if she was in the Rat's Nest? Something didn't add up.

As Jet realized this, he suddenly felt a tight line wrap around his neck. Jet instinctively reached for it, and suddenly a surge of energy surged through Jet, causing his muscles to seize and contract.

ZAAAAAAAP.

He involuntarily fell to his knees and strained.

"You know, when we were pitched the idea of trying to bait one of you young heroes, I didn't think it would actually work," the woman said.

Jet sputtered and strained. His mind commanded his arms to let go of the line and grab his sword to cut the line. But he couldn't. He gripped the line so tightly that his nails felt like they would tear through his gloves and into his skin.

"But here we are, one junior hero later," the woman continued. "I guess I win the prize for staking out the Rat's Nest."

The tightening line yanked Jet onto his back. He struggled to fill his lungs, and panic set in. He started being dragged back to the woman, his legs kicking out in a futile attempt to stop himself.

"You young optimists always want to fix all the bad things in the world, all the things you see as a problem," the woman said.

Jet could see her from his upside-down position. She held a red line in both hands, and Jet saw her face. Her chin was angular, and her eyes bright. She was wearing makeup that brightened her features, and Jet could tell even in his extremely pained state she was classically beautiful.

"The thing is, little hero, I like those problems," she said. "They're good for me and good for business."

She reached under her dress, pulling out a long red dagger. Jet coughed, trying to let out a cry for help. But Paladin wasn't anywhere near, Jet figured. Paladin was probably half-way to stopping Xanor. Again, as in the bunker, he was on his own. Jet needed to find a solution. Jet thought of only one thing, and he wasn't sure if he could do it.

It took all his willpower, but Jet shut his eyes and forced himself to let go of the line. The energy still seized through him, causing his body to spasm. Jet did his best-possum impression. It took a few seconds, and the energy stopped flowing through the line.

"Really? You're not even going to let me enjoy it?"

The line slacked a bit, and that was all Jet needed. Jet spun on the ground and kicked up onto his feet. He dragged the woman forward, but before reactivating the energy, he grabbed his sword and cut the line. Jet gasped for air and reached for his neck. It was hot, and he sensed a few cuts around his neck. But he was still alive. The woman's expression went from surprise to one of amusement.

"Oh well then, you have some fight in you," the woman stated.

"Oh, I've got enough to take you down," Jet commented through gritted teeth.

"Really?" she asked with a raised eyebrow.

Jet perceived behind him a clicking sound followed by the whir of energy. He checked over his shoulder. The three goons he knocked out were back on their feet, and in their hands were large energy rifles, trained on Jet. He turned back to the woman in red.

"Whatcha want us to do, Cassandra?" one thug asked.

Cassandra, the woman in red, smiled.

"Well, I suppose I can't have all the fun. Just don't miss and hit me," Cassandra instructed.

One goon fired at Jet's feet. Jet jumped out of the way, the discharge of the rifle causing a loud *BOOM*, followed by a second explosion as it hit the ground.

Jet planted his feet against the wall and launched himself towards the first one who fired. With a slash of his sword, Jet cut the rifle in half, and then he jabbed forward at the thug with his hand. He hit the thug in the neck, causing him to gasp for air.

Dodging another rifle blast, Jet spun and charged forward at the shooter. The thug's rifle was primed, and Jet shot forward with a hand. The barrel of the rifle lifted, and a blast fired into the night sky.

FOOM!

Jet then kicked the thug in the knee and brought the pommel of his sword across the thug's face.

WHAM!

Just as the thug dropped, Jet heard a rifle discharge. He didn't have time to move again, and he brought his sword up to cover his body.

FOOM BOOM!

The blast hit his sword and sent Jet flying back into the wall of the alley. He hit it with a hard crash, denting off stone and brick. Jet then fell to the ground.

Between the line of energy that attacked his body and the blast, he didn't have much strength in his body. Jet strained to stand but found he couldn't. Cassandra walked over to him and lifted his head ever so slightly so he could peer her in the eyes.

"Well, you had more fight than I thought," she commented. "But it wasn't enough to take me down."

She reached back for her dagger when a sudden crashing sound caught her and Jet's attention. They both turned to notice the third thug, who Jet was hit by, suspended in the air by the collar, in Paladin's grip.

"Step. Away," Paladin instructed.

Cassandra smiled smugly and took a step back.

"Well, this junior hero has a senior one looking out for him. Adorable," she said as she backed away from Jet.

She sheathed her knife back under her dress and took a few more steps back.

"I'll keep that in mind moving forward that this one has some red tape," she said.

There were several tense seconds as Cassandra smiled slyly at Paladin. Jet couldn't help but wonder why she looked like she was still in control with Paladin right there.

"But you know what will happen if he causes too much trouble, don't you?" Cassandra asked.

There was a long pause from Paladin.

"I do."

With that, Cassandra turned and walked out of the alleyway. Paladin watched her for a few moments before kneeling and helping Jet to his feet. Jet's whole body ached. His muscles felt like they were on fire after the energy coursed through his system. The blast didn't hurt that badly, but more to the point, it knocked him over, which proved to be the tougher part to get over.

"Thanks, Paladin..." Jet said, but Paladin held up one finger and cut Jet off.

Paladin's whole body heaved with angry huffs. Jet eyed around nervously, not sure what was about to happen.

"Not here. Roof. Now," Paladin instructed.

A moment later, Paladin stood with his arms crossed and his back to Jet as he gazed at the water treatment plant. Jet looked around apprehensively, not sure why they weren't back on their way to Xanor's lair.

"Shouldn't we be going?" Jet asked.

"He's long gone, Jet," Paladin said quietly.

His voice was low, but it was trembling with an anger Jet hadn't heard before. Jet was more confused than scared at the moment.

"Did he know we were coming?" Jet asked.

Paladin dropped his arms to his side, and he looked over his shoulder.

"He did," Paladin said, and then paused. He turned as he

finished saying, "He did, the moment there was a plasma blast that fired off in a nearby alley!"

Paladin practically roared at Jet. His anger, his disappointment. It was like nothing Jet had ever seen before. Jet for a moment felt himself cowering, but then he thought back to what made him make the decision, and he stood back up tall.

"Look, I screwed up the plan, and I'm sorry, but I thought someone was in danger," Jet said. "Isn't that why we do this?"

"We do this because we try to save the most people we can," Paladin said back through gritted teeth. "And tonight, the way to do that was to stop Xanor from summoning an army of Constructs. Now we've lost that chance."

"Then," Jet tried to say, patting his hands against his sides. "We stop the army when they come. We can do it. We have the other teens, and we're awesome; we can do it when it happens!"

"You don't get it!" Paladin shouted. "Those were Brigand goons. I was okay with you going up against them last night because you got to meet some new people, but we need to pick our battles with them. Now not only do we have Xanor to worry about, but the Brigand also has a target painted on our back as well!"

"What about the Constructs targeting me?" Jet asked. "Aren't I in constant danger already, anyway?"

Paladin was silent for a moment, breathing in and out.

"I don't know," Paladin remarked. "However, we can keep ourselves safer by ensuring we're picking our targets better. And The Brigand isn't a safe target."

Jet considered Paladin's words for a few moments. At a fundamental level, he understood what Paladin meant. That would make life harder for them, and more dangerous. But something didn't sit right.

"So?" Jet asked.

Paladin reeled backward in shock.

"What if that was an actual mugging tonight?" Jet asked. "What if someone's life were in danger? Would you still be telling me I did the wrong thing?"

Paladin stared at Jet for several moments. He took off his helmet, and Jet saw how red Paladin's face was. His eyes burned with a fury Jet never seen. Jet felt a tug in his chest.

"Aren't we supposed to be superheroes?"

Paladin's fury lightened slightly, and he stopped glaring so hard at Jet.

"Jet, when I said in the bunker you don't understand this city...this is what I meant," Paladin explained. "Sometimes stopping crime is the wrong thing to do. It can have repercussions you can't understand."

"Stopping crime is the wrong thing?!" Jet shouted. "Make me understand these repercussions, Paladin, because if I'm not out here to be a superhero, what the hell are we doing?"

Paladin raised a hand, and Jet felt his voice trapped in his throat.

"Enough, Jet, enough," Paladin said. "We're not going to get anywhere else tonight."

Paladin turned and glanced back towards the water treatment facility.

"You're benched," Paladin said.

"What?!" Jet cried out.

"I should have done it earlier tonight. You're not focused. Your focus has been lacking since our first night out. You're not ready," Paladin continued.

"I...but," Jet tried to argue.

"This isn't forever," Paladin said. "We were just too early. I should have let you adjust to school life first before dragging you out to this. Give it a week, and we'll try again."

Jet wanted to argue and fight with Paladin, but he felt so

small. He felt like Paladin, like the city, was crushing him. As if he didn't even have a voice to fight back with.

"Go home," Paladin said. "You know the way. I'll speak to you in a few days."

Jet gripped his fists in anger. But he turned away from Paladin and left. He couldn't hear Paladin's sad sigh as he did.

ISSUE 3 EPILOGUE

"WHAT ARE WE GOING TO DO WITH HIM?" PALADIN asked over the phone.

Quinn was in the dark, sitting in his recliner facing the end table and the window, which he hadn't moved from in almost an hour. His dinner still sat unfinished on the table, and after Jet left that night, Quinn slowly walked over to his chair and sat, where he contemplated his words with his nephew.

Paladin called a few minutes earlier, and Quinn left his phone on speaker, letting it sit on the armrest of the chair.

"I don't know," Quinn replied. "He's young and eager, but he's so unafraid that he's going to get himself in trouble."

"My thoughts exactly," Paladin sighed. "Do you think you can make sure he stays home the next few nights? I don't want him to get any bold ideas."

Quinn glanced at the table sitting beside his chair. Sitting there was a picture of him and his younger brother, Richard, on Richard's wedding day.

Richard was taller than Quinn. He had grown past him in high school. He was also skinnier than his chubbier older brother, his features lean and narrow, but still built with a solid frame. His hair was black and wavy, much like Quinn's.

Jet got his brown hair from his mother, Valerie. Everything else, though, he received from his father.

Richard was always more of the risk taker between the two, always the one more ready to go on an adventure and take a chance on a stranger. He had a way of seeing the good in opportunities, in people. Whereas Quinn was cautious, Richard seemed more carefree.

Quinn was always envious of his brother for that, his ability to shine a light wherever he went. His brother's death extinguished a bright light in Quinn's life until Jet arrived, and it dragged Quinn out of the dark.

"I don't know if I can do that," Quinn quietly commented.

There was a long pause on the phone, where Quinn imagined Paladin scowling at him.

"I can't stop him from being who he is, Paladin," Quinn said. "I can try to push and prod him in the right direction, but I have let Jet be who he is."

"What happens when that has consequences, Quinn?" Paladin asked back.

Quinn's gaze went back to the picture of him and his brother. He inhaled through his nose and out through his mouth.

"I'll talk to him, Paladin. I can't promise more than that," Quinn said.

Quinn heard Jet stomping his way to the front door. Quinn quickly hung up on Paladin and listened as Jet swung the front door open with an angry force. He heard Jet mumbling angrily under his breath and realized how mad he was through his breathing. Before Jet stormed off to his room, Quinn called after him.

"Jet. Just come here for a minute," Quinn said.

There were a few brief angry huffs before Jet walked into the living room proper. He sat down hard on the couch, ripping his mask off his eyes as he looked at his uncle. Quinn saw how red his nephew's cheeks were, how bloodshot his eyes were.

"I just spoke with Paladin..." Quinn began.

"Great," Jet interrupted. "So now you think I'm a screwup too for trying to help people? Wonderful!"

To this, Quinn leaned forward and more addressed his nephew.

"That's not what I think," Quinn quickly said. "I think you have a heart of gold in a city made of rust."

This caught Jet off guard, and he relaxed more fully on the couch.

"This is just a setback for now," Quinn continued. "Paladin is our expert superhero, and we must trust what he says. So please, for your sake as much as mine, take him seriously. You'll be back out there before you know it."

Jet frowned, but nodded and stood up to go to his room. Quinn wanted to say 'love you buddy,' or something along those lines, but the words got stuck in his throat. For the third time, he looked at the picture of him and Richard.

"Miss you, buddy."

ISSUE 4

BREAKING RULES

CHAPTER 16
DIFFICULT REALITY

As his math teacher droned on about the quadratic formula, Jet stared into space in the classroom. He was still feeling angry and raw about being benched the other night.

It was two nights ago, and Jet still couldn't think about anything else. Everything he was supposed to have learned that day went in one ear and out the other. There was only static interference in his brain stemming from his frustration with Paladin, making it hard to concentrate on anything.

As Jet saw it, he still did nothing wrong. Yes, he fell into a Brigand trap. However, he genuinely thought someone was in immediate danger. Shouldn't it have taken priority? Wasn't being a superhero about helping as many people as he could?

That was what Alpha used to say, and Jet wanted to live his life by that mantra for as long as he could remember.

So he spent the last two long days at school. While Jet enjoyed the school part of school, going to classes and learning new things, he could admittedly do without the homework. What made it so excruciating, however, was that he still felt like a social pariah. Jet did not know that spending five years in a bunker would make him out of touch with his peers.

He was even placed in a few group projects, but he felt like his suggestions and input went unwanted. Comparatively to other students, they would at least acknowledge Jet existed. Jet had a hard time looking forward to the day, knowing he didn't have patrol in the evenings and he was going to feel ostracized during the day.

He didn't notice Alan glancing over at him, looking confused. Jet was normally so vocal in the classroom, asking questions, but in this case, Jet didn't say a word. In the absence of sound, it was like there was a black hole where Jet sat.

There was a sudden break in the fog around Jet's mind as a booming voice came in over the school's intercom. Jet nearly fell out of his chair in surprise as everyone in the room popped into motion.

"LOCKDOWN, LOCKDOWN, LOCKDOWN!" the voice called out.

Jet watched around the room as students got out of their chairs and moved towards a wall. There was a profound sense of resignation that overcame the room. Unsure of what to do, Jet hesitantly stood up, following Alan.

"Lockdown?" Jet asked quietly.

Alan nodded and motioned for Jet to follow as the teacher began walking to the door of the room.

"Yeah, they're pretty common. I'm surprised one hasn't happened yet since you got here," Alan commented.

"Why is it happening?" Jet asked.

"Usually, the convenience store down the road is being robbed or shaken down by Brigand. Sometimes it's..."

The rattling sound of gunfire cut Alan's sentence off outside the window. The entire mood of the room shifted to panic and fear as everyone who had been meandering to the wall suddenly broke into a sprint.

Students hit the floor, sitting in crouched positions, some holding one another. The teacher broke into a dash towards the door, quickly scanning the hall before slamming it shut.

"Sometimes it's a lot worse," Alan muttered.

Jet sat with his back to the wall, looking out at the window as he heard screeching tires, gunfire and sirens erupt from outside. His mind was spinning with the cacophony of noise and motion, unsure of what to think. The teacher quickly joined the students along the wall, and Jet couldn't help but glance around at his classmates. Everyone's faces showed intense fear, mixed with another emotion. Almost a familiarity with what was happening.

"Has this happened before?" Jet asked.

"A couple of times...this school year," Alan sighed quietly. Alan bent his knees close to his chest and rested his arms on them.

Jet looked from the window of the classroom to Alan.

"Has anyone ever gotten hurt?"

Alan's head slumped downwards.

"My first year here...yeah. A stray bullet went through a window," Alan responded.

"Did they..."

"No...no, they lived," Alan said. "But they're in a wheelchair for life."

Alan sniffed and glanced away from Jet.

"Some other schools haven't been so lucky."

Those words hit Jet hard, but he could tell Alan no longer wanted to talk. He didn't know. How could he know? He spent five years in a bunker. All that time, things in Vinton got so bad that students were afraid to be in school?

Jet sensed a tug to go out there and do something about the crime that was no doubt taking place outside the school.

He knew he couldn't. If he did, there would be questions from the authorities, or the Brigand might seek retribution from a very public action. He wasn't sure how he would do anything about it.

As he glanced at the faces of everyone in the room again, how could he not do something? How was it possible for someone with his power to do nothing?

Jet lay in bed, staring at the ceiling. Darkness fell, and Jet didn't bother to turn any lights on. He told Quinn he was going to bed, but truthfully, he wanted to be left alone. So he lay fully clothed on top of his sheets, his hands behind his head, and his right leg crossed over his left, which was bent at the knee.

On a Friday night, most teens would be out with their friends, seeing a movie, or getting into trouble. Jet realized he wasn't a normal teen, despite the lack of super-heroing over the last few days. Instead, Jet thought about earlier in the day. Back to the chaos and fear the lockdown created.

He loathed his inability to change what occurred. He couldn't have stepped outside to stop the crime. That he lacked the means to make those students feel safe. It ate at him that his classmates were in peril. He had the power to do something.

But he was benched. He wasn't allowed to go out and fight crime. Paladin was his mentor, his leader, and even if he was mad at Paladin, he wasn't about to defy him in broad daylight. The longer Jet lingered on the thought, however, the more he wondered why he couldn't. Paladin wouldn't give him a good reason not to go out and save people.

Everything Paladin said was about stopping Xanor, but would stopping Xanor really do anything about the gangs?

They seemed to be the ones causing the most harm to everyday people. As Jet debated for the moment about going out and trying to make a difference, the thought occurred to him that other than going out and trying to stop crime when it happened; he had no way of knowing when it was going to happen. He would only cure the symptoms, not the disease.

Jet sighed and scratched his nose. He was uncertain about his next course of action. Listen to Paladin, who may know better, or try to make a difference. He felt stuck. It was like he left one bunker to be in a metaphorical one.

Just then, his phone buzzed. Jet wasn't used to the sensation of receiving a text, so it stunned him. Regaining his senses, Jet reached into his pocket and pulled out his phone. Unlocking it, Jet gazed at his phone screen to see he received a text from Hunter.

> Hey. Got the scoop on a Brigand shakedown happening tonight. I texted others. Meet at the jewelry store from last time in 30? Let me know.

Jet stared at the text for a long time. The idea excited him, but he was benched. He wasn't supposed to go out on patrol without Paladin.

However, Paladin also didn't have to know, Jet figured. The realization sent guilt down his spine, but Jet also didn't spend five years training to make one mistake and not use it. Jet looked at his floor and saw the costume. Quinn also thought Jet was asleep, so he wouldn't worry about him.

Jet glanced back at his phone. Teens on Friday nights got into trouble with their friends, right?

CHAPTER 17

BREAKING CURFEW

Jet punched out a Brigand goon, sending him crashing into a computer keyboard, then the floor. Jet spun to dodge a baton from slamming him, letting it crash into more computer equipment.

With a flick of his sword, Jet sent the baton flying out of the thug's hand. Jet kicked the thug back, making the thug stumble. Siege grabbed the thug by the back of his collar and slammed him into a table.

Siege turned and grabbed a thug who approached him and tossed him back out the window of the one-story building. Behind Siege, a thug tried to sneak up on the tall teen, but Hunter promptly bashed him in the back of the head. Before he collapsed, Hunter grabbed him by the neck and used him as cover as a thug tried to swing horizontally with a baton.

The baton slammed into the thug's torso. Hunter let the body drop and then lunged forward at the thug who attacked him, grabbing his wrist. He forced the baton into the thug's torso, shocking the thug into unconsciousness.

Hunter tossed the baton up into the air, and it suddenly flew towards Sting. Sting ducked and let it fly past at a thug who raced towards her. It hit the thug square in the forehead, and he collapsed mid-run.

Sting fired her energy blasts at the roof, dropping some rubble on the thugs, who took cover behind some desks and were readying guns. They let out guttural groans of pain. Sting turned as one more thug ran towards her, but Jet ran in and swung his sword with the blunt side of his blade. Jet baseball batted the thug into the far wall of the room, sending him crashing through several rows of computers.

The group caught their breath, all the Brigand soldiers who were stealing computer equipment from a local start-up out cold. Jet looked at Sting and then at the other two. The adrenaline was still coursing through him, and he scratched the back of his head.

"Are there any other sites being hit up tonight?" Jet asked.

Hunter chuckled and exchanged looks with the group. Siege and Sting both nodded with a shrug of their shoulders. Hunter took off his hat for a moment and rustled his curly hair.

"Yeah, I might know one."

The group stopped two more raids that night, the next one another Brigand one and the final one being a Shinogi one. The gangs didn't stand a chance against the combined might of the four teen heroes. There were no gang members with special powers or technology that enhanced them to prove a real challenge. The lack of it didn't make it any less fun for Jet, as by the end of the night he felt more fulfilled than he did any other night that week.

After midnight, the group except Hunter sat on the edge of a rooftop, looking over downtown.

"That was awesome!" Jet exclaimed. Sting sat on his left and Siege on his right. Neither responded right away, and Jet glanced between the two of them.

"Was it awesome or am I just that lame?"

Sting laughed a little at that and looked at him.

"It was a little awesome," Sting replied.

Siege grunted a little in response and folded his arms.

"We don't do this because it's awesome. We do it because it's right," Siege said.

Sting glanced at Siege and moved her head around as if she were inspecting him.

"Hey, Siege, is it cold?" Sting asked.

Siege didn't respond right away, but after a moment, he furrowed his brow. He seemed confused by the question and looked back at Sting.

"What?"

"I'm wondering if it's cold up there on your high horse," Sting followed up.

"Ha! Burn!" Jet laughed.

For a second, Siege appeared even more disgruntled, but the smallest hint of a smile appeared on his face. Sting then looked to Jet, and even though her entire face was obscured, Jet sensed the incredulity coming off her.

"Burn? Who says that anymore?"

Jet shrugged his shoulders in response, his cheeks turning slightly red.

"I dunno, I've watched a lot of That 70s Show DVDs while I was in the bunker," Jet replied.

Before anyone else could say anything, Hunter approached the group from the back.

"Wow, you sass literally everyone, don't you?" Hunter asked.

The group turned to see Hunter with two bottles of pop in each hand. He walked over to sit next to the group.

"No one is safe from the wrath of Sting," Sting replied cheekily.

Hunter sat down and passed out glass bottles of soda.

"What are these for?" Jet asked as he eyed his bottle.

"I figured we could celebrate all our victories tonight," Hunter said. "Thanks to us, the gangs are going to have a harder day tomorrow."

Hunter looked out at the glow of Vinton with pride.

"We keep it up. Each day for them will get harder until they don't have a tomorrow," Hunter said.

There was a quiet pause as everyone contemplated that optimistic thought.

"That was kind of a dark way to say that," Jet commented. "You made it sound like we're going to kill them."

Hunter nodded his head with a chuckle, realizing his mistake.

"Yeah, next thing you know, Hunter will be the next mob boss of Vinton," Sting chipped in, drawing laughs from Hunter and Jet.

Siege was mid-drink, and the comment made him choke. This made the others laugh at Siege harder. When he finally stopped coughing, he acknowledged the group with an indignant smile.

"Shut up, shut up, shut up," Siege instructed.

They stayed there for over half an hour, chatting about their nighttime adventures. Jet wasn't sure he had ever laughed like he did that night talking with the four. Between Sting's snark, Hunter's non sequitur comments, Siege's grumpiness, and Jet's own ignorance, the conversation flowed into many laugh out loud moments.

Jet didn't get home until after one in the morning, sneaking quietly into bed. He planned to sleep in as late as he could. He knew he would need to get as much rest as he could because they made plans to do it all again the next night.

CHAPTER 18

A NEW ROUTINE

On Saturday during the day, Jet worked on homework and watched television. Saturday night, Jet and his new friends stopped a Brigand attack on a Shinogi safe house, raided a Shinogi warehouse for information, and handily defeated a Brigand force who were trying to rob a bank.

On Sunday during the day, Jet watched more television and went shopping with his Uncle Quinn. Sunday night, Jet and his new friends fought against a Brigand platoon that was in a shootout with the police and stopped an assassination attempt by the Shinogi on a politician.

Before Jet could really think, he was back in school. His foot tapped incessantly all throughout the day, knowing that in the evening he was going back out again. One of his classmates, who sat beside Jet in math, leaned over to him.

"Hey, would you mind stopping that?" he asked as he pointed at Jet's foot.

Jet realized what he was doing and stopped.

"Sorry," Jet whispered.

A few moments later, it picked up again. The student audibly groaned, and for a moment, Jet felt the weight in his chest again. However, he could push past it more easily than before as he thought about his weekend and his plans for the night.

School continued as normal for the rest of the day. Jet was excited about class but looked down upon by his peers. Jet threw himself entirely into his classwork and the lectures. He knew the next day he needed to deliver a presentation on Macbeth. While it was an assignment to do in pairs, Jet opted to do it alone. As the class all worked away on the assignment, chatting in their pairs, Jet sat alone, writing his presentation.

That night, after eating dinner, Jet stood up from the table. He hurried to the sink to scrape his dish and started cleaning up after dinner. Quinn watched Jet with a raised eyebrow, confused about what was happening.

"Gotta work on my presentation for tomorrow. I'll be up in my room, then I'll be in bed! Night!" Jet said as he hurried out of the kitchen and up the stairs.

Quinn watched his nephew depart and shook his head. For a moment, he contemplated what to do, thinking Jet was likely disregarding his instructions from Paladin. Whatever Jet was up to, he seemed happy. Quinn wanted to let that last a little bit longer.

"Teenagers," Quinn said to himself with a small smile.

***

"Alright, for real, it's a school night, so I can't be out as late," Jet said to the group.

"You still go to school?" Siege asked.

"You don't?"

Siege shook his head.

"The Order advanced me through. I earned my high school diploma last year," Siege commented.

"Nice," Hunter chipped in, who was overseeing a building

with binoculars. "I'm doing mine online. I'm still about a year or two out."

Sting walked over to Jet and patted him on the back, a little rough.

"I'm in the same boat as Blade Boy over here," Sting chipped in. "Though I'm usually up late anyway."

Hunter quickly let out a low whistle, interrupting the conversation. The other three walked over to the edge of the building and saw two big black armoured trucks pull up.

"How about we go to school with them? Eh? Eh?" Jet asked the group.

The three of them all groaned. In the next fifteen minutes, they capably dispatched the Brigand raiding force.

***

"So, while I'm still not at the end of the play, we can see early on that Macduff is an important character in the play because he is the one to stand opposed to Macbeth. Already from where we are, his role is more and more prominent, especially as Macbeth has targeted him," Jet said, reading off his notes.

The class stared at him with vacant eyes, uninterested in what he had to say. This made Jet tremble, feeling extremely self-conscious. However, one quick glance at his teacher revealed he didn't need to be, as he watched with a finger to his chin inquisitively. Jet swallowed and kept going.

"See, to quote our teacher, we're watching as Macbeth's star falls, but Macduff's is rising to replace his. That, at least, is my theory for the ending of Macbeth," Jet finished.

The teacher nodded and walked forward, causing a few of the students in the room to snap to attention.

"Excellently done. You supported your argument with some good points," the teacher said. "I have one question for you. If Macbeth is our main character, what do you think will happen with Macduff finally confronts him?"

Jet pondered for a moment and shrugged his shoulders.

"They all go for ice cream? Or gelato? Gelato is big in Europe, right?"

The comment made the teacher laugh, and despite most of the students rolling their eyes, a couple also chuckled.

Jet received back a math exam he aced on the Friday of the week before, passed the fitness test in gym with unsurprising flying colours, even though he had to hold back from breaking the equipment, and received a high grade on the lab he did in chemistry.

The next day at lunch, Jet sat alone while he ate. He got used to the idea of eating alone, but he was currently flying high on his success in school and his nighttime crime-fighting to let the loneliness get to him.

However, as he took a bite, someone suddenly sat down next to him by his locker. Jet glanced over to see Alan joining him for lunch. Alan passed Jet a chocolate bar from his lunch kit, which Jet looked at in confusion. Alan sighed for a moment and gestured for Jet to take it.

"For saving me, those few weeks ago," Alan said.

"I mean, Alan, I didn't do it to be..." Jet said.

"Just take the stupid chocolate bar," Alan instructed with a small smile.

Jet smiled back and took it from Alan.

"So what's it like being a superhero?" Alan asked.

Jet stared wide-eyed at Alan for a moment, but then remembered he had first met Alan by saving him on the street. He even excitedly told him he was going to have a costume, so it wasn't too surprising that Alan pieced at least some of it together.

Jet smiled and took a bite of the chocolate bar as he pondered the question.

"It's fun. I mean, not always fun, but I find it fun," Jet responded with a mouth full of chocolate.

Alan looked to the ground for a moment, lost in thought. His mouth opened and closed a few times, as it appeared as if he was trying to formulate a question.

"Do you...find it tough at all? Knowing what to do and when to do it?"

Jet stopped chewing for a moment and pondered the question. It felt like it was the very thing he was wondering ever since he left the bunker, if he and Paladin were truly doing the right thing then, and if he was doing it with his friends. There wasn't a simple answer.

"Well...yeah, I guess. But lately I've been doing what felt right. I don't know if we're making a difference, but it feels like it," Jet replied. "So I'm going to keep at it until I know otherwise!"

Alan nodded in response, the cogs in his mind visibly turning. Jet watched him for a moment and felt a sudden need to pay Alan back for the chocolate bar. He tried to offer him a grape from his packed lunch, which Alan politely declined. When Jet awkwardly tried to offer him the entire bag of grapes, Alan let out an incredulous laugh.

CHAPTER 19

EVERYONE'S TRUTHS

By night, Jet was the costumed crime-fighter Blade Boy, battling crime in the city of Vinton. By day, Jet was a slightly eccentric high school student. Jet wasn't sure which identity he preferred, but for the first time in his life, Jet was thrilled with the direction his life was going in.

On Wednesday night, the four teens rested after stopping another drug trade near the Rat's Nest. As per tradition, they were drinking from glass bottles filled with soda Hunter picked out for them. Jet, Hunter, Sting, and Siege sat on a nearby rooftop of the convenience store.

From their perch, the wind was calmer than on the usual peaks of the skyscrapers, and they looked out and saw the large high-rise buildings of downtown Vinton. The lights in some buildings appeared like little stars dotting downtown, and there was only the occasional sound of traffic. They were sitting quietly for a few minutes before Hunter broke the silence.

"So, is this what you expected?" Hunter asked.

"What do you mean?" Jet questioned.

"Being a superhero. Going out on patrols. Fighting bad

guys. All those years in the bunker to think about it. Is this how you imagined it?"

Jet sat and contemplated. It was the same question Quinn asked roughly a week ago, and Jet wasn't even more unsure of his answer. He was flying high with how well everything was going lately, but he couldn't deny there was still a bit of a knot in his stomach at the question. His mind went to conversations he had with Paladin, to the conversation he had with his Uncle Quinn, the school lockdown, and then to the countless gang members they had battled that past week.

"I dunno, I guess? I didn't expect so much...bad."

"Bad?" Hunter asked with a tilt of his head.

"Like, there's us. We're the good guys, and we're trying to help people. But here in Vinton, we're pretty outnumbered, and there are a lot more people trying to take advantage of everyone else. Bad people," Jet remarked.

It made Jet think about Macbeth in a lot of ways. There were so many villainous characters and only a handful of good characters. Something that he once said was unrealistic was becoming a reality for him.

"I guess I didn't think there would be so much bad. I thought there was more good."

Siege snorted at this and shook his head.

"You're figuring out how the world works."

"What's that supposed to mean?" Jet asked with a raised eyebrow.

"These bad people, as you call them, they see us as the bad people and themselves as the good ones," Siege said, still staring out at the city.

He took a small drink from his soda as Jet looked at him. Sting looked from Siege to Jet and, seeing he was visibly confused, bumped Siege in the shoulder with a hand.

"Dude..." Sting muttered to him.

"But, but they're doing the bad things. The things we all

know are bad," Jet said, somehow entirely missing that interaction between Sting and Siege. "I spent years in a bunker, and I know it's not socially acceptable to blow up the city."

Jet continued to stare wide-eyed at Siege. Siege looked from Jet to Sting and rolled his eyes. After letting out a slight sigh, Siege turned to Jet and elaborated. For the first time since meeting Siege, Jet noticed he was trying to keep his patience in check, as these resigned revelations came from Siege.

"Look, you've watched a lot of movies, right? That's what you said?" Siege asked. Jet nodded, so Siege continued, "Everyone's life is like their own movie. They all have their own narratives, where they're the star. Sometimes bad things happen to them that put them where they are to do bad things, or sometimes they're born that way. But they're still the star of their story. People or ideas that get in the way or disagree with them are the villains in their stories. That's the way it is."

"That's kind of a cynical way to look at it," Jet replied.

"Why? Are you not the star of your story?" Siege replied. "I'm the star of mine. Hunter is the star of his and Sting, hers. It's human nature. Here in Vinton right now, we've reached a boiling point where these stories are clashing to create these conflicts that need people like us."

Jet considered Sieges' words for a few moments. Sting sighed and looked at Hunter, who shrugged his shoulders.

"Well, guys, maybe it's time..." Sting tried to interject, but Jet interrupted her, addressing Siege's last comment.

"I mean, you're not totally wrong. I guess I see myself that way, but I think there's more to it," Jet responded. "Maybe these people who I call bad guys are just people who get in my way or disagree with me and they're not bad guys...I think they've reached a point where they're so desperate that force is the only way to stop them from hurting others."

"That doesn't sound much better," Hunter chipped in.

Jet conceded with a nod and then said, "Maybe there is a better way, but I think to assume that's how people operate is to sell them short of what they are capable of. Maybe people need to learn how to listen again, to have empathy for other people's stories. Remember that we aren't so different."

There followed a long silence. Hunter glanced back at Sting, seeing her entire form almost decompress. Hunter narrowed his eyebrows in confusion, but he turned to see Jet place his bottle beside himself and fold his hands together.

"It's probably harder than just beating the bad guys up, but if we can turn bad guys into good guys, isn't that worth it?" Jet asked.

Hunter laughed and then stood up and cracked his back.

"Well, that's the problem right there. It's this us vs them mentality you two both have," Hunter remarked.

Jet and Siege both turned to regard Hunter.

"Take it from a black guy who has been dealing with being a black guy his whole life. Dividing people into different categories, white or black, good or bad, it creates this duality which breeds conflict," Hunter explained. "As long as you treat people differently because they fit into a different category than you, you're unintentionally creating the conflict."

Sting turned to glance up at Hunter for a moment. She let the armour peel away from herself, revealing her brown skin, and just examined her own hand for a moment.

"Sure, that's probably an oversimplification because I can't speak for everyone, and everyone's story is different, like you said Siege. Viewing people who differ from you as only that, differing from you, will always get you off on the wrong foot. There's common ground everywhere," Hunter continued.

Hunter sat back down, draping one leg over the side of the building while tucking one knee in closer to his chest.

"Just treat people like they're people," Hunter commented.

Jet and Siege looked over the side of the building for a few more moments. Sting let the armour reform around her hand, but she remained silent.

"It makes it harder to do what we have to do when everyone is a person," Siege said, a hint of sadness in his voice.

Jet let out a little smile at this and shook his head.

"No, I think if anything, that makes it easier," Jet argued.

"How do you figure?"

"Because it makes defending the people who can't defend themselves easier because they're people too. Whether the people we have to fight are people, sometimes whatever their story is, however they got there, they're able to do harm to others, and they need to be stopped somehow. We must do what we can in that situation to save the people who can't save themselves," Jet said. "Sometimes if that means providing some empathy to the guys threatening to do something bad, then that's what we do."

"You going to listen to the bad guys into submission?" Sting asked.

"If there's a risk of someone innocent being hurt, I won't hesitate to crack a jaw or two. And I'll admit I find it fun," Jet said with a sheepish smile. "I enjoy fighting. If, for example, I can help people to learn to empathize with someone different, I'll also try my hardest."

"Isn't that why we dress up like superheroes? Aside from the whole secret identity thing. To be better? To help encourage and inspire people to be better than what they are?" Jet concluded.

"I'm wondering if it's maybe people who aren't superheroes who need to step up," Siege responded. "Maybe it's ordinary people who need to be setting this example better."

Those last words sat with Jet as the four peered over the city they called home. The four remained silent for several moments, considering the moral quandaries. For a moment, the four enjoyed being in each other's company, teens of a similar spirit who were struggling to find their place in a city intent on tearing them apart.

"Man, I have watched Breakfast Club and Fast Times before, but I never knew how good it felt to have a deep, meaningful conversation at three in the morning with buddies," Jet commented, completely ruining the moment.

Hunter laughed out loud as Siege groaned. The two got up and walked away, Siege muttering under his breath about the immaturity of Jet and working with amateurs and about how they weren't friends, while Hunter continued to laugh. Sting waited for a moment, her eyes locked on the city. With a sigh, she stood up and followed the others.

Jet shrugged his shoulders and gazed up into the night sky.

"Well, I thought it was meaningful. And it is three in the morning, so whatever," Jet commented to himself. He then stood and followed the three others, leaving the Vinton nightlife to glow ominously.

CHAPTER 20

THE FINAL WARNING

Jet walked home from school a few days prior, having learned a route which only took him about twenty minutes to get home. It weaved through several back alleys, over a bridge, over the top of a highway, and through an elementary school field near Quinn's house.

A bright blue sky stretched overhead, windless and still, allowing the late summer heat to soak into the earth. Quiet was the norm on his journey home, so Jet often talked to himself to stay entertained. Jet was walking through the field with a little pep in his step, shuffling his feet while singing a little song to himself.

"Blade Boy and the awesome friends...fighting bad guys until the end...! Blade Boy is the coolest one...he's their number...one?" Jet stopped singing for a moment but continued his little shuffle forward. "Can I rhyme one with one? Is that allowed?"

A sudden chilly wind bristled through Jet.

"Your little dance is the only thing that shouldn't be allowed here."

Jet nearly jumped out of his pants at the voice, spinning

around mid-air and turning to face the source of the voice. Behind him, with his arms crossed, was Xanor. Jet immediately turned from scared to determined as bent his knees and curled up his fists.

"Pretty low ambushing me here without my sword, but don't think I'll go down without a fi..."

Jet caught himself as a thought dawned on him.

"Wait...do you know who I am?"

To this, Xanor smiled, but not with a hint of malice. It was more bemused, introspective. Like a warm memory crossed his mind.

"It wasn't hard to figure out," Xanor explained. "None of your friends are doing an excellent job of hiding your identities. If the gangs really put their minds to it, they would figure it out too."

Jet allowed himself a quick grimace, but he caught himself and stood tall once more.

"So why not take us out where we live, huh? Since we've been taking the fight to the corruption in this city's heart and beating it back...isn't that why you're here? To take me out?" Jet spat at him.

Xanor snorted with a laugh.

"You're sounding like him, you know that?"

"Who? The guy who's about to kick your butt?"

"Paladin."

Jet froze. He didn't stop to think about it, but 'beating back the corruption in this city's heart' was certainly a Paladin expression. He hadn't seen Paladin in weeks. What brought that on?

"And no...I'm not here to take you out. I'm here to talk. To give you one final warning," Xanor explained.

"Final kind of implies there was a first warning," Jet commented. "Unless sending Constructs to kill me counts as warnings, but that's kind of an aggressive warning."

Xanor stuck his hands in the pockets of his trench coat. He glanced over at the field. An elementary school with yellow and red brick walls and a red roof was located down the hill from them. Xanor gazed at it for several moments, and although he was trying to remain stone-faced, Jet could see something in his eyes. Maybe a hint of regret or longing.

"I didn't send those Constructs after you," Xanor calmly said. "But they were mine. Someone took them from me."

All of Jet's defenses dropped. He stood up fully and stared at Xanor.

"I...huh? What?"

The man turned to acknowledge Jet and took a step forward.

"I know you and Paladin believe I sent them after you, but I did not. I never have. Someone else has hijacked my Construct's programming and sent them after you. I don't know why, but my best guess is to get you out in the open," Xanor explained.

"Who would want me out and kicking names and taking butts-I mean, wait, kicking butts and taking names?" Jet stuttered. "That seems like a dumb plan."

Xanor conceded with a small nod.

"Unless that's what they wanted. They wanted superheroes to make some noise in the city to draw him out," Xanor continued.

It took Jet a moment, but the distant expression in Xanor's eyes reminded him of when he had seen it once before in Paladin's eyes. It was when he had talked about an individual whose name escaped Jet at that moment.

"Who is this...him? Paladin has mentioned him before... uh...Mary...Martha..."

"Marath," Xanor completed for him. "Before Marath showed up, Vinton was a fairly normal city. There were superheroes, supervillains, and organized crime. About five years ago, Marath joined the Brigand. Everything changed."

"You're telling me one guy turned Vinton into a dystopia?" Jet questioned incredulously. "Nuh uh. I don't remember Vinton as being perfect, but it takes more than one dude to scare the entire city stupid."

"You've never met Marath. And if you're not careful, you will," Xanor stated. "This is your last warning. Stop interfering with the gangs, or he will come for you next."

With that, there was a flourish of the black and gold dust behind Xanor. The giant batlike wings sprouted from his back like they had back at the factory. Before he could take off, Jet had one more burning question.

"Why do you care? Aren't you Vinton's premier supervillain?"

Xanor stared hard and long at Jet for several seconds. Without another word, his wings flapped mightily and Xanor took off into the sky. Jet watched him leave, more confused than when Xanor first arrived.

Xanor seemed calm, almost peaceful. There was no menace or malice in his approach. That did not match the description the nightly news wove about him. Nor the first night he saw Xanor in the warehouse, where Xanor almost appeared demon-like. This seemed to be a middle-aged man who was worried about his safety.

Jet thought back to what Paladin told him. Xanor was once upon a time a superhero. He had turned heel and become a supervillain, but for reasons Paladin didn't divulge. Could there still be some good in Xanor somewhere?

"Treat people like they're people," Jet commented to himself, remembering Hunter's words.

Jet was determined to treat Xanor like he was the scum of the earth, but Xanor warned him of an impending danger. Maybe there was more to him than Jet realized.

Or...it all could have been part of a more elaborate play. Maybe the gangs were getting frustrated with his and his friends' progress dismantling them, and Xanor was sent with a story of a boogeyman to scare them away from it. Jet wasn't worried about some phantom that seemed to have scared everyone else.

Jet smiled and nodded, firmly believing that no one person could make a city a worse place to live. The optimist in him believed only people acting selflessly had that kind of power... some kind of guy named Marath didn't have it.

All these adults were afraid of genuine change, and it was a change Jet planned to bring. With his friends at his side, there was nothing Jet couldn't do.

ISSUE 4 EPILOGUE

The last of Xanor's Constructs faded to dust as Paladin sheathed his sword. At Paladin's feet lay the Construct Pylon, slashed to bits by his sword.

Paladin glanced around the room, a tight corridor of boxes, shelves, and windows placed high on the wall. He finished battling through the wave of Constructs in the large room over, and he battled his way through the warehouses' back alleys to find the Construct Pylon.

As Paladin examined the surrounding room, he realized what a sneaky maneuver this was on Xanor's part. By hiding the pylon and making Paladin search for it, it could generate more and more Constructs every time he destroyed one. This created the illusion of more Constructs in the warehouse, and thus more Chaos Energy being stored, than there really was.

But why? Paladin wondered as he retraced his steps. Was it just to keep him busy one more night?

Paladin destroyed several Construct Pylons in the past week, and he noticed the number of Constructs guarding them was less and less.

Was Xanor running out of Chaos Energy? Or was there a

greater, substantially bigger Construct Pylon hiding somewhere?

When would he bring Jet back into the fold?

Paladin was walking through the empty warehouse when the thought crossed his mind. He stopped moving, the light of the moon through a window casting a shadow over him. Jet would have loved this battle, Paladin thought to himself.

The Constructs constantly pouring out of the hallways, the seemingly never ending sight to them. It would have been a challenge Jet would happily rise to and surpass. Jet would have figured out where the pylon was before he did.

With a sigh, Paladin reached into one of his pouches and pulled out his phone. Though cracked and dented from recent fights, his phone was in his hand, and he could easily afford a repair or replacement. He never seemed to have the time. It always came down to time. Opening his phone, he scrolled through old photos for a moment until he landed on a picture of Jet.

It was Jet four years ago. The first time Jet used his sword in combat training. He was so excited to try using his dangerous weapon he insisted Paladin take a picture. Jet always seemed like nothing could hold him back, that he would always be ready to tackle the next big problem or challenge. However, that's exactly what Paladin was doing, holding him back.

Jet wasn't wrong to save Cassandra. Paladin knew that. Saving an innocent person was always the right thing to do. It was unfortunate; it was a trap that proved all of Paladin's fears right. If the gangs targeted Jet, if they sent Marath...then not only would Paladin lose one of his dearest friends, a boy Paladin saw as a younger brother, but Paladin truly believed Vinton might lose its greatest champion. That was how much Paladin believed in the boy.

By not letting Jet even try to take part, was Paladin turning

Jet against him? Was Paladin risking making Jet into a cynical, jaded teen? Was he risking snuffing out that light?

Paladin let out an audible groan of frustration and put his phone back in the pouch. There were no right answers. There never were. Ever since he took it upon himself to be Vinton's only superhero, he faced dead end after dead end in his attempts to make the city a better place for people to live. Whether it was the gangs, or Xanor, or other supervillains who tried to stake a claim in the city, nothing seemed to improve.

Except, Paladin realized, except for Jet. He watched Jet grow, become more competent, and challenge ideas he disagreed with. Jet was on his way to becoming everything Paladin always wanted to be. Paladin needed to acknowledge he played a role in that.

Maybe it was time. Paladin decided as he left the factory that he would go see Jet the next night. He just wanted to do a little digging into what the gangs were up to after hearing rumours that several of their safe houses were hit first. Then he would bring Jet back out onto the field, and together, they would save Vinton.

Paladin truly believed that.

ISSUE 5

THE CITY STRIKES BACK

CHAPTER 21

FALLEN IDOL

"Hey Jet! Can you come down here for a minute?" Uncle Quinn called from the first floor.

Jet left his room and did a small wall run along the curve of the stairs on his way down. He thumped onto the ground and looked up with an eager smile at Quinn. His expression abruptly changed, however, as he saw Paladin sitting on the couch. He wasn't in his full armour; rather, he was wearing a black tank top and his sweatpants he wore back when he and Jet trained in the bunker. He sat forward, his hands folded together.

Quinn sat at the table with his chair leaning out to face the couch. He rested one arm on his table and his other on his legs. Quinn had a small smile on his face, as opposed to Paladin, who had a more nervous expression. Jet glanced between the two of them in confusion until Paladin seemed to snap to and see Jet standing there.

"Jet," Paladin said. "Please sit."

Jet eyed the chair nervously and sat down carefully. He realized in the moment he watched none of the videos Paladin sent him that week. Despite being benched, Paladin continued to send Jet videos with ideas of things to try. There was a slight panic that Paladin would ask him about those videos, but Jet remembered Paladin's anger last time he saw him. It was of greater concern.

"Hey Paladin," Jet said. "Are...are you still mad at me?"

A smile cracked on his face, and Paladin shook his head.

"I was never really mad at you. I was just frustrated," Paladin said.

Paladin sat up straighter to address Jet fully.

"You see, Jet, in truth, I think you were right. In fact, my heart knows you were right," Paladin explained. "You were right in the bunker when you wanted to leave. You were right when you questioned whether we were doing the right thing as heroes."

Jet peered at his mentor in confusion. This was not the anger he was used to from Paladin. However, Paladin's warm smile faded.

"The other half of the truth is...doing what's right isn't always what's best for the city," Paladin explained. "In Vinton, we suffer from the death grip of a few different things. The biggest one is Xanor and his Construct horde. Without him, if all we target is the gangs, then we're running a larger risk."

Jet cocked his head to the side.

"What?"

"I explained to you that once upon a time, Xanor was a superhero," Paladin continued. "I told you the theories of why he changed, but I never told you exactly why."

Paladin inhaled through his nose and out through his mouth.

"He did it to control the gangs."

Jet sat back and stared into the blank space. Several quiet moments passed, and Paladin exhaled. He sat further into the chair, clasping his hands together again.

"He told us he was getting sick for a while, that his powers were draining away at his health. When he came up with the solution of siphoning his own powers away to make Constructs, he also realized he was building an army," Paladin explained. "With an army like that, he could use fear to control the gangs instead of trying to put them away. If he became the true-crime boss, he could reign in crime."

"That's not a solution. That still creates crime," Jet argued. "It's just sinking to their level."

"I never said I agreed with it," Paladin quickly replied.

After a tense pause, he continued, "However, it's worked. The gangs have...have a hitman. One who was notorious for picking off heroes. When Xanor entered the scene, the assassinations stopped. Mostly."

"Mostly?" Uncle Quinn prodded.

"I don't know what kind of deal they struck, but the assassinations have almost stopped. They only happen when people interfere too much with the gangs," Paladin explained.

Jet fought back a gulp. So exactly like what he and his friends were doing.

"If their business that Xanor allows is interfered with, then they send Marath," Paladin explained. "He's a force of nature. I've only seen him in combat once, and it was enough to show me I never wanted to face him myself."

"Has it worked?" Quinn asked.

Paladin glanced at Quinn quizzically.

"Has it reduced crime?" Quinn asked. "Not to get high and mighty on you, but things still seem pretty bad from where I'm sitting."

Paladin nodded in understanding.

"We haven't had a dead superhero in two years," Paladin muttered. "That's something."

Jet couldn't believe how much he hated Paladin at the moment. How much the weakness in Paladin's voice betrayed Jet's view of his mentor.

"It's why I'm still working on bringing Xanor down, eventually," Paladin said. "If it's done right, done carefully, I can unbalance the elements in the city, and hopefully avoid being on Marath's list."

Paladin then looked at Jet.

"You deserved that explanation, Jet. I've been afraid to tell you, but it's time you knew. I'm sorry. I wish I told you all this long ago, maybe back in the bunker, but I wanted to protect your innocence."

Jet stared at Paladin, probably harder than he meant to.

"Why would you be afraid to tell me?" Jet asked.

"Because, Jet, I still wanted you to see me as the superhero you saw me the first night," Paladin said. "However, we're beyond that now. I need to trust you'll follow my lead out there. It's only fair you trust me, and you can't do that if I'm keeping secrets from you."

Jet glanced at the floor. Somehow, knowing the truth made it worse. Knowing why Paladin kept him at arm's length, why Paladin kept him in the bunker so long. Was it because he was afraid of Marath? Was that really why?

"Well," Jet said, trying to find the words. "I guess it all makes sense."

Jet said it with such a lack of conviction, Quinn leaned back in his chair and bit back a sigh. Paladin's expression hardened. He closed his eyes and nodded.

"That's what I came over to say, at least," Paladin said. "Tomorrow night after dinner, we'll go on patrol."

Paladin looked at Jet, but the teen continued staring into space. He patted his legs and stood up.

"I'll see you tomorrow night, Jet."

After Paladin closed the door on his way out, Quinn let a quiet minute pass. Quinn glanced from the door to Jet and back to the ground.

"You okay?" Quinn asked.

"Yeah. Yeah, I'm fine," Jet said.

Quinn continued to stare at Jet for a few moments longer. Then he rubbed the back of his head and stood up and continued to clean the kitchen. Jet's eyes were a little glazed over, his mind still feeling like it was stuck in neutral.

His stomach felt as if it were filled with bile. His eyes felt hot, and his arms felt like they tingled with a pulsating heat. It seemed like Jet's entire world was turned upside down. His perception of Paladin, his hero, his big brother, was shattered.

All he thought of were those students' faces during the lockdown. How could Paladin, the man who mentored him, tried to teach him right from wrong, lecturing about superhero philosophy, do nothing when there was fear like that in the city? How could he preach to be better, pose like a hero, when he did nothing to make Vinton safer from the actual threats?

Paladin wasn't a hero, Jet thought to himself. He was a disgrace. He was Jet's hero no more.

CHAPTER 22

CONFLICTING IDEAS

"Hey Blade Boy," Hunter said, waving his hand in front of Jet's face.

Jet shook his head, snapping into reality. He zoned out again, thinking about Paladin. He wasn't really sure when he arrived at the rendezvous point that night, but he was standing around waiting for Hunter to make the call to go into a Brigand safe house.

"Oh jeez, I'm sorry," Jet commented. "I totally spaced."

"All good," Hunter said with a raised eyebrow. "It happens."

Hunter walked back to the edge of the building. Siege nodded towards Jet, grabbing his attention. Jet walked to the edge of the building to join them.

"Hunter was saying in fifteen minutes we should head in," Siege explained. "That's when the guards change and we'll have the path of least resistance."

Jet blinked and rubbed his eyes a few times.

"Um, about that," Jet said.

The group turned to peer at Jet for a moment. He

considered telling them what Paladin relayed. It was information they probably needed to hear. However, his anger at Paladin overrode it.

"Ah, never mind," Jet said. "Sounds like a plan."

"No, it doesn't."

Everyone turned to see standing behind them was Paladin. Jet's heart plummeted into the very deepest pits of his stomach.

"It took me a while to track your trail of destruction and figure out where you would hit next," Paladin said. "But I finally stopped you before you caused more chaos."

"Destruction? Chaos? Last I checked, we were stopping those," Sting interjected.

"No, you don't get to talk now!" Paladin yelled, anger in his voice as he pointed at the entire group. "You don't know what you've done!"

Everyone visibly shrank at the comment. The powerful teenage superheroes, who were standing tall not a moment before, reverted to the kids who were in trouble.

"I told him," Paladin said as he pointed at Jet. "Now I must tell the rest of you. In Vinton, when you prod the gangs, you're inviting something worse."

"There is an ecosystem here, and when you don't proceed cautiously, you disrupt it and bring something way worse down on all of us," Paladin continued.

Hunter at that moment stepped forward.

"Look, with all due respect, Paladin, seriously. But I'm following my dad's plan for taking these gangs out, stopping their operations and taking them down on a structural level," Hunter said.

Paladin stopped and breathed in through his nose.

"Your father, whom I knew, planned to take them down quietly. I agreed to his plan. His plan worked. His plan didn't involve getting into nightly brawls with the gangs."

Hunter backed down, turning quiet. Paladin breathed heavily, anger seething from him.

"You all need to leave now. Or I'll make you," Paladin said.

"You can't stop us from doing this," Siege said.

"I'm not!" Paladin shouted.

Jet felt every muscle clench. He didn't know Paladin could get this angry.

"I would never stop you from doing what you believe is right," Paladin said, physically trying to calm himself down. "I realize now, once I knew there were other teens active in the city, that I should have taken you all under my wing, and not assumed that Jet would help rein you in."

The three teens all turned to Jet, and he felt his face flush a deep red. There went his secret identity.

"I won't make you wait long. Tomorrow night, this roof. I'll show you my plans for taking down Xanor and then the gangs, and we'll come up with something that will work for the city," Paladin explained.

"But for now? Tonight? Go home. Go home before I do something we'll all regret," Paladin finished.

The group all shared a look. Siege wasn't happy about it, but he was the first to depart as he leaped down from the building, followed by Sting, who glided down. Hunter was the last to leave, going to the building's rooftop access.

"You really knew my father?" Hunter asked before he left.

Paladin didn't take his eyes off Jet, but he glanced to acknowledge Hunter. Paladin nodded.

"He was a good man. I'm sorry you lost him."

Hunter nodded in response and closed the door behind him.

There were several excruciating, quiet minutes after they left. Jet continued to wait for Paladin to tear him apart.

"Look, Paladin…" Jet began, but Paladin cut him off.

"I hoped that by coming here tonight I would help curtail

the behavior," Paladin said. "I don't want to control you, Jet, but when I realized a group of teens disrupted the gang activities, I knew you had to be involved."

His voice was calm, but there was definite sadness.

"I guess I hoped you still trusted me," Paladin muttered.

Jet wasn't sure what snapped in him at that moment. He never yelled at Paladin before in the five years he knew him. But the anger, frustration, reached a point of tension where it snapped irreparably.

"How can I trust you when you don't tell me the truth?!" Jet yelled. "That all this time you kept me in the bunker because you were afraid!"

Jet slapped his chest and gestured out to the city.

"Other than the Constructs we hunted down, I haven't seen a single one these past two weeks! Were they ever really hunting me?!" Jet screamed.

Paladin stood tall and peered down at Jet.

"I don't know why they stopped hunting you," Paladin continued to speak.

"I think you were always scared because you knew that this is what I would do! That I would try to make a difference!" Jet countered.

Paladin said nothing in response.

"If you weren't such a coward, then maybe Vinton would be a better place to live for everyone, not just you!" Jet shouted.

"Enough!" Paladin finally yelled back. His tone was hard, definite, and rough.

"You don't know the full extent of what I've sacrificed for this city. For you, Jet," Paladin shouted at Jet. "You don't understand how any of this works, you're too young. Any time, any time someone pushes forward too much, they die here, Jet. I can't afford to die yet, not when the city and so many others, like you, need me!"

"You're selfish then!" Jet shouted. "We put on these costumes and take on these personas to be selfless. We know there's a chance we can die doing this!"

"Actually, you put on those costumes to hide," a third venomous voice said.

Jet and Paladin both turned to see the source of the voice, as the first few pitter-patters of rain fell around them. Immediately, Paladin's entire demeanour changed from one of solidarity to one of fear.

Standing across from them was a man with long red hair reaching down past his shoulders. He was wearing a long red coat that he left open, extending to just before his knees. Covering his chest seemed to be black kevlar like armour with a blood-red dragon curled over in the middle of it. He was wearing black pants with long black boots. In one hand was a long, clear, slender sword that reminded Jet of a katana but longer, and it shimmered like a diamond. His eyes were a bright shade of green, almost neon.

"You hide because you are afraid of the consequences of your good intentions," the man said while walking forward, one hand displaying air quotes over the last few words. "You pretend to be good, to be gods because you can't imagine a world where you might be wrong. Maybe being 'good' is wrong."

Jet glanced from the man to Paladin, back to the man. Every word dripped with a biting poison stinging at Jet's core. He walked with such swagger in his step, such confidence, almost bravado, that Jet couldn't help thinking the man was right. He shook his head, realizing he disagreed with pretty much everything he said.

"I'm sorry. Who are you?" Jet asked as he took a step towards the man.

The rain began falling harder, but it was as if none of them felt it as they became more and more drenched. Faster than Jet could think, Paladin outstretched a hand and prevented Jet from walking any further.

"Me, I'm the consequence," the man said. "Or as you may have heard me called in the darkest alleys, in the whispered breaths of terror, I am Marath."

CHAPTER 23
WRATH OF MARATH

Jet's eyes widened. His feet and legs locked into place. He couldn't move. No ethereal force-controlled or compelled him. He realized it was terror.

"Now, the Brigands and Xanor agreed these teenage superheroes had to go," Marath said, stopping walking. "They disagreed on body count, but I think one dead teen plastered all over the news will be more than enough to scare the others straight. What do you think, Paladin?"

Paladin said nothing in response. Marath's lip twitched upwards into a smile.

"Or will it be a dead adult superhero? The last bastion of hope in Vinton? I'm sure the gangs would also be fine with that."

Jet's eyes darted from Marath to Paladin. In his peripherals, he saw Paladin's hand was blocking him from advancing. It was trembling.

"So what will it be? Get in my way and be the last dead superhero in Vinton? Or let the boy die and live to fight another day? The choice is yours, Paladin," Marath said, his voice teasing.

Silence reigned for several moments. Jet almost grew angry that Paladin's immediate response wasn't to fight back, to stop Marath from either.

"Jet," Paladin whispered. "Run. I'll hold him as long as I can."

Marath closed his eyes and let out a breath.

"Very well. If you can't choose two dead superheroes, it is."

Marath charged forward, moving faster than Jet thought possible.

"Run!" Paladin yelled, and suddenly he was gone too, returning the charge at Marath.

They moved so fast, Jet lost his breath for a moment. By the time Jet caught his breath, only seconds later, so much happened his head spun, and the world snapped into hard focus as the chaos and ferocity before him exploded into a kinetic battle.

Paladin's feet splashed through the puddles formed by the rain, while Marath seemed to have an almost ghostly charge. With a horizontal swing, Paladin lashed out at Marath.

Marath seemed to flow over the top of the attack, like water passing by a rock, rolling over the top of Paladin's back. Marath, with his back to Paladin, quickly raised his sword, knowing Paladin already spun around with a second swing.

TING!

Marath's quick parry reeled Paladin back, and Marath pivoted on one foot and quickly slashed upwards. Paladin leaped backward, and Marath rushed in to close the gap.

Knowing he couldn't stop another attack head-on, Paladin backflipped upon landing and dodged a follow-up swing from Marath. Marath spun low and vaulted forward and slashed again.

Paladin had enough time on the landing to bring up his sword and block the blow. The sheer momentum Marath came at him sent Paladin skidding backward. Water splashed up around him as Paladin slid. Marath grinned and stood up tall.

With a growl, Paladin charged back forward. Marath remained in a neutral stance as Paladin took several swings at him. Marath seemed to dodge the attacks, even though Jet barely saw Paladin swing his arms, his sword only leaving gold blurs in the air.

At the end of one attack, Marath grabbed Paladin's wrist and held his attack in the air. With a burst of speed, Jet could only compare to an arrow being fired. Marath jabbed the butt of his sword into Paladin's side.

TUNK!

Paladin keeled, and Marath raised one foot up high, high above his head, and swung it down hard on the top of Paladin's head. Paladin fell to the ground with a grunt and a hard crash. With a flourish, Marath prepared his sword to stab down.

Paladin suddenly found the will to move, and he quickly rolled away, somersaulting backward into a standing position. However, Paladin was unprepared as Marath left his sword embedded in the building's roof, but then Marath kicked at it, dislodging and sending it up into the air.

With pinpoint precision, Marath kicked at the pommel of the sword and sent it like a bullet towards Paladin. Paladin had enough time to raise his sword to block the blow, *WAHTING*, but the impact sent Paladin off his feet.

He found his footing, but Marath was too fast. Marath was upon him in a moment, having caught his sword out of the air and now swinging in at him. With his sword, Paladin blocked Marath's blade, which was inches from his throat.

As Marath grinned, Paladin grimaced. Shifting a foot to lie over Marath's, Paladin used his superior position to push back and repel him. Marath took several steps back and chuckled.

Paladin stepped forward and feinted a blow towards Marath, his sword coming in from high. Marath seemed to fall for the feint, so as Paladin let go of his sword and dropped low, he swung his other fist into Marath's stomach.

It was Marath's turn to go skidding backward. However, Paladin was left unsatisfied. Before he landed his punch, Marath blocked the blow with one of his hands, prepared to take the full force of the attack. Neither Jet nor Paladin saw Marath move fast enough to block the surprise blow.

Jet snapped out of his funk at the temporary lull in the battle. It was only a second or two, but it was enough that the two combatants weren't moving. With a growl, Jet gripped his sword.

"Oh, screw this," Jet muttered, still angry with Paladin. "I'll protect myself!"

Jet ran into the battle. Paladin turned his head to see Jet charging in and outstretched a hand towards him.

"Jet, no!"

At the moment, where his concentration wasn't on Marath, Marath swooped in. He elbowed Paladin hard on the side of the head, sending Paladin sprawling out.

"Oh, let him try," Marath said. "If I can't decide on who to kill, I'll just kill you both."

He turned to see Jet charging in, and Jet leaped forward with abandon. He figured if he hit Marath with enough force, he could at least stagger him. Marath didn't move and let Jet approach.

As Jet neared, he swung with all his might, hoping to send Marath backward like he watched Paladin do to him. Marath only raised his sword to block, and Jet was sure he had him.

TUNK!

However, as the hit connected, Marath didn't budge. There was a moment when Jet's feet were in the air, and his and Marath's eyes met. His calm demeanour only heightened the intensity of Marath's.

However, before Jet could roll away, Marath stopped his momentum and countered, returning all the force to Jet. Jet went flying backward in an uncontrolled flight.

Marath shifted Jet's direction again by grabbing his foot and slamming him hard to the ground. Jet sensed his ribs crack and his muscles groan in agony as he cracked the roof below him. Jet let out a gasp of pain, but Marath picked him back up and slammed him into the ground again as his world darkened.

Before Marath punished him further, Paladin was there and slashed at Marath. Marath leaped back to dodge the swing, and then was suddenly working harder than before to block Paladin's onslaught.

Paladin attacked with renewed vigor, his swings faster and stronger than before. As Marath parried and blocked, he teased his adversary.

"Well, if I knew hurting the boy would have gotten this much effort out of you, I would have done it sooner!" Marath said between attacks.

"You'll never get the chance again!" Jet called out.

He came in from Marath's side, slashing wildly. There was a moment when there seemed to be no way Marath could block both blows. The surrounding rain seemed to cease for a moment as all three clashed.

KAH-TING!

With unexpected speed and grace, Marath held Paladin's sword at bay with his own, and he stepped down hard on Jet's sword, sending it straight to the ground.

There was no physical strain present in Marath, no exertion present. Only an eerie calm. The rain fell harder than ever as Marath swung back at Paladin, sending Paladin backward. With his foot, he kicked Jet in the head as Jet tried to bring his sword to bear.

Jet reeled backward, and as Paladin tried to recover, Marath moved towards him first. Marath swung twice, forcing desperate quick blocks from Paladin. Although Paladin tried to step in and parry, Marath's forceful blow shattered Paladin's guard, throwing him onto his back.

Jet regained some sense and slashed in at Marath with three quick swings, but hit nothing as Marath dodged with his back still to Jet, sensing his movements. He spun and swung upwards, and Jet brought his sword up to block the blow.

Jet reeled as the sheer strength of Marath's attacks rattled his muscles and bones. He watched as Marath's smile grew ever so slightly. And then Marath unleashed a volley of attacks in such rapid succession, his sword blurred into a flurry of lines that seemed to cut the air itself.

SWISH SWISH SWISH!

Jet held his sword out in front of himself and blocked most of the blows, knowing that if Marath ever went for an attack that would aim for a critical spot, he could kill him instantly. But Marath seemed to toy with Jet, wearing him down as it took all of Jet's strength of resolve to continue enduring the hits.

Just as Jet felt like he couldn't take anymore, the attacks stopped, and Marath suddenly disappeared. Jet felt his whole body tremble as he lowered his sword cautiously, looking for Marath. How could he just be in front of him and then vanish? Jet felt a presence behind him, and realizing Marath had looped around behind him, Jet spun around.

BAWOOM!

Before Jet had time to react, he received a punch to the stomach from Marath that was so strong, so powerful, the rain around Jet blew back. He felt his ribs crunch and his stomach contort. Then he was off his feet.

Jet flew backward off the building. He heard Paladin call his name, but then his back hit the opposing wall, and then Jet was tumbling into the alley below. His world faded out before hitting the ground.

Paladin stood up, having struggled to get to his knees. He began moving towards Jet but suddenly felt a sharp jab through his ribs. He fell back to his knees and felt the blade extract as Marath walked around in front of him.

"You should know better than to turn your back on your opponent," Marath mocked.

Anger seethed through Paladin's helmet. With a roar, he stood and swung at Marath with abandon, as Marath leaned back in time to dodge it. Paladin jabbed forward with a punch, which Marath grabbed mid-air.

Marath swung back at Paladin, and Paladin blocked it, holding the attack in place. He felt Marath push in, but Paladin matched the strength. Marath raised an eyebrow in curiosity, impressed with Paladin matching his strength.

"If you haven't been able to tell, this is not the battle to hold back in," Marath said over the top of the sounds of the clashing steel. "You should have been trying to kill me with everything you have the whole time."

Paladin gritted his teeth.

"I won't make that mistake again!" Paladin shouted.

He pushed through, finally overpowering Marath. Marath leaped backward, soaring through the air over the gap between buildings. Paladin chased, leaping between buildings and chasing Marath as the two continued their battle on the next building.

As the air rushed over his head, Jet's world snapped back into focus. All around him, it smelled of garbage. Right in his line of sight was a banana peel, and as he tried to stand, he sensed his weight shift. Looking around and seeing garbage bags and other assorted trash, he realized a dumpster broke his fall. Still, he sensed the fight was still happening, and he tried to scramble out of the dumpster.

As he did, he felt his body twinge, and he surged with pain. He gasped for air and then fell out of the dumpster, landing on his back. His entire core ached with extreme pain he never felt before. His ribs had to be broken. There was no other explanation for it.

Jet counted himself lucky to still be alive after falling into the alleyway, and with the strength he could muster, he did his best to stand. He wasn't sure what else he could do, but he knew he needed to help Paladin.

Paladin and Marath continued to trade sword blows, their swords clashing and sparking in the night sky. They maneuvered around each other, moving so quickly Paladin could barely follow. He needed to keep pushing through, or Marath would kill him instantly. They clashed in the middle during one exchange, interlocked for a moment, before they both leaped backward and charged in again.

Marath swung low, and Paladin blocked the attack. He tried to shoot a knee up into Marath's torso, but Marath leaped back and stepped in again with a downward swing. Paladin knocked the attack with his sword and spun and swung again. Marath blocked the attack with his sword and skidded backward.

With an upward swing, Paladin lunged forward. Marath backflipped, passing by the edge of the sword. His foot caught Paladin's chin and hit it with such force it dislodged Paladin's helmet.

Paladin stumbled backward, his helmet loose. Marath landed and dashed forward. Taking advantage of his disoriented opponent, Marath grabbed Paladin's helmet and yanked it off his head. Paladin broke free, his vision blurring, and as he turned to Marath, Marath suddenly bashed him in the head with his own helmet.

BASPLICK!

A kick sent Paladin backward, making his world go hazy. Paladin felt himself tumble backward and fall into an alleyway.

He crashed into a landing, and although his body groaned in protest, he needed to stand as Marath gracefully landed in the alley across from him. They were in a tight, contained space, which meant Paladin's bigger sword would be less helpful than Marath's slender one. It was a kill zone, where Marath meant to finish him.

Marath dashed in, and Paladin just brought his sword to bear in time. It was there in that alley that the two had their last dance, their swords bouncing off each other. They fought as only trained warriors could.

With every attack there was a counter, for every feint a prepared follow-up. The two struggled and exchanged for minutes, neither gaining ground nor giving any. For a moment, there was a glimmer of hope, as Marath seemed to struggle for breath. Paladin intended to take full advantage.

He stepped in, swinging down low. Marath moved his leg out of the way in time. He then, with a sharp flick of his wrist, swung up, abusing Paladin's use of momentum. Paladin felt his sword leave his hands as Marath disarmed him. His sword flipped through the air behind Paladin, lodging itself into the ground, showing the reflection of the battle.

Then Paladin, who was a superhero for over ten years, who battled villains on the streets of Vinton, who lost friends and loved ones in his pursuit of justice, felt a pain he never felt before.

Marath drove his sword deep through Paladin's chest, piercing his heart. Paladin gurgled as his body tried to react, but all his pain sensors were on overload. Marath leaned in close, placing his mouth near Paladin's ear.

"And now, with you dead, there is no one who can stop what is coming," Marath whispered.

Marath then slashed outwards to extract his sword.

Paladin's blood painted the nearby building's wall. Falling backward, his eyes glazed over. He collapsed onto his back, into a puddle on the ground.

Marath stood over his victim for a few moments until he heard panicked running coming from the street near the alley. He gripped his sword tightly for a moment, but then loosened it.

"Be glad you will not be here to see what happens to the boy. For it will be longer, and far, far worse," Marath stated to Paladin.

With two quick jumps, one vaulting off the side of the building, Marath was on the roof.

He watched as Jet neared the alley his fallen mentor was in and smiled before departing.

Jet ran as fast as he could, his hands clutching at his ribs. He heard the sounds of battle just an alleyway down, and he hobbled his way into it. As he reached the entrance, he became dizzy, as he needed to lean against the side of the building while panting to avoid falling over. Once his vision was corrected, he saw the body of Paladin lying in the alley.

All his pain washed away with the rain. Dread flooded his mind. Ignoring his body screaming at him for doing so, Jet ran to Paladin's side. He slid onto his knees by Paladin's chest and saw Paladin's labored breathing. Jet realized it wasn't the rainwater soaking through his uniform.

"Paladin! Paladin!" Jet clambered. He checked Paladin's pulse and felt how faint it was. He didn't know how much time he had. Given his armour, attempting CPR on Paladin was hopeless, and its effectiveness was uncertain. The slits in Paladin's armour and the bruises marking his face looked fairly definitive.

Jet pushed the thought from his mind. He couldn't give

up on Paladin. He couldn't. Jet scrambled into one pouch of his uniform, fumbling through the buckles that he once laughed at. The costume he judged so harshly. That Paladin made for him. He brought out his phone and immediately dialed for an ambulance.

"I have a superhero down! We're off of 7th Street and… and…I don't know where exactly. We're in an alleyway, and there's a lot of blood! Hurry!" Jet started crying as soon as someone picked up on the other line.

Paladin found the strength to lift a hand and grabbed the wrist of the hand that held his phone. Jet peered at his mentor, who stared at him with the smallest of smiles.

"Please! Hurry!" Jet cried again before hanging up.

He dropped his phone to the ground, letting it splash into a puddle, not thinking twice about it.

"It's…it's okay, someone's going to come and help you and you're going to be okay!" Jet said to Paladin.

Jet watched in his mind's eye all the training he did with Paladin. All the frustrations he had with his mentor fell by the wayside in the face of the good times. Faced with Jet learning to fight, Jet catching up on curriculum, of Jet and Paladin watching movies together and playing board games together on nights Paladin didn't patrol. Jet watched that all slip away as the face of his mentor, of his friend, grew pale.

"You have to be okay," Jet whispered into Paladin's hand.

"Jet," Paladin muttered, his voice labored. "It will be okay."

Jet glanced down at his mentor, tears in his eyes. The words he could muster became lost in a lump in his throat.

"I was wrong," Paladin said. "All these years, I've been wrong, and I see it now."

Every word wheezed out of Paladin, but he seemed to have enough strength left to say this.

"I was afraid...afraid of what would happen to me...that I became blinded," Paladin said. "Because of you...because of who you are...I wanted to be better...but I was still afraid."

Paladin gripped Jet's hand so tightly, Jet almost had a surge of hope Paladin would pull through.

"Don't be afraid. Just...be you. You are the strongest...of all of us. In you...in your heart...I see the strength...the love... the hope that you need to save Vinton," Paladin said. "To save...us all."

Paladin's grip softened, and his eyes began to shut.

"You...can be...the greatest...hero...my...hero..."

Paladin's hand went limp in Jet's grip. Jet quivered as he gazed at Paladin. His eyes hadn't closed over completely. But he stopped breathing. He was completely still. A small smile marked his face.

Jet's head throbbed in pain. His stomach surged in agony, the pain pulsing every time he took a breath. He shook in disbelief. The world was falling out from under him. It felt like the deepest darkness was swallowing him up. Like the light was going to be forever out of reach.

Jet stared at Paladin for a few moments until a few sobs bubbled out. Then he let out a long, painful wail at the loss of his best friend, his mentor, his hero. He yelled until his voice was hoarse, until his throat was raw and sore. With such force, he clenched his knuckles that his nails drew blood from his palms.

When there was no more he could muster, he buried his head in Paladin's chest. All the angry feelings he felt earlier towards Paladin converted into a deep, undeniable guilt, making his heart feel like lead.

After all the awful things he said to him, Paladin still stood tall and defended him from Marath. After he denounced his hero, his hero died protecting him.

Jet cried. He cried until he felt like he couldn't anymore. There was nothing he could do. Paladin wasn't going to wake up. His world was changed forever. The world was a worse place without Paladin in it.

Vinton lost its last superhero. And it was Jet's fault.

CHAPTER 24

A HERO'S SENDOFF

It was all over the news the next morning. Paladin's real name was Brian Hickman. He was a doctor in his residency at the Vinton Memorial Hospital. How he balanced it with super-heroics and training Jet, they would never truly know.

Authorities ruled his death a murder and are investigating to find the killer. However, they would never find Marath, Jet knew. They all already knew who had done it, but no one would lift a finger in the face of the powerful gangs and their assassins.

Jet had. And he paid for it.

The next several days passed as a blur to Jet. Uncle Quinn had given Jet a strange tonic the next morning, and while Jet thought he might check himself into a hospital to be looked at, it was only a day or two of rest until he felt healed. It was as if Quinn's tonic sped up his likely already expedited healing factor. Jet wasn't sure if he had quicker healing, but he guessed. He didn't think much about being a superhero.

Jet spent most of the time in his room. He laid in his bed, staring at the ceiling as the weight of guilt threatened to crush him. Marath was there for him to kill Jet. But Paladin was the one who died. Vinton's last superhero, gone because of him.

It was twofold: the crushing weight of costing the city a great hero, and the heart-shattering realization that the person he was closest to was dead because of him. Jet honestly couldn't decide which feeling was worse, but both fought for purchase in his heart. His eyes were often swollen and red that week.

Or he spent his time sitting on the floor, looking up at the news articles of superheroes lining his walls. After returning from the bunker, Jet put them back where they belonged, a daily affirmation of what he wanted to be. Staring up at them in the wake of Paladin's death, Jet couldn't help but feel like the goal would never be achievable.

Paladin's last words to Jet made him feel responsible for stepping up and being what Vinton needed. How could he? In doing what he felt was right, he brought a nightmare down on top of him. How could he live up to Paladin's legacy when he was the reason it ended early?

In looking at those news articles, Jet saw the legacy of superheroes, their marks they left on the world. Stories of leadership, good vs. evil, and hope were all the trademarks of the world's most famous superheroes. In Vinton, none of those things were possible. Leaders were killed.

What was good and evil anymore?

All of Jet's hope was gone.

Jet glanced back up at the news article of Alpha. In the deepest pit of his core, he felt a twinge of light. A twinge of hope. Jet shut his eyes, curled up into himself, and held onto that hope with all of himself. It felt like it was all he had left.

He may never live up to Paladin's legacy, never be the hero his mentor was. With a bit of hope, maybe he could still crawl back to himself. Maybe.

It was less than a week when they held Paladin's funeral. In a cemetery located south of downtown, where they buried old war heroes, hundreds of people from throughout the city assembled to pay their respects to Paladin.

The day was overcast, and the threat of impending rain loomed overhead. The cemetery was built in a valley between hills, both sides of the graves surrounded by bright green rolling hills and large oak trees.

There were several rows of chairs to seat roughly sixty to eighty people, but then behind them people stood and watched from afar, lining the hills of the cemetery.

Jet, dressed in a suit that Quinn bought, sat with his uncle only a few rows from the front. In the front rows that were saved for the family, Jet saw several people who were approximately Paladin's age, siblings, or cousins, Jet reasoned, as well as a few people older than Quinn, likely aunts and uncles, and his parents.

Jet did not know Paladin had such a big family. He realized he didn't know Brian Hickman, the doctor, with family members and friends. He knew Paladin, the hero. He was probably one of the few people who did.

"Brian believed in putting others before himself, always," said a minister who stood by Paladin's casket. It was left open, and he lay there dressed in a nice suit with his hands folded over his chest. His smile remained.

"Whether he was a doctor, a superhero, or a son and brother, Brian put others' needs before his own with such abandon, all who knew him always worried for his wellbeing," the minister continued. "He was known for smiling or waving it off. For dismissing it, not out of carelessness, but because the idea of others being worried about him cut against the core of who he was."

"Brian Hickman was clearly talented, clearly gifted. So much so that he took the entire city under his watchful eye. Those who knew him, who truly knew him, knew he never did it to prove anything to anyone. You see, Brian wasn't a superhero."

Jet raised an eyebrow and stared at the minister incredulously for a moment. He was ready to be angry at the minister's nerve to say something like that, but then the minister continued.

"Those who knew him would tell you he was always a hero. To everyone around him. Today, that's how we'll all remember him," the minister finished.

Jet glanced downwards and reflected. Paladin didn't need to take Jet under his wing and train him. He didn't need to protect him and his uncle from the Constructs. And he didn't even need to continue Jet's education. But he did because the minister was right. Paladin, Brian, was a hero.

They shut the casket as the minister continued to speak. They lowered Paladin's body slowly into his grave, and the sounds of crying and sobbing could be heard among the crowd. Some remained stoic and were the rocks for others, but others gave in and let themselves feel the weight of the moment.

A life lost, a hero's life in the line of duty, would never be easy to accept.

Jet shut his eyes so tightly, hoping that when he opened them, it would all have been a bad dream. But as he opened them, he knew it wasn't possible. He couldn't change what happened. Nothing could. As Jet watched Paladin's casket descend into the ground, he felt the sensation again of his heart shrinking in his chest.

"In you...in your heart...I see the strength...the love...the hope you need to save Vinton," Paladin's words echoed in Jet's head.

But how? How could his shrivelled, barely visible heart possibly carry all those things?

Those questions pounded in Jet's head. He held his chest tight, searching desperately for the hope he found earlier in the week. More than ever, it was hard to find.

Once the ceremony was over, most of the assembled crowd left, but many stayed to pay their last respects to the family. Quinn had tried to get Jet to leave, thinking this would be too hard on the youth. But Jet had insisted he talk to Paladin's family. He had something he needed to tell them.

As Jet waited his turn to shake hands with Paladin's family, he took note of who they were.

Standing in a row, clad in their black formal attire, were Paladin's brother, sister, and mother. His brother had blonde hair and stood probably half a foot taller than Paladin, who was already very tall. His face was less regal looking than Paladin's, but he still had a strong chin line and soft eyes.

Paladin's sister had brown hair like him, and she was closer to his height, likely a little shorter. Her face was skinny as well, like her siblings, but she had round cheeks, unlike her brothers.

Last in the line was their mother. Edith, Jet recalled from the ceremony. She was considerably shorter than her children, her hair silver. She wore thick-framed glasses and a black beret on her head. Her whole body seemed frail, like she was going to fall apart at any moment. However, her face carried the same warmth that Paladin's always did.

As Jet approached, a conviction suddenly rose in him. Paladin died because of his irresponsibility. If he wanted to be better, to return to himself, he knew he needed to take accountability. With a deep inhale, he readied himself.

Jet shook hands with Paladin's siblings, and Uncle Quinn spoke for both of them, telling them how sorry they were.

When Jet reached Edith and shook her hand, he inhaled sharply, making Edith tilt her head in concern.

"Ms., I have something I need to tell you," Jet said.

Quinn and Paladin's siblings looked at Jet in confusion. Edith stared at Jet, and Jet swallowed hard before continuing.

"Paladin, Brian, was training me to be his sidekick. He's been training me for five years," Jet explained.

Edith's face lit up a bit upon Jet saying that.

"So that's what he's been doing those nights he wasn't patrolling," Edith said, her voice warm, but tired. "It's a pleasure to meet you."

Jet nodded and wanted to break down into tears then and there, but he forced himself to push through.

"You see, on those last few nights, Paladin asked me not to be a superhero, and I ignored him. I ignored him, and because of that, the gangs punished me...and he stopped them," Jet said through choked back tears. One tear breached through, and Jet quickly wiped it away while he continued to talk.

"He stopped them from punishing me, and they killed him," Jet said, his voice quivering. "I'm the reason your son is dead, and I am so, so sorry."

Jet could no longer stop the tears. They poured from his eyes. He wished he could vanish, just disappear from the world. Nothing could have made him feel worse than in that moment.

Quinn put a hand on his nephew's shoulder, and the siblings exchanged quick glances before the sister covered her mouth in awe, not sure what to say. Edith's warm expression faded, and she watched Jet for what felt like an eternity.

"Oh, you poor thing," Edith said.

Jet's eyes opened, and he looked at Edith.

"Come here," Edith motioned with her arms, and she brought Jet in for a hug.

Her arms were skinny and weak, but they felt like a heavy

warm blanket during a chilly night. Jet brought his arms up and returned the hug.

"I'm sorry...I'm so sorry," Jet cried into her shoulder.

She brought Jet back within a shoulder's reach, and the warmth returned.

"I can't imagine how hard this must be for you," Edith said. "You must feel so lost."

Jet knew she was the one this should have been hard for, that she was the one who was suffering more than him. She just buried her son. But despite himself, he couldn't help but nod his head.

"Listen to me. My son was an amazing hero. But he wouldn't have picked to train you unless he saw something amazing in you too," Edith said. "You might feel lost now, but you need to follow your heart to wherever that leads you."

"That is what my son would have wanted you to do," Edith continued, and paused for a moment. "It's what he knew you would have done. Don't continue onward for him. He's at rest now."

The idea of that struck Jet's core. How could his mother be so at peace with her son's death?

"Continue onward for yourself. Be who you're meant to be. That was what he wanted," Edith said.

Jet left the conversation in a haze. He hugged Edith again and apologized to Paladin's siblings one more time before moving on. He wiped away his remaining tears and put his hands in his pockets. Quinn followed behind Jet, giving his nephew some space.

After a few moments, Quinn told Jet he would wait in the car, seeing Jet needed a little more time. Jet found a tree a short distance away from the funeral and leaned against it. He let himself have a small cry there as his head swam.

How could he just be 'who he was meant to be?'

All that time, fighting alongside the other teens, being in

school, that felt like who he was meant to be. However, it resulted in Paladin's death. His actions, being that person, was the reason for one of the worst things to happen to him. How could he keep doing it when that happens?

"Hey, Jet," a voice called from the side.

Jet wiped away a tear and looked. Standing in a row were three teens his age, two boys and a girl. Even if Siege hadn't shown them his face before, Jet could have discerned it was the three heroes he had been fighting with.

Siege seemed to almost be popping out of his suit he was wearing. Hunter appeared very similar in a plain dark suit, but without the hat and mask on, Jet saw his curly black hair and softer features.

The girl was a bit jarring to see, as Jet finally saw Sting's lean facial features. She was pretty skinny underneath all the armour, and her brown eyes glowed. A black bandana covered her head, and she wore her long black hair in a braided ponytail.

For a moment, Jet wondered how they knew it was him. Or how they knew his name. But he remembered Paladin outed his secret identity to them, likely accidentally in his anger, and Jet nodded. He walked over from the tree towards the group, not really sure what to say.

"Hey guys," Jet said awkwardly. "Thanks for...thanks for coming."

"Of course," Sting said. It was one of the few times her voice didn't drip with the sarcasm Jet came to expect. "We're so sorry."

Jet looked up at her, and she looked sadly back at him.

"Thanks...Sting," Jet said.

"It's Jazleen," she said, her eyes closed.

The other two boys regarded her curiously for a moment. She opened one eye and looked at them, and sighed and rolled her eyes.

"Oh whatever, I'm Sting, the butt-kicking superhero when my suit is on, and I'm Jazleen, the butt-kicking Sikh girl when my suit is off, alright? Don't make a big deal out of it," she commented.

Her tone was still sad, but a bit of the glibness in her voice returned as she addressed the two.

Hunter managed a small smile and nodded in understanding.

"Jet, we want you to know this is just as much our fault as you might blame yourself," Hunter said. "If we didn't act like a wrecking ball, with or without you, then Marath wouldn't have come after any of us."

Jet appreciated the sentiment, but a thought nagged its way to the surface.

"Yeah, but if I hadn't gotten involved, then Paladin would still be alive," Jet argued.

"Then it would have been one of us," Siege countered. "Or all of us."

Siege sighed and, as Jet glanced at him, he noticed the large man wasn't able to make eye contact with Jet. He finally turned to look Jet in the eyes.

"This was because of the evil people in Vinton, and no one else," Siege finished.

Jet scratched the back of his head for a moment and gave it some thought.

Why couldn't he just blame Marath for Paladin's death? Marath was the one who did it. Why couldn't he just blame the gangs or Xanor for Paladin's death? Did they order it? Why couldn't he blame anyone but himself for it?

Then, Jet saw past Siege's shoulder, standing a decent distance away from the funeral up on a hill, was a man wearing a long black trench coat. He had only seen that man twice before, but the haircut, his figure, and more than anything, his sheer presence, informed Jet of who that was.

"Hey, give me a second," Jet commented, and pushed past Siege.

He didn't see the three teens turn and watch him leave, nor did he see their confused expressions. His walk was determined and may have even been a run for all Jet knew. It felt like an eternity to reach the man, but also it felt like no time had passed when he was suddenly standing in front of the most hated man in Vinton.

"What the hell do you think you're doing here?" Jet demanded.

The man looked curiously at Jet, inspecting him for a moment. Xanor offered the teen a small nod.

"How dare you come here today?" Jet hissed.

Every impulse wanted to scream at the supervillain in front of him. But every instinct also thought to stay quiet, not wanting to make this day any more dramatic for Paladin's poor mother.

"Brian was a good friend," Xanor said, looking past Jet to where the funeral was wrapping up. "He deserved better."

Anger swelled.

"Then why would you order his death, you sick freak!" Jet insulted.

"I didn't," Xanor curtly replied.

The response caught Jet off guard.

"You and your friends angered the Brigand and the Shinogi. They asked for my permission to kill you," Xanor explained. "I asked Paladin not to interfere and let it happen. Clearly, he ignored me."

"You can't blame us for what happened to him. If you were once a superhero, why didn't you stop the gangs once and for all? Then Paladin would be alive, and Vinton would be a better place!"

"Heh, a better place," Xanor chuckled. "Just because I can stop the gangs from killing superheroes doesn't mean I can stop them outright. All I truly do is keep their assassins off your back."

"Unless you don't."

Xanor stiffened at that and continued.

"Nor should I shut down these gangs. The power vacuum that would open would far more endanger this city than it is right now."

"What are you all so afraid of?" Jet asked. "You and Paladin, my uncle, you're all so afraid of something that none of you want to change the way this city works. You're all so afraid that you'd let everyone else suffer!"

Xanor nodded towards the funeral. Jet looked back at it and saw the grieving people. Paladin's mother. His tombstone.

"Life is fleeting," Xanor said. "We want to protect everyone. We want the best for everyone. But not everyone gets that. In the end, we can only protect what our power lets us protect. One of the wisest things you can do is to learn and accept your own limits. I have, and Paladin did until you pushed him."

Images of Paladin flashed through his mind. The hero who saved him from the muggers, from the Constructs. Who he fought alongside, who posed dramatically on rooftops. Paladin was a hero, Jet thought to himself, a hero who pushed Jet to be better at every turn. Not whoever Xanor thought Paladin was.

"But we should want to be better, we should do better," Jet argued.

Xanor sighed.

"As much as at one time I would have agreed with you, I've learned one very important thing. All things exist in a balance," Xanor said pointedly to Jet. "Just because you have good intentions, just because you think you're right, it is not a reason to disrupt that balance, or you risk making everything worse for everyone."

"Now, because of this, I'm forced to do something dramatic," Xanor continued. "If the city rallies around superheroes again because of Paladin's death, the gangs will push back harder and I won't be able to stop them. I need to maintain this balance, and if you're smart, you and your friends will stay away."

"Yeah? Well, what about those people who things already suck for? Do we leave them behind?" Jet shot back.

"All things exist in a balance," Xanor finished, and then he walked away.

How could that be a justification? How? Things need to be bad for some people so they could be good for others? How could that be the way the world worked?

A hand gripped Jet's shoulder, and he turned to see Quinn returned to him. Standing a short distance behind Quinn were his friends, all looking on at him with concern. Jet didn't realize he was trembling; he didn't realize his eyes were red.

Almost involuntarily, he hugged his Uncle Quinn tightly. For just a moment, he needed to escape from this world he didn't understand anymore. This world was determined to batter his beliefs and throw them in his face.

Jet knew it would only be for a moment, and he would have to face reality again. He would have to figure out his place in this confusing world.

CHAPTER 25

"Well, it's all here," Hunter said, slapping down a file folder onto the kitchen table.

The file folder was thick with paper, creating a weighty sound as it hit the wood.

"Paladin's plan, which includes notes from my dad, to bring down the gangs once Xanor was taken care of," Hunter said.

Siege and Sting sat at the kitchen table where Hunter stood. Quinn sat in the living room, watching the news as testimonials continued to flood in from citizens about their experiences with Paladin.

Quinn expected a flood of news coverage that night, but invited the teens for dinner after the funeral. It was secretly to keep them from doing anything else reckless, but Quinn also knew the sense of community would help them with their guilt.

Jet sat in the recliner that faced out the main floor's large window, separating himself from the group. He said barely a word since they returned, and he just continued to contemplate everything Paladin, Edith, Xanor, and Marath had said to him. He couldn't make sense of anything.

Siege reached across the table and grabbed the file folder that Hunter had tossed down. Hunter sat down and bit his lower lip, deep in thought. Siege flipped through a few pages, but they visibly made no sense to him. He looked to his side and saw Sting was watching him with a raised eyebrow. Feeling judged, Siege closed the file folder and pushed it back towards Hunter.

"Well, would it have worked? Will it still work?" Sting asked, saving Siege the embarrassment of admitting his confusion.

Hunter tilted a hand side to side in a non-committal manner.

"Maybe. I mean, yes, it probably would have worked," Hunter said. "But now that he's gone, and my dad's gone... there were a lot of factors in play that I'm not able to follow. Names and contacts I don't recognize."

Hunter placed his hat on the table and rubbed his temples.

"I guess that falls on us to pick up the pieces," Hunter lamented.

"If we can," Siege said, his tone pessimistic. While normally the group would curtail the tone, at that moment no one disagreed with him.

Jet closed his eyes and sighed. Things felt hopeless.

Why should they bother trying? Even if they try a measured approach, even if they go about things more carefully, what are the odds they make things worse again? What was the point of trying to make things better when there was the chance things could go worse as they had?

Somewhere deep, deep inside Jet's core, there was a small dissenting feeling that fought back against that sensation. As upset and angry, and hopeless as he felt, something that was true to Jet's nature pushed against those thoughts. Jet wanted to feel sad, he wanted to feel helpless, but something wouldn't let him sink totally into that abyss.

"Uh, kids?" Quinn said.

Jet turned in his seat, distracted from his thought process. The three at the table also looked over, and most of them stood up and walked closer to the television. They could see the main plaza downtown, known as Hero Plaza, a large concrete space filled with modern art and benches, from the perspective of a helicopter camera.

There was a ticker at the bottom of the screen reading in all capital letters: VINTON IN TERROR. Spotlights illuminated the area, and as the group leaned in close to see what exactly was happening, they saw it.

There were so many of them, they almost looked like one writhing mass. But as the spotlights shone over them, their brownish-grey colours and deformed figures were visible. A moment of horror gripped the room as they realized how many Constructs were now crammed into downtown.

"This has been the scene in Hero Plaza downtown for the last fifteen minutes as Constructs swarmed in. They have so far done immeasurable property damage, but reports show civilians were allowed to flee the center and no harm has come to anyone yet," a news anchor said over the footage.

"He doesn't want bodies...not yet," Jet commented, thinking back to the conversation he had with Xanor. "He's trying to scare the city, not bring the Guardians down on himself."

The angle shown on the camera suddenly changed wildly, flipping upwards in an almost nausea-inducing manner. Standing at the top of a large skyscraper with a Chaos Energy generator that must have been three times the size of the one Jet saw before was Xanor.

He was wearing his brown trench coat again, in the same attire he had been wearing when Jet first saw him. He spoke, but the noise still muffled his words. It cut mid-sentence, and the group had no choice but to hear the helicopter's propellers over the top of Xanor.

"...the would-be heroes of this city have led me to this moment, to an act of terror I would never dare otherwise commit! Superheroes are not something to be admired! They are not to be revered! As an act of good faith, I allowed the civilians who were downtown to evacuate before my Constructs entered, but if the city council does not rush the outlawing of superheroes in Vinton, I will unleash this flood upon the city! I will hold the heroes and city council accountable for the damage they cause!"

Xanor turned with a flourish and walked away from the edge of the building and out of view. The anchor then took over, reiterating most of what Xanor just said. There was a tense pause in the room. No one was sure what to say. Quinn looked from the television to the teenagers, whose eyes remained locked on the visuals from downtown.

"What...what do we do?" Sting asked.

"Do you think the city council will push it through?" Siege asked, directing his question towards Hunter.

Hunter lifted a hand and waved it from side to side in uncertainty again.

"It's hard to say. If something isn't done by us, it'll destroy any goodwill we can ever try to build up, or we'll be outlawed by the city. On the flip side, if we do something, then we risk the Constructs ripping the city apart, and that will definitely destroy our reputation forever," Hunter commented. "That's more what this is about. He's trying to turn the city against us, one way or another."

"What an absolute ass," Sting chipped in, crossing her arms.

Jet gripped his hand tightly as he realized what it all meant. If Xanor couldn't make the city hate them, if he couldn't scare them into their holes, then he wanted the Constructs to kill them. It was their choice to intervene, not his. He was trying to wipe his hands of the guilt of forcing the superheroes of Vinton to stop one way or the other.

Siege rested his hands on the couch and leaned in on them. He seemed to contemplate for several moments. Hunter likewise leaned back onto the kitchen table. There was a long, quiet pause. Sting looked at the boys and then rolled her eyes.

"Oh, whatever," Sting remarked.

Siege and Hunter both looked at her, and Sting extended a hand. Jet also turned, and his eyes widened as they watched Sting's suit emerge from her skin, starting from her hand. It overlapped her clothes, and folded on top of itself again and layered into the form the group had been used to seeing. It covered her entire body but stopped at her neckline. She glanced at the boys in the room.

"You guys were going to decide we were going to go fight anyway. The more time we spend overthinking it, the less we have to stop this maniac," Sting said.

Siege stood up, and his face had turned resolute.

"You're right, we can't afford to waste the time. Even if we can't win the battle here, I intend to go down swinging," Siege commented.

Hunter scratched the back of his head and sighed.

"Well, screw it. Let's do this. Let's be superheroes," Hunter added.

Jet glanced at the floor. It took several moments, but eventually the others looked Jet's way, waiting to see what he said. As he felt their gazes boring into him, Jet inhaled and looked up.

"I...I don't know. What if we should stay out of this one?" Jet asked.

No one answered for several seconds, and Jet felt a need to justify his question.

"I mean, being superheroes, what have we accomplished? Paladin's gone. We're the reason this is happening," Jet said, motioning to the television. "I don't think we win this one by being superheroes. Not in Vinton."

Hunter and Sting looked on at Jet, and sadness painted their faces. Jet knew he was always the eager one, but he never realized how much of an impact that must have had on the others until that moment. Siege crossed his arms.

"So what, you want us to give up?" Siege asked.

"I...no, I just want us to consider..." Jet stuttered out.

"You're not the only one that has lost something in all this," Siege interrupted with a pointed finger. Anger etched his face.

"If we surrender now, if we let Xanor have his way, we are sending the wrong message to this city! We need to show people that when the chips are down is when we rise! That's what the superheroes you love so much do!"

Jet inhaled slowly and looked back at Siege.

"I thought you said that people need something more," Jet shot back.

Siege looked about ready to explode, but Quinn suddenly stepped in between them.

"Look, kids, I can't condone you going downtown. I think you do what you feel you have to do. My nephew, though...he needs some time," Quinn said. "I'm going to ask that if you guys are going to go...please go now."

Siege's glare shot up to Quinn, and he quickly looked away in frustration. He said nothing else to Jet and Quinn, but Jet sensed Siege's rage permeating from him.

"Come on, I need to grab my armour," Siege said as he grabbed his belongings and headed for the door.

"Yeah, I don't have that problem," Sting said, her small cheeky smile returning.

She looked Jet's way one last time and gave him a small

smile before her suit formed around her head, her hair being folded up around her head as it did.

"I'm pretty much dressed already," Hunter commented, winking at Jet.

Jet managed a small smile in reply to that, thinking back to their conversation about The Spirit.

"Banter later, move now," Siege instructed.

A few moments later, they were gone. The noise of the television continued to drift through the house, and Jet remained standing. Every instinct in his body told him to race after his friends and go help.

Wasn't this what he wanted his whole life to be a superhero? To race off and stop evil like this?

The moment was right in front of him. His head held him back; every doubt and insecurity he had froze him in place. He never thought he would question if stopping a supervillain was the right thing. So much changed.

He learned so many things in these last few days that made him question his own resolutions on the line between right and wrong. His heart felt like it still knew what was right, but he couldn't reconcile that with the thoughts circling in his head.

Quinn found the television remote and turned it off. He sat down on the right side of the couch and patted the other side of it for Jet to sit down. Jet remained still, not even noticing Quinn at first.

"Jet, grab a seat," Quinn instructed.

Jet looked at his uncle and raised an eyebrow. His uncle, who he had seen as cowardly after the night he was dropped off at the bunker after he hid during that confrontation in the streets when he met Alan, was now a source of solidarity. Quinn gave Jet a gentle smile, and for a moment Jet was a small child again, and his uncle was all he had.

Jet nodded and sat down next to Quinn. They were both

quiet for several minutes, and Jet's head continued to swim. Quinn just waited, and eventually Jet let down his guard enough.

"I don't know what to do, Quinn," Jet finally said.

"I feel like any decision I make is the wrong one, and trying to make things better just made them worse and now my friends are putting themselves in harm's way but I'm too scared to help even though I know they need me and I just..." Jet said, word vomiting until Quinn interrupted him.

"You know, Jet, I've really enjoyed having you at home with me," Quinn interjected.

Jet's mouth remained agape. Whatever words he was going to say next were lost in space. He glanced up at his uncle. He was slightly offended at being cut off, but he wanted to hear what Quinn had to say.

"When I first adopted you after your parents passed, it was tough because I was dealing with my grief and suddenly I had a child in the house. But we grew together. I learned how to take care of you, and I watched you become a young boy with such a beautiful view of the world. The world was a place filled with superheroes and light and good, and evil could never overcome that. As an adult, it filled me with hope even as I watched things in this city get worse and worse. I knew if our next generation was like you, then we would be okay. Even after you left for five years, isolated and alone with just Paladin and me on occasion, you never lost that sense of optimism. You still believed this world was a good one," Quinn said.

"Then you saw what this city truly was, and even as you learned more and more, still you refused to change. It was stubborn to a fault," Quinn said. "Yes, it had consequences. Brian is gone, and we can't get him back."

Jet stared at the floor, his guilt and shame washing over him.

"If you think that this is what it takes to knock that sense of wonder, that optimism in you, out of you, then you're selling yourself short," Quinn commented.

He leaned over and rested a hand on his nephew's shoulder. Jet looked back at his uncle, and the two locked eyes. At that moment, Jet saw a sense of strength he never seen before in his uncle.

"This world is good. It just needs someone to fight for it. Even though I don't like you putting yourself in danger, I believe that person is you, Jet. However you choose to fight the fight, I think your hope, your resolve, is your greatest strength. And truly, that makes you stronger than any of us," Quinn said.

Quinn continued to look at his nephew for a moment longer, and then he stood up and walked into the kitchen. Jet sat on the couch and contemplated.

As far sunk as his heart felt at the moment, it felt uplifted. It seemed like there was a hand reaching out to him, to pull him from the darkness he was falling into. Jet needed to reach out and grab it.

He just had to reach.

ISSUE 5 EPILOGUE

A few short blocks away from the sounds of the battle in the Hero Plaza was a large skyscraper, home, Vinton's premiere energy conglomerate, Equilibrium Enterprises. They specialized in technologies and research that harnessed the Chaos Energy that was native to Vinton, Chaos Energy that had long pooled in the Vinton Reservoir.

While the VGB researched and studied most of the energy deals with the Alberta and Canadian governments, as well as deals under the table, allowed Equilibrium Enterprises to profit and provide jobs for many of Vinton's citizens.

Equilibrium Enterprises' large, bright green, overlaid E's made it easily spotted above many of the city's other buildings. The building housed almost the entire domestic business, from research and development to manufacturing.

Equilibrium Enterprises also housed the core operations of the Brigand gang.

In a long-running operation, the very seed of Equilibrium Enterprises was rotten. What had started as a cover operation had blown up into a massive industry, and it allowed the

Brigand leadership to control much of Vinton from the shadows. When their legitimate strategies failed them, they could supply their foot soldiers with the advanced weaponry or tech they might need to take what they wanted by force.

At the very top of this tower was a penthouse adorned with the finest furniture and luxuries one could afford. The lighting bounced off the golden trim of the penthouse's built-ins and the black onyx floors, adding to the room's luxurious feel. Large windows faced out towards the city, slung on the outer corner walls, from which the glow of Vinton could be seen.

Standing at that window was a man wearing a dark leather suit that fit tightly to his form. He was a tall, fit-looking man with trim, neatly spiked black hair. He was wearing black gloves, and in one hand he held a glass of scotch, which he swirled as he listened to the news.

A large flatscreen television was on the wall behind him as he looked out the window, as Cassandra sat on the large black leather sectional couch.

"Sounds like the teens decided to show," Cassandra commented, her smoky voice wafting through the penthouse.

The man said nothing. He continued to stare. From the penthouse, you could just see the edge of Hero Plaza. Helicopters circled the area with spotlights on the scene. They were too high up and at the wrong angle to see what was happening, but his eyes remained fixed on it, regardless.

"All of them?" he asked, his voice cold and raspy.

Cassandra was draped along the couch, resting her elbow on the corner of the sectional as her legs lay along the couch. Her red dress stuck to her closely, and her blonde hair flowed down her shoulders. She looked at the television closely, and then shrugged.

"Can't tell. The news doesn't want to get too close. Sounds like only three," Cassandra replied, uninterested.

The man grunted and then turned to face the television himself.

"What the hell is he thinking?" the man muttered to himself. "Five years...for five years we've had an excellent system going and now this?"

He took several steps towards the couch, taking a drink from his glass.

"If he wins, he'll have more control of the city council, maybe more than we do," the man continued. "If he loses-then the Shinogi are bound to act up again. We'll be back at war. There'll be blood in the streets."

He finished his drink and crossed his arms.

"What changed, Xanor?" the man whispered to himself. "Why now?"

"Might be Paladin's death," Cassandra replied, having listened to her boss despite his hushed tones. "Doesn't want those kids to get any big ideas?"

"We've had superheroes killed before," the man quickly retorted. "No, this is...this is different. Something...or someone...has affected him."

There was a pause, a silence between the two.

"Do you think it's the boy? The one Marath didn't finish?" Cassandra asked.

"The one he let get away," the man corrected. "Marath doesn't do half-measures. I don't know what happened, but that's our deal. I don't push or pry. He kills indiscriminately."

The man let his hands fall to his sides. He turned back to the window.

"Maybe it's time I pried," the man remarked.

Then the news suddenly changed with a breaking update. Cassandra regarded the television more closely, and her eyes slowly widened.

"Vince," she said. "You should see this."

Vince, the principal shareholder of Equilibrium

Enterprises, the leader of the Brigand, turned back to television.

On the news, they were showing a video of a new arrival at the scene. Standing on top of a building on the very edge of Hero Plaza was a fourth teenager.

ISSUE 6

BATTLE FOR THE HEART OF VINTON

CHAPTER 26

JET THOMPSON

Jet could hear the carnage of the battle below. He heard the shots from Hunter's guns. Sting's kinetic blasts. Siege's hammer smashing into the ground. And most disturbingly, the weird, strangely unrhythmic sound of the Constructs as they clashed against the teens.

The hum of the helicopters overhead threatened to blot out all the other noises, but Jet focused his listening on the sounds of the battle.

The helicopters continued to spotlight the battle below; the lights flashing around wildly. Jet stayed further back on the roof of the building he was on, purposely staying out of the light. He wasn't ready yet. He clutched and unclutched his hands.

Jet let his mind drift back to fifteen minutes before, fifteen minutes before his sprint across the city.

The news report on the television spotlighted his three friends. They arrived with minimal fanfare and got to work immediately fighting Constructs. Quinn stood at the bottom of the stairs, watching the battle unfold, before looking upstairs.

After a moment of hesitation, Quinn walked up the stairs and towards Jet's room. Jet sat on his bed, his Blade Boy costume sitting on his lap. The sword leaned against the opposite wall, but Jet focused on his costume.

Quinn stood in the doorway and looked at his nephew, and a moment later, he crossed his arms.

"They've reached the fight," Quinn said.

Jet nodded. He didn't move from his spot, didn't change where he was looking. It took him a moment to articulate what he was thinking, but he was speaking more to himself than to his uncle.

"All I've ever wanted to be was a superhero," Jet said. "Even before I knew I had superpowers. I idolized them. I wanted to be like them. So when I finally got the chance, I jumped in headfirst without looking."

"Maybe...maybe it wasn't an entirely bad thing. Some bad things have happened, and they've been my fault because of that. I've learned. I've learned that while I love superheroes, while I still want to be a superhero, I need to be something more," Jet continued.

"Something more?" Quinn prodded.

"This world is good. But you're right. It's one that has to be fought for And that's what superheroes are for. They're meant to be what's right and good. They're meant to be the truth. It's more complicated than that. I understand that now. There's more than one truth. So I don't think people in Vinton need to see a mask or a costume. They don't need to see what that's supposed to represent. They don't need an idea. An idea can be disagreed with. An idea can be wrong," Jet stated. He shook his head and added, "it doesn't matter if it's wrong or not. If people don't like it, they'll see it as wrong."

"So you need to be something more than an idea," Quinn said. "What does that look like?"

"I think that means I need to be honest. I can't be just a superhero, a good guy, because then I'm a bad guy to others. I need to be me," Jet said. "Because even if people don't like me, if they don't agree with me, at least it's still me, not just an idea. They can argue about what the truth should be, but they can't argue with the truth of who I am. That I'm fighting for a wonderful world, but we can always make it better. I can show everyone this hope, this truth, my truth, that I'm fighting for, and I can and need to do this just like me."

"That's who I am," Jet finished, looking up at his uncle finally.

Quinn looked at Jet, and for a moment there was an air of sadness between them. While Jet hadn't directly said what exactly he was going to do, Quinn had enough of an idea to know it was going to have repercussions for the two of them. But Quinn smiled and nodded away from Jet's room.

"Well then, what are you waiting for?" Quinn asked. "Get out there and show this city what that means."

Jet smiled at his uncle. He let himself droop for another moment, but smiled again.

"You know I've enjoyed living here again too, right?"

"I know Jet," Quinn said. "I trust you. Now go do what you feel you have to."

CHAPTER 27

BATTLE IN HERO PLAZA

Back on the roof downtown, Jet inhaled and exhaled. It was time for him to be himself. And to show the city what that meant.

Jet stepped forward. Walking towards the edge of the building, he peered down and saw his friends fighting the Constructs. Hunter was standing in place and letting the Constructs come to him, firing in all directions, ducking and sidestepping when he needed to, when some would get too close.

Sting bounced around the Constructs, kicking, punching, and firing her kinetic blasts in frenetic fashion. Siege also stayed on the move, taking big wide swings to wipe out hordes of Constructs at a time. A few would get in close, but he pushed them back and attacked. Though formidable, the teens were soon overrun.

Jet felt a helicopter spotlight illuminate him and felt he was on camera. People all over the city would have seen him just like he wanted, an ordinary teen wearing an unzipped brown hoodie with a green shirt underneath. He was wearing blue jeans and sneakers. He had a leather strap across his torso, which he used to keep his sword sheathed. His hair blew in the wind the helicopter's blades created.

Even though the building was lower than the one Xanor stood on by a considerable amount, Jet looked up and saw Xanor standing on the edge, peering down at him. Jet inhaled and then gripped his sword tight.

"My name is Jet Thompson!" Jet shouted at Xanor. He unsheathed his sword and pointed it upwards at the villain. "And remember it, because I'm going to carve it into your butt!"

Jet leaped off the rooftop and descended into the battle below.

A fall from that distance would be a death sentence, but Jet had a plan. As he rapidly descended and it felt like his belly button was going to pop out of his back, he watched the Constructs close to his location.

With as much strength he could muster, he threw his sword downwards. His sword drove straight through one Construct, dissolving it to ash as the sword embedded itself in the ground.

THUNK!

Jet reached for his sword, grabbed it, and flipped himself over the top of it in a dizzying twist of his momentum. He flipped forward, slamming his feet onto a Construct in front of him to brace his impact and sending it into the ground.

As Jet landed, his sword ripped out from the ground with a terrifying amount of force, and controlled it to swing it up and over his head, and he slashed down, cutting a Construct in front of him in half.

He caught his breath for a moment, even as more and more Constructs neared in on him. He allowed himself a small smile as the exhilaration of the action kicked in.

"Wasn't sure I could do that," Jet commented.

With a blinding charge forward, Jet cut through several

Constructs that were too slow to keep up with him. As he ran deeper into the mob, he parried blows from incoming Constructs, spinning as he moved, almost dancing his way through the Constructs. Just as one almost closed in on him and he turned to combat it, a green energy blast tore through it.

KAZAP!

Sting jumped into the place where that Construct had just been, and she and Jet moved together through the crowd, attacking the Constructs in their way. Between quick bouts, she turned to him as they continued to move.

"So, decided to join us?" Sting asked.

"Yeah, it took me long enough," Jet said back with a smile. He slashed through a Construct, ducked under an incoming attack, and hacked at the attack while saying, "Just had to figure some stuff out, you know?"

Sting nodded and flipped over a Construct. She pointed her hand down and fired a blast straight through the Construct, and when she landed, she backpedaled to keep pace with Jet.

"For sure. We're glad to have you, Jet," Sting said.

Jet grinned.

"Glad to be here."

The two stopped moving and turned to face downtown. Sting pointed in the direction they could hear Siege fighting.

"You go help the big guy and I'll help Hunter," Sting suggested.

"Then meet in the middle?" Jet asked.

Sting nodded and vaulted away. Jet watched her for a moment, but then spun around and cut through a Construct that tried to sneak up on him. The cacophony of noise and lights from the helicopters made the already chaotic mass of Constructs more overwhelming, but Jet was in his zone.

Surrounded by tall buildings, standing in the lower inlay of the plaza, Jet grinned. This was where he was meant to be.

Siege slammed his hammer through three Constructs that closed in on him, quickly bringing his hammer back around to block a blade that swung down on him. He pushed back and reached forward, grabbing the Construct by the top of its head and swung it like a bat into several others, disintegrating a few while knocking the others backward. He heaved a heavy breath, having been at this for longer than he was used to.

Suddenly, he felt a heavy weight slash against his back, and he lurched forward. His armor had protected him from the attacker behind him, but the force had still beneath to make Siege recoil. He spun and swung his hammer upwards, hitting the Construct from the bottom and propelling it upwards, sending it flying backward into the crowd.

Siege thought he had a moment to gather his bearings when he felt a heavy on his shoulders as a Construct leaped on top of him. It buckled him to his knees, and thinking quickly, Siege dropped his hammer. He reached up with both hands and wrestled the Construct off himself, slamming it into the ground in front of him. He punched his fist down through the Construct to finish it, but three other Constructs tackled him.

They pushed him down onto his back, and Siege was forced to bring up his arms to defend his face as the Constructs piled on him, some using their weight to keep him pinned while others slashed and railed against his armor. Siege knew he could force them off if he could find his footing, but the Constructs attacking him from every side were enough to keep his body recoiling enough he could summon the strength. Just as he thought he considered every option, there was a loud call from the side.

"Hey uglies!" Jet shouted.

The Constructs and Siege all looked to Jet, who was

standing with one foot resting behind the other, pointed down, and he was leaning on his sword like an umbrella. Siege furrowed his brow in confusion.

"Don't you know its improper etiquette to attack like ten Constructs versus one person? The max is like five Constructs to one person. Honestly, Xanor would be ashamed of you," Jet asked.

The question seemed to confuse the Constructs. Even though they weren't capable of logical thought, the mention of Xanor seemed to halt their process, like a computer program crashing because of an illogical error. Siege realized quickly, however, that the minor distraction created the moment he needed to recenter himself.

With a tremendous show of strength, Siege jumped to his feet, sending the Constructs off him. He quickly ducked low, grabbed his hammer, and swung out at the Constructs that were attacking him.

WHAM!

His hammer drove through several, and as he turned to attack the others, Jet dashed through and slashed them in half, creating a small gap in the Constructs.

Jet stood up straight and looked back at Siege, and Siege's eyes went downward for a moment, visibly feeling guilty for how he had yelled at Jet earlier. With a swallow, he met Jet's eyes and nodded.

"Thanks," Siege said.

"Don't mention it," Jet replied. "Come on."

Jet motioned for Siege to follow, and the two hacked and beat their way through the Constructs towards the middle.

Sting, meanwhile, caught up to Hunter much more quickly. Hunter continued to fire on all cylinders, his arms outstretched in both directions as he fired at the Constructs advancing.

BAM! BAM BAM BAM! BAM BAM!

He braced himself perfectly for the recoil, using each bullet's momentum to strategically reposition and aim at his next target. Sting landed behind him, and for a moment, the two were back to back and sent out volleys of projectile attacks into the crowd.

Sting leaped away, bounding and leaping off the Constructs to create more kinetic energy while destroying them like they were Goombas from a Mario video game.

Hunter's guns suddenly each clicked, their ammo empty, as several advanced in towards him. While spinning, he unloaded his guns and pointed the bottom of his guns out towards the Constructs, sending the empty clips out like they were projectiles. Seeing more Constructs advance in, Hunter threw his new ammo clips up into the air and sheathed his guns.

Once they were away, two new Constructs quickly advanced in. Hunter sidestepped a sword slash and leaned back to dodge another. As he stood up, he unsheathed his guns and held them upside down as his two new clips slid right into place. He quickly locked them in and flipped them as he leaped up into the air over the top of the two Constructs' simultaneous attacks as they each slashed horizontally.

At the apex of his jump, he fired each gun, two bullets that put down two Constructs, and they dissolved away as he landed.

Hunter allowed himself a quick smile as Jet and Siege joined him.

"Man, you always gotta make everything look so cool," Jet commented, parrying a Construct's attack, which Siege quickly batted away.

"There's no point in doing this without some flair," Hunter replied.

The three watched as the few Constructs they destroyed were replenished by three times as many. They each readied their weapons when Sting suddenly bounded through, green energy crackling off her.

"I'm going to try discharging a super enormous amount of energy, but I need some help to generate enough of it," Sting informed.

Jet scratched the back of his head and asked with a small, ashamed smile, "Anyone else up for a round of volleyball?"

After a quick exchange of looks, followed by a small groan from Siege, Hunter nodded for Jet to go one way and for Siege to stay put.

"The serve!" Sting yelled as she leaped up and down towards Siege.

Siege brought his hammer in from down low, swinging upwards. The flat side of his hammer met with Sting's feet, and she launched herself up into the air. She gracefully flipped up through the air and descended towards Hunter. Hunter clasped his hands together and caught Sting's feet in the ball of his hands.

"The volley!" Hunter shouted as he launched her up again.

Sting skyrocketed up in the air, the green energy surging off her. She turned and kicked her feet up into the air as Jet propelled himself off a Construct to meet her in the air.

"And the spike!"

WHACK!

Jet slapped down at Sting with the flat side of his sword, and she rocketed towards the ground. Right before she hit the ground, she released her energy, discharging a large amount of energy in a massive area attack.

BAAWWWOOOOOOOM!

Dozens of Constructs were instantly vaporized by it, and Hunter was almost blown off his feet, not being weighed down by the same armour as Siege.

The explosion pushed Sting back up in the air, and she

landed on her feet, though barely. She was a little wobbly, and Siege quickly rushed over to help her stay on her feet.

"Thanks, never done something quite that big before," Sting commented.

Jet and Hunter quickly met up with the other two, now standing in a decently open space. Even though the attack and their efforts destroyed a lot of Constructs, there seemed to be no end to their number. Jet looked up at the skyscraper Xanor was on and remembered seeing the Chaos Energy pylon there.

"This will not stop until we destroy the pylon," Jet commented. "I need to get up there."

Hunter looked at Jet incredulously.

"By yourself? We're not sure how strong Xanor is, and you want to fight him on your own?"

Jet quickly motioned to the surrounding Constructs.

"We need you guys here to keep these things down here and not swarming over the city. Anything less, and it won't be enough," Jet argued.

"Jet, don't be crazy," Sting chipped in.

Siege stepped forward, drawing their attention.

"You got this?" Siege asked.

Hunter and Sting both looked at Siege incredulously, but Jet smiled and nodded.

"I got this," Jet answered.

There was a moment of quiet, but the group seemed to fall in with Jet's confidence. Seeing that, Jet took a step forward as he sheathed his sword, knowing he'd need two hands.

"Can you give me a lift?" Jet asked Sting.

Sting nodded and reached out, pulling a metal grate out of the ground. She held it just up in the air enough for Jet to reach out and jump up onto it.

Seeing Jet was stable, she rocketed it upwards and Jet soared through the air. Her power didn't reach far enough, and Jet jumped off the grate towards the building. His hand grabbed a ledge and used that to vault himself upwards. He was nearing the top and found a small foothold he used to keep bounding until he reached one last handhold he used to flip himself up and over, landing gracefully on the roof.

As he oriented himself to his surroundings, his eyes focused on one thing. Standing across the rooftop with his back to Jet, much like in their first meeting, was Xanor.

It was time to end it.

CHAPTER 28

SHOWDOWN

THE ROOF HUMMED WITH ENERGY. BEING CLOSER TO it than before, Jet saw the full scale of the Chaos Energy Pylon that Xanor brought downtown.

Almost identical in design, with its rod-like structure and the three triangular stands, it dwarfed the other one by at least twenty feet. Instead of the blue electricity of before, purple and green electricity crackled out of it and danced in the sky, creating an ominous glow all around them.

The building they stood on must have taken up roughly a city block, making a large space for them to fight in. The buildings on either side of them were larger by several stories, with two-way, two-lane streets separating them.

Mixed with the wind from the higher altitude, Jet's sweater and hair blew almost violently around him as the noise was deafening. Apprehension gripped Jet for only a moment, but he pushed through and swallowed hard. He knew it was the moment to back up everything he had been saying.

Jet sheathed his sword as he stood up fully. As much as he knew Siege was joking when he asked if Jet would talk villains into submission, he figured he should at least try to negotiate with Xanor first. Maybe it had just been because it was a funeral, but Xanor seemed reasonable enough when they last spoke. It may not have been too late to end this without further violence.

Or Xanor would just sucker punch him and kill Jet instantly. It was a gamble.

"Xanor!" Jet called out as he walked across the roof. Despite the noise, his voice rang out true over the cacophony.

Xanor's shoulders heaved up and down with an audible sigh, a weight descending upon him. But he didn't turn to acknowledge Jet.

"Come on, this can end without anyone getting hurt. Namely you," Jet kept going.

Jet was roughly ten yards away from Xanor, and still Xanor did nothing. Jet grimaced, and his eyebrows furrowed.

"Prove you're better than me since you're so convinced! Do the right thing here!" Jet shouted.

That finally grabbed Xanor's attention. He turned to face Jet, scowling at the youth. Jet didn't back down, his face resolute. They locked eyes for several moments, neither backing down.

"The right thing? I suppose you mean joining forces and stopping the gangs together?" Xanor asked. "I suppose you mean finding the solution where no one is hurt?"

Jet finally broke gaze as he rolled his eyes and shrugged his shoulders.

"I mean…is that such a bad-sounding thing to you? The idea that no one has to suffer?"

Xanor scoffed and shook his head.

"No, it sounds perfect. Ideal," he calmly said.

"This isn't a world of ideals. It's a world of truths, and the one fundamental truth is we can't stop suffering. We can't stop the pain! All we can do is try to aim it, direct it away from the people who matter most to us," Xanor finished.

"But that's not the truth," Jet responded as he looked down. His eyes went up to Xanor again.

"We can't stop pain and suffering. But everyone should matter to us," Jet said. "I might like or love some people more than others, but everyone matters. Friends, families, strangers. Even the gangs, and even you."

"It's when people like you and the gangs decide that what matters most to you is more important than anyone else that we have crap like this," Jet gestured out to Hero Plaza. "If you're so convinced you're right that this is the only way to keep people safe, then you're blinding yourself. You don't want to accept what you're doing because you would know it's wrong!"

Xanor took a step forward.

"You don't know what I've done!" Xanor shouted. "You're a child! You don't know what I've done to keep this city safe! You don't know what I've sacrificed to accomplish this! I have given all of myself to this cause because I truly believe it is right, and every day I feel that suffering! I know what I'm doing to the people of this city, but because of me, at least they're safer than before I began."

"They might hate me, might despise me, but I'm saving them," Xanor continued through gritted teeth. "I don't need to be lauded or loved for it. I am doing the best I can for this city, and I will not have a child tell me what I'm doing is wrong!"

"There it is," Jet replied calmly, a small smile on his face.

Jet's calm statement surprised Xanor. The teen closed his eyes for a moment and let out a small breath.

"Look, I'm not the smartest guy around. I don't have plans for how to fix this city, or the world, or anything like that. Some days I think it's a miracle I tie my shoes together. But I know the difference between right and wrong," Jet said. "I also know now that the line is sometimes blurred. So if someone were to tell me I was wrong, I would at least listen."

Xanor's eyebrows furrowed.

"I have listened. I had to learn to listen. I listened to Paladin's lectures. I listened to my Uncle Quinn. And I've listened to you," Jet said. "A lot of what you said I've disagreed with. But it pushed my convictions, and showed me what it is I need to do. Because I'm here to say now, you're not wrong."

"You did what you thought was best. And I don't know what you've sacrificed to do it, but it must have been a lot to make you such a dick. But maybe you're right. Maybe because of you, the city is in a better place than it was before it started. But listen to me like I've listened to you," Jet ramped up.

He left a long pause in the air as the two stared at each other.

"This world is good. It deserves better than this. And you can do better," Jet concluded.

"Enough!" Xanor shouted. "If you want to prove so badly what an amazing hero you are, I'll give you that opportunity!"

Xanor spread his arms outwards and looked upwards. Chaos energy rippled from the sky. As the electricity in the air heightened, it swirled in a circular pattern. As it sped up, the colors solidified, and Jet watched as grey ash, much like the ash the Constructs dissolved into, floated downwards from a funnel of clouds to surround Xanor.

Much like the energy in the sky, it spun in a circle around Xanor, and as more and more of it descended, it obscured Jet's view of Xanor. It solidified itself around Xanor. As Jet watched, he could see brief flashes of Xanor's face between streaks of the ash.

"I will show you how much better I can be. When I kill you for the world to see, the heroes, the gangs, everyone will remember their place in my city!" Xanor proclaimed.

For a brief moment, the ash slowed down in its circular

motion. The moment it stopped, it seemed to hang in the air. Then, as if it were magnetized, it snapped inwards towards Xanor with blinding speed. Jet almost lurched, thinking for a moment there was a mistake, that Xanor suddenly killed himself.

However, Jet then watched as the ash transformed into a gold suit of armor that encased Xanor. It made Xanor look almost twice the size as before, with a thin etched black design that swirled all over the armour.

The helmet was round, with three black lines on each side running horizontally inwards towards the nose. In each hand was a long golden blade, not as big as Jet's blade, but they were still alarmingly big. Jet watched as from its back spurted four angular golden metal wings, and Xanor raised from the ground, floating in the air with both swords at the ready.

Jet glanced up at Xanor and slowly unsheathed his sword. The two continued to lock gazes, Jet now unable to see Xanor's eyes, but he knew they were still under that helmet somewhere. He shifted his stance and snapped his sword into a fighting stance.

"Let's go," Jet muttered.

In a blur, Xanor swooped in. Jet had a moment to bring his sword up and block the incoming attack. They clashed, Jet resolute as Xanor crashed into him. Xanor continued to push, and Jet felt his feet sliding backward as Xanor pushed. The armoured villain pushed Jet across the building as Jet attempted to dig in his heels. Jet had a moment to look over his shoulder and saw the edge of the building.

Thinking quickly, Jet leaned backward as he disengaged his sword. It resulted in Xanor flying over the top of Jet, zooming past him. Jet quickly stood back up as Xanor banked to the right and then flew back in at Jet.

Jet braced himself, and as Xanor swooped in for another attack, Jet braced himself for another push. But it was a feint as Jet sprang up into the air, over the top of Xanor. Jet swung his sword downward, colliding with Xanor's back.

WHACK!

The force slapped Xanor onto the ground and sent him rolling. Jet landed and sprinted towards Xanor. Xanor quickly stood on one knee as Jet charged in. The golden warrior went on the defensive, crossing his blades as Jet swung in.

Xanor used his right sword to parry Jet's sword upwards. Thinking Jet defenseless, Xanor thrust in with his left blade. To Xanor's surprise, Jet was already spinning around the thrust, using his momentum from being parried to carry him.

Jet brought his sword down from up high and thrust the pommel of his sword down into Xanor's temple.

DUNF!

Xanor stumbled back for a moment, but as Jet attempted a follow-up, Xanor suddenly flew up from his crouched position. As Xanor did, he exerted a burst of energy, which halted Jet's charge just long enough to give Xanor a chance to go on the offensive.

Xanor swooped in and unleashed a barrage of swings. Xanor would swing with both blades from the right and then follow up with a left-handed jab and then a right-handed swing.

TING! CLANG! TING!

Jet deflected the attacks as they came, pivoting and angling his sword to catch Xanor's as they came in. Xanor slashed in from up high with his left, which Jet blocked, and then Xanor again attempted to thrust, thinking Jet vulnerable.

Jet saw it coming and kicked outwards, hitting the flat side of the blade and sending the attack off to the side.

Despite the speed, ferocity, and power behind each attack, Jet was surprised how easy it was to block the attacks. They came in hard and fast, but there was seemingly no skill behind it. In terms of fighting prowess, Xanor didn't hold a candle to

Marath. Jet had better sword fights with some Shinogi soldiers, even.

Right as Xanor attempted to cross his blades and slash down with such force to power through Jet's defense, Jet saw his opening. Jet leaped back, just out of the reach of the attack.

Jet leaped forward and launched an uppercut. Throwing as much force as he could into the attack, Jet felt his fist connect with the bottom of Xanor's chin.

BAM!

The hit sent Chaos Energy blasting off half of Xanor's helmet, revealing his shock and surprise. Jet couldn't help but grin. Xanor was sent sprawling onto his back, and Jet landed from his attack.

Jet needed a moment to catch his breath as he watched Xanor sit up. His one visible eye locked onto Jet with pure anger, and then from his seated position, Xanor flew upwards.

Chaos Energy swirled back and reconstituted the half of Xanor's helmet. Xanor then lifted his blades in the air, and Jet watched as more Chaos Energy swirled around at the tips of the blades.

Xanor pointed his swords towards Jet, and Jet watched a blue glow sparkle from the point of the swords as there was a high-pitched whining noise. It didn't take long for Jet to guess what was coming.

THOOOOM!

The teen dove out of the way right before a blue laser would have shot through him with a loud metallic noise. Jet landed into a roll and then had to stop himself as a second laser blasted right where he would have been. Jet spared a short moment to glance at Xanor, and he saw Xanor aiming his swords at him, the lasers coming from the swords.

THOOOOM!

With another one-shot in and Jet leaped backward and flipped. Jet landed on his hand and sprung backward again, just narrowly avoiding a laser. As he landed, Jet began sprinting forward.

He realized the same thing, Jet thought to himself. Xanor knows he's not a match for me up close. The lasers kept him at a distance, forcing Jet back as another laser interrupted his run. Jet had only a moment to think, but he thought back to his training. Xanor forced him to play by his rules. Jet needed to force it back onto his own.

As another laser hit the ground, Jet listened for the whine and started counting in his head. As soon as he heard the metallic echo of the incoming laser, Jet started counting again. And then a plan formed.

It took about three more lasers for Jet to find his footing, but once he did, Jet began taking diagonal strides forward. Timing each leap with the lasers, Jet started moving ahead of them, giving himself the time between the warm-up and firing of each laser to advance.

Jet approached Xanor, zig-zagging his way forward. Xanor realized how close Jet was getting and let out an audible growl in frustration. Then he angled his two sword tips together, and the hum of the charge began significantly louder.

THOOOOOOOOOOOOOM!

Jet prepped his dodge but wasn't ready for the laser to be significantly more powerful, the blast impacting the roof and detonating as a minor explosion that rocked Jet forward off his feet.

Jet landed into a roll, and he needed to spring up to avoid being shot through on the ground. However, the blast made his moves sluggish, and he wasn't quick enough to dodge a follow-up laser that singed his arm as he was still in the air. Jet grimaced with shut eyes, and as he reopened them, he only had a moment to bring up his sword as Xanor suddenly lunged in.

CLANG!

The attack connected with Jet in the air and sent him soaring backward, far back towards the edge of the roof.

It took some quick thinking, but Jet stabbed his sword into the ground and used it to slow his descent. The sword dug through the roof, and Jet realized it wouldn't be enough. A quick look forward revealed Xanor was already diving in to finish him. A desperate play came to Jet's mind.

With all the strength he could muster, Jet dug his sword deeper into the ground, forcing it to stop. His momentum was still carrying him, so Jet swung himself around his sword with all the strength he could muster. He swung the sword around and let go of the hilt, sending himself flying back towards Xanor.

Xanor didn't expect Jet to fly back at him feet first.

WHAM!

Jet kicked Xanor out of the air, sending him sprawling backward. Jet bounced off the attack and flipped into a landing. Xanor's swords went flying out of his hands, and Jet saw his opportunity. Before Xanor could get off his back, he leaped up and landed on Xanor's stomach, slamming him into the ground.

Jet placed one foot on either side of Xanor and unleashed a volley of punches. Chaos dust blasted off Xanor with each punch, quickly reforming to protect Xanor before each hit, but there was a small glimpse of Xanor underneath each time.

With a roar, Xanor outstretched a palm and a pillar of energy blasted forward. It would have taken Jet's head off, but he leaned back in time to dodge the attack.

However, Xanor took the opening and used his other hand to fire another blast of energy that connected with Jet's stomach. It hit Jet like a truck, slamming him and sending him skyrocketing backward while knocking all the wind out of him. Jet went tumbling backward in the air, and even though he was discombobulated from the hit, he knew he was going to go off the side of the building. He would not catch himself this time and needed a strategy.

KATHWAM!

Like a gold blur, Xanor charged in. Not content to let Jet fall to his death, Xanor tackled Jet in mid-air and crashed him into the building across the street. Jet hit the wall with a hard crash, pain reverberating through his body. Xanor held him in place with his hands on his shoulders and then let go with one hand and placed the other on Jet's chest.

THOOOOM!

More energy burst forth, enveloping Jet and drilling him further and further into the building. Jet felt his ribs crushing in as the energy pounded him, and strength left his body. Xanor finally had his edge, Jet realized, using his sheer power to overwhelm him.

Jet gave him one opening, and that was all it took. As Jet looked over Xanor's shoulder, he saw across the way to the Chaos Energy Generator.

Like a light bulb turned on above his head, Jet remembered what Paladin had told him. For Xanor to use and control the Chaos Energy like he was, he had to store it in Generators. If the Generator was destroyed before Xanor reabsorbed it, the energy would disperse and be lost.

Xanor, in his aggression, left a far bigger opening. In his right hand, Jet still held his sword. He knew as soon as the energy blast ended, he was going to drop. Jet was going to have to act fast.

With as much strength as he could muster, Jet swung his sword up and hit Xanor's palm. Xanor reeled back in shock and pain. Just as Jet dropped, he reached out and grabbed Xanor's ankle with his left hand. Jet felt himself snag in the air, his momentum broken as Xanor kept him suspended.

If Xanor recovered fast enough, Jet would be in an even more precarious position than before. So with all the strength in his upper body he could muster, Jet swung Xanor downwards, flipping over the top of himself. With extreme coordination, Jet slammed Xanor back into the roof, head down, and stabbed his sword in the wall to catch himself.

KA-BAM!

Xanor let out a guttural groan as he was embedded in the building's wall. Jet's sword let Jet catch himself. The teen planted his feet against the wall, and with all the strength in his lower body, he ripped his sword out of the wall and leaped for the original roof he was on.

The jump was further than any Jet attempted before, the length of two three-lane roads.

Just as Jet was scared he was going to make it, his sword caught in the wall and slid down, Jet eventually slowing to a stop. He was several stories down from the roof, but at the very least he wasn't concrete pizza. Then there was the metallic whir of a charging laser.

His chest burned with pain, but Jet had no choice but to use his upper body strength to extract his sword and then heave himself upwards, narrowly avoiding another laser blast. The laser burned into the wall right where Jet's head had just been, grazing his ankle instead.

Jet cleared a couple of stories and was still a few below where he needed to be. He reached up again, but a laser blasted and he barely got his hand out of the way, almost causing him to lose his other grip. Jet pivoted his head and saw Xanor charging in, swords pointed right at him.

It looked all over for Jet at that moment. To Xanor's surprise, Jet smiled. Jet let go, and Xanor crashed into the building. Then Xanor lurched again as Jet grabbed Xanor's ankle. Xanor then went downwards as Jet heaved himself upwards, throwing himself upwards.

That was the momentum Jet needed to clear up to the roof of the building. Jet stumbled to a stand as he landed, his ankle almost giving out from the pain. He collapsed to one knee, having a moment where his life wasn't in immediate peril, and all his sustained injuries caught up to him. He breathed shallowly, his ribs not letting him expand his lungs fully. But Jet looked up to see the Chaos Generator, and he knew he was almost done.

THHHHHOOOOOOOOOOOOOOOOMMMMMM!

However, Xanor blasted a massive laser upwards, red and larger than any Xanor had fired previously. It tore through the building diagonally and sent Jet sprawling forward to avoid being disintegrated by the blast.

Rubble and debris fell away as a chunk of the top few stories of the building gave way and went tumbling towards the street below. Jet landed on his stomach and turned just in time to see Xanor fly through the destruction he created, taking a prime position in the air. He floated above Jet and then pointed his swords together again, and Jet watched as a red ring materialized in the air around the tips of his blades.

Jet struggled to his feet, getting up just in time to avoid a blast that tore through the building like paper.

THHHHHOOOOOOOOOOOOOOOOMMMMMM!

Xanor sustained it and chased Jet. Jet did his best to keep running, but he knew Xanor was tenacious. Xanor would not give him the break he needed to destroy the Chaos Generator, and he needed to incapacitate the villain long enough to do it.

As the laser blast continued to dig through the building and shoot up rubble and debris in its wake, Jet came up with a desperate play. It would take more precision than anything he did before. Baseball wasn't exactly a pastime in the bunker.

Jet dove to the right and planted his feet, grabbing his sword like a bat. As the blast changed direction and turned towards him, Jet shifted his focus to the chunks of buildings that were blasting upwards in the destruction's wake.

Seeing one that looked big enough, Jet swung the flat end

of his sword at it, angling it as best he could. He focused on the angles he would need to make this work, and his sword connected the rubble at the right spot on the sword and a flat enough piece of the debris.

The debris flew up to Xanor. For a moment, it skidded along the tip of the laser, but it stayed true and hit its target.

TUNK!

Xanor's head knocked back in shock as his laser ceased, the debris exploding on impact. Xanor reeled back in the air in shock, flipping backward over top of himself. He fell a few feet in the air before he could right himself, and as he shook his worldview back into focus, Jet was in his face. Jet leapt up high, reached up with his hands, and grabbed Xanor's head. He threw Xanor's head down and thrust his knee up, connecting them both with an ugly sound.

WHAM!

Xanor fell again, and as Jet descended, he grabbed Xanor's ankle one last time and threw the villain hard onto the ground, sending Xanor crashing stomach first onto the ground.

KABAM!

Xanor lay for only a moment before trying to stand, but Jet was suddenly over the top of him, grabbing Xanor's head with his left hand before letting out one more brutal punch into the back of Xanor's head.

BAM!

Xanor collapsed onto the ground, motionless.

Jet heaved for breath, but he knew he probably didn't have long. He ran towards the Chaos Generator, picking up his sword from where he had left it. It wasn't far between him and the Chaos Generator, and Jet could make it and destroy it.

However, his vision became obscured by the brown tinge of Chaos Dust. It swirled around his feet, and Jet involuntarily was lifted off the ground. He felt a crushing weight slowly push in all over him as the Chaos Dust seemed to cling to him in air. His sword slipped from his grasp, the Chaos Dust clinging to it and pushing it out of reach in mid-air. Jet turned his head for a moment to look at Xanor.

Xanor had his hand outstretched towards Jet, but his armour was gone. Jet turned to look back at the Chaos Generator before the dust completely obscured his vision.

There was a loud snapping sound, and the Chaos Dust formed into a large concentrated ball in the sky.

Xanor struggled to stand, his hand now a fist. He held it up towards the large Chaos Dust sphere he created in the sky and clenched his hand tight. The villain never turned his back on it as he walked between the sphere and the Generator.

Even though Xanor knew Jet couldn't have survived the attack, he didn't want to take any chances. He didn't feel good about that victory, but he needed to win.

Jet Thompson couldn't have survived.

CHAPTER 29

SIDEKICK NO MORE

Jet's vision was hazy. All he could feel was intense pressure all over his body. As his vision corrected, he saw all around him was a brownish-grey mass that was trying to crush him.

It pushed in constantly, attempting to break his bones and smash him into a paste. The pain was unlike anything he had ever experienced before. Jet let out a small painful yelp, the air struggling to leave his body.

At the end of his vision, he could see his hand still reaching out. Following his hand's reach, Jet could just see the hilt of his sword. It was so close. So close to being in his grasp. Maybe, maybe if he could reach out and grab it, he could use it to break free.

Jet felt his body extend towards it, reaching desperately for it. It was like trying to move through an extremely viscous liquid while a force crushed the life out of him. Jet gasped and wheezed and struggled. It felt like his arm was going to pop out of its socket. The sword was so close. He needed to move only a couple of inches. It felt like he was one good movement away from grabbing it and freeing himself.

But his body wouldn't move. It wouldn't obey him like he wanted to. The sword remained out of reach. Jet let out a sigh, and he felt his body give out, strength leaving. The sword seemed further away than ever before.

He couldn't do it. At the end of it all, Jet couldn't finish the job. Despite all his training, all his power, all his ideals, all it took was one attack of a power he couldn't hope to match to end him. To halt his journey in its tracks. Jet felt tears welling up in his eyes, and he blinked them away.

Maybe this wasn't the worst way for this to end, Jet thought to himself. The news must have shown the battle he had with Xanor. The rest of the team could rally. Xanor would have been weakened. Something would change after this. It would have to. Jet's sacrifice would still propel the city forward.

But what was what Jet wanted? He wanted to change; he wanted to make the world a better place. But was this going to be enough, or couldn't Jet do more? Did this have to be the end of the journey? Couldn't Jet still do more?

He reached again, but it was an even more futile attempt. He felt no closer to the sword. It remained out of reach. Jet felt a sob boiling up, and he pushed it down. If this was it, this wasn't how he was going to face it.

Not with tears, not with crying.

Despite every impulse telling him to cry at the direness of the situation, Jet wouldn't let himself. It wasn't what a hero would do.

Instead, Jet shut his eyes. He tried to envision the future of the city after this battle. Tried to envision a better world than the one he was leaving behind. Siege, Hunter, and Sting could save the city without him. They would defeat Xanor and topple the gangs. They would restore the city and make it a better one.

Jet let out a quiet sigh of contempt as the mass of Chaos

Energy pushed in harder than ever before. He thought of all the students in his classes. All the other people in the city would be saved because of this. It wasn't what he wanted, but it was enough. He thought about Paladin's family, his brother, and his sister. It was enough. He felt the darkness pushing in. It was enough.

He thought of his Uncle Quinn.

If you think that this is what it takes to knock that sense of wonder, that optimism in you, out of you, then you're selling yourself short.

Jet's eyes slowly opened. The words came back to him, piercing through the darkness.

You are the strongest...of all of us. In you...in your heart...I see the strength...the love...the hope that you need to save Vinton.

Then Paladin's words. Paladin's dying words to Jet, the last things he ever said in the world. Jet felt a swell in his chest.

You might feel lost now, but you need to follow your heart wherever that leads you.

Paladin's mother, Edith, at the funeral. Energy and strength flowed back into Jet. He pushed back against the mass, crushing in.

Be who you're meant to be. That was what he wanted.

Jet reached for his sword again. It still felt out of reach. It was going to take one more push to get there. Jet wasn't sure if he had it in him. But he had to try.

I think that your hope, your resolve, is your greatest strength. And truly, that makes you stronger than any of us.

With a gasp of air, Jet felt his hand clutch around the hilt of his sword. There was a moment when everything seemed still, everything seemed calm.

Jet let out a primal roar.

NEEEAAAARRRRAAAAAGGGH!

From outside the Chaos Energy Ball, streaks of light burst forth. Xanor stuttered back in surprise as the ball exploded in a blaze of light. Jet remained suspended in the air for a moment, his body outstretched as his sword had just slashed through the energy and dissipated it.

Jet landed on the ground in a crouched position. He and Xanor locked eyes. All the Chaos Energy was still above Jet, swirling in the dust. It was free and open.

Xanor realized the imminent danger he was in. But he had no time to react, as he suddenly had to lean back and dodge. Jet threw his sword in a vertical spinning circle right at Xanor. Just like Paladin had taught him.

Xanor dodged out of the way, but he quickly realized he was never the intended target. It would never have hit him. He didn't see it connect, however, as he turned back to Jet, he received a solid punch in the jaw knocking him to the ground. Jet continued his run, following his sword as it embedded itself in the Chaos Generator.

Sparks crackled and surged, but it wasn't enough yet. Jet dashed up to it and extracted his sword. With a spinning leap, Jet jumped and slashed at the Generator, tearing through it. It buckled and crumpled underneath itself, short-circuiting.

Suddenly, in the sky above it, an explosion of Chaos Energy detonated, creating a vortex that almost looked like a small galaxy.

Jet landed facing toward Xanor as the winds suddenly changed direction, flowing into the vortex of Chaos Energy. No longer with a focal point to control its sheer volume, the energy was set to coalesce and detonate.

From the streets below, Constructs disintegrated, their dust flying on the wind through the air up towards the vortex. The three teens down below had to brace themselves. The debris on the gravel on the ground was being lifted, too.

Xanor tried to crawl away. He felt himself being lifted towards the vortex as well. The Chaos Energy within him comprised the same gathering in the vortex. That would be a death sentence. However, as he felt himself being lifted off his feet by the forces of the Chaos Energy, he was suddenly snagged. Xanor turned and saw Jet holding him by the collar.

Jet planted his feet firmly, one hand on his sword that was on the ground, the other holding Xanor. The wind heightened and strengthened, forcing Jet to brace himself. Jet stood tall in the face of it. It seemed like the moment of anarchy would never end.

When suddenly it did. The wind died down, and Jet had just enough time to look at the vortex of Chaos Energy, green and purple, and blue. The energy seemed to form into a strange crystalline shape for a moment before it exploded in a large green color. The explosion took out the rest of the Generator and a chunk of the building with it. It knocked Jet and Xanor forward, Jet landing on his stomach and Xanor on his back.

Several quiet minutes passed, where only the hum of helicopters, sirens from fire trucks and police cars could be heard. Jet shook his head and slowly stood up. His body felt like it was on fire. He was alive. He did it. Jet stood shakily tall, breathing in slowly.

Jet turned to see Xanor lying on his back, finally defeated. Against all odds, Jet had taken down an opponent far stronger than himself. Even though Jet knew destroying the Generator would have exhausted most of Xanor's power, he still cautiously moved towards the villain. He wasn't sure how many fights Xanor would have left and didn't want to take any chances.

To Jet's surprise, Xanor's face had completely changed. Where once Xanor had a hair that flopped over one side of his head in a floppy mohawk, now it covered his full head in a tussled mess with grey sneaking into the edges of it. Wrinkles and crow's feet marked his skin, and a bushy grey and black beard covered his chin. Once Xanor had looked like someone in his late thirties, now he looked far more middle-aged, at least in his fifties.

Seeing Xanor was still breathing, Jet commented, "So I knew some people did stuff to make them younger, but I didn't know there was a cream that effective."

Xanor's eyes slowly opened in response. He groaned and felt his face, letting his hand flop back down to the ground.

"Damn it," Xanor said. Even his voice sounded raspier, more tired. The older man turned onto his stomach and lifted himself to his knees.

"Any more fight in you, or can I take you in now?" Jet asked.

Xanor heaved and shook his head for just a moment. Jet crouched down low to get on his level and peered at him in confusion.

"Just...just please," Xanor said. "No one...no one can know this is who I am."

Jet scowled in response.

"Wow, all that high and mighty talk..." Jet said, but Xanor cut him off.

"I have a wife and son in the city," Xanor continued. "If they knew...if the gangs knew...they'd never be safe."

Jet glanced downward for a moment.

"I have no more fight in me," Xanor said. "But don't take me in. Take in Xanor."

The old man grunted and strained, and Jet watched as Chaos Energy came from Xanor's person. It was a small amount of dust compared to the sheer volume earlier, but it lifted and covered Xanor's face. It molded to Xanor's head, and Xanor looked like the villain Jet recognized.

"Just know, Jet Thompson, when I am gone, you'll have far worse to contend with," Xanor said, his voice returning to what Jet was used to. "You may call what I've done cowardice, hiding behind this mask, but even the other teens know to hide their identities. To face what this city will throw at you with me gone, and to do it in plain sight...I don't envy you."

Jet gave a brief nod, digesting the words. Then he shrugged his shoulders and stood up. He grabbed Xanor's arm and lifted the defeated villain to his feet, slinging one arm over his shoulders so he could carry the villain.

"I'm not out for envy," Jet replied. "I don't know how bad it's going to be, but I'll face it as me. There's no one else I'd rather be."

CHAPTER 30

MOVING FORWARD

THE NEXT DAY, JET STOOD OVER PALADIN'S GRAVE. His sword was sheathed on his back. He was wearing his street clothes, but underneath were bandages and braces that held him together. It was all done by patchwork from Hunter on the fly, so Jet knew he'd have to get himself looked at soon.

It was too soon to return to Quinn. Even with some precautions in place, Jet knew he was probably being watched like a hawk and needed to lie low for a little while.

Jet had the other teens, whose identities were unknown, hand over Xanor to the police. It was roughly sixteen hours since the battle ended, and Jet was biding his time to wait for his next steps. He had the beginnings of a plan in place, but he would be lying if he said he thought it out entirely.

"I know this is kind of the opposite of how you would have done it," Jet commented, looking down at Paladin's grave. "You would have had a plan all figured out and kept yourself secretive to keep everyone safe. I'm still trying to do the latter. I need to be true to who I am."

Jet breathed in through his nostrils and out through his mouth.

"I think that to do that...I need to be out in the open a little bit. I need to be a bit of a target. Better me than someone who can't handle it, right?" Jet chuckled a little bit, but then felt a pang of sadness.

He crouched in to be closer to the grave. After the funeral, Jet didn't take the time to properly pay his respects at Paladin's grave, or at least he felt like he hadn't. He had been such a mess from everything going on; he felt like there was still one more thing to say to his mentor.

"Thank you, Paladin. I wasn't the best student, wasn't the best sidekick. But I'm going to take everything you taught me and use it to make this city a better place," Jet commented. "This world is good. I'm going to fight for that. I'll do so by doing everything you taught me. Thank you."

Jet then stood back up and turned to see Hunter approaching him. He took a quick cursory glance around for the other two and didn't see Siege or Sting anywhere.

"What? Did I paint too big of a target on my head last night?" Jet asked.

Hunter laughed and shook his head.

"Siege is held up with something he won't say, but Sting is stuck at school. Those two aren't day people," Hunter commented. "Speaking of, I guess you're officially full time now, huh?"

Jet nodded in response.

"Yeah, I can't let a school become a target because I'm ticking off the wrong people. So I guess my education is on hold for now," Jet responded.

"I, uh...I do an online program," Hunter remarked. "I can get you hooked up."

Hunter almost seemed embarrassed by it, but Jet smiled in response.

"That would be awesome. I still don't know why I need to

know physics if I break those rules all the time anyway, but I still want to find out how Macbeth ends!" Jet exclaimed.

Jet then walked past Hunter, leading the other teen to turn and walk with him.

"Did you look at the thing?" Jet questioned.

"By thing, I'm assuming you mean paperwork about your uncle. Yeah, I did. Paladin must have had friends in high places to pull it off. While Quinn is your legal guardian, you'd only know to find that out by looking in the right place," Hunter explained. "Most searches to your place of residence or Quinn's is a wild goose chase buried under a mountain of Guardian paperwork. Some officials might look into it, but he should be safe from the gangs for now."

Jet nodded, feeling relieved.

"So, you've got a plan?" Hunter asked.

"Nope! I'm assuming you do?" Jet asked back.

Hunter chuckled.

"I have the start of one. We'll go slower from this point on, but we'll take down the gangs. As legally as possible," Hunter explained. "I'll start the legwork, but for now, you and the others focus on stopping crime. We'll do base raids when the timing is right, not just because it's fun."

Jet stopped walking, making Hunter turn to face him.

"That's it? Just stop normal crime for now?" Jet asked.

"I'll try to point you toward any Brigand or Shinogi operations that could endanger lives that come on my radar, but like I said, we'll be playing smarter, not harder," Hunter replied.

"What if, like, there's any big supervillains that come out of nowhere?" Jet asked.

Hunter smiled at him.

"I think after last night, that's more about your department. You're the superhero after all," Hunter said.

Hunter then departed, promising to text Jet more info

later, including the link to the online school. Jet stood dumbfounded for a moment, but gradually an enormous grin came to his face.

He would carry the guilt of Paladin's death with him forever, the responsibility of living up to his legacy forever a painful reminder. But there was a warmth coming back.

Jet sensed some of the old him returning, the joy of being a superhero returning. It wasn't how he thought it was going to feel, the weight of responsibility and existential looming dread of making the right choices forever present in the back of his mind.

But getting to help people, protect them, and ensure that they felt safe, reassured Jet he was making the right choice. A part of him was forever sad he would never get to have a proper superhero identity, no true codename or alias, like all the superheroes he admired. No flashy costume to wear. It would just be him.

But he would be enough. Deep somewhere in his heart, memories of the things Paladin, Edith, Uncle Quinn, and his friends had said to him gave Jet the confidence to know that he would be enough. Jet would be the superhero Vinton needed. While before it was his deepest desire; it was now his mission.

And Jet was up to the task. With a smile on his face and hope in his heart, Jet could do it.

About half an hour later, Jet was hurriedly cleaning out his locker at school. He already removed the yellow caution tape that was plastered over it. He figured he would be part of a police investigation now and he had to act fast to get his stuff and get out. He snuck in when he figured it was least likely for there to be a large police presence.

There was still quite a large police presence, but at the

moment, they were interviewing teachers and staff, leaving Jet's locker unguarded. There were only a few things Jet was looking to get from the locker, but they were important enough to Jet to take the risk. Right as Jet crammed a book in his backpack, a voice to his left startled him, and he sent the book flying in the air.

"Hey, Jet," Alan said upon seeing him.

"Oh, hey man," Jet responded upon grabbing his book off the floor.

"I saw you all over social media this morning," Alan said. "You're trending."

"For real?" Jet asked, feeling surreal. "Huh. Well, more reason for me to hurry and get out of here."

Alan scratched the back of his head for a moment while Jet continued to work feverishly. Finally, Alan seemed to find the words he was looking for.

"Hey listen, I think what you did last night was super cool. I saw some clips from the fight that got posted, and I think it was pretty amazing," Alan continued.

Jet said a quick thanks, not pausing from his task. Seeing he would not get Jet to stop, Alan more forcefully continued.

"Seeing you last night, I feel you know how to use your powers really well. So, I was wondering if maybe...you could try to help me figure something out." Alan went on.

Jet finally stopped what he was doing and turned to Alan.

"What do you mean?" Jet asked.

Alan quickly checked around, and not being able to see anyone in the vicinity, he raised an open palm and a small fireball materialized out of thin air. Jet jumped back a little in shock, and then suddenly the fireball turned into a ball of cold, freezing air, and then a small bolt of electricity. Alan closed his hand.

"I have these superpowers, and my dad was supposed to teach me how to use these, but he ran off years ago. I've always wondered what it would be like to use them properly. If I could do more for the surrounding people. I guess I've always wondered if I could be a superhero too," Alan said wistfully.

Jet looked from Alan's hand up to Alan, realizing what was being asked of him.

"And well...now I know a superhero. So I know this is a huge ask, but I'm guessing I'm asking if you can train me. If I could be...well, if I could be your sidekick."

ISSUE 6 EPILOGUE

Quinn woke up to a quiet household. He came down from his room and started his pot of coffee in a daze. He wasn't sure what to think, but he had already known Jet wouldn't be home. He knew he wouldn't see much of Jet anymore.

Thoughts buzzed around in Quinn's head. He heard the words Jet said. He knew on a logical level Jet cared, but at that moment all he knew was Jet had taken the superhero life over the normal one. The life with him.

His legs felt like molasses. His chest was heavy. He knew Jet would come by periodically, but Jet also wanted to keep his uncle safe. A thought that contrasted with the feeling Quinn had that his nephew didn't care for him.

Jet was a boy, and worse than that, a teenager. The more logical thought that took over all others to Quinn was that Jet was never going to properly express to Quinn what Quinn wanted to hear.

That Jet cared.

With a sigh, Quinn sat down. That was the first time he saw it. Sitting on the table across from him was a package that was poorly wrapped in red paper. It wasn't entirely covered in the paper, revealing a wooden exterior, and the tape was strewn all over the package. Quinn reached across the table and pulled the package in close.

It didn't take long for Quinn to realize it was a picture of some kind. But as Quinn unwrapped it, he realized the frame was familiar. It was the frame he had put the Alpha news article in from Jet's birthday all those years ago. He didn't have the same love of superhero history that his nephew did, but he knew how much Jet loved that stuff. So when he could do that for Jet's birthday, he dished out the extra money for a nice frame.

Jet hugged the framed news article so tight when he opened it, Quinn remembered. Even when Jet returned home, it was the first thing that was hung back up. It was his prized possession.

That's why it was so shocking what was in the frame. The Alpha news article was still in there, but it was only visible due to how large it was. The headline: Rise of the Superhero was still visible, but in place of the picture of Alpha and overlaying most of the text was the picture of Quinn and Jet for one of Jet's birthdays.

It could have been an accident. Jet could have slipped the picture over the top of the news article by accident. But then why would it have been wrapped?

A few teardrops fell onto the glass of the frame.

Quinn placed the frame in the living room, right next to the picture of him and Richard. So whenever he sat down to watch Jet's exploits on the news, he could see the picture and he would have his answer. He would know how Jet felt.

He knew his nephew was doing incredible things.

EPILOGUE

Xanor sat in his prison cell. A power dampener rested along his neck, but the way he remodeled his face held. No one would ever know who he was, and his family would be forever safe. That was all that mattered.

When the Chaos Generator was destroyed, it was like a fog had lifted. Something had always pushed him, edged him closer to aggression than he would have liked. Attacking the entire city?

That wasn't what he wanted to do. There was a wave of deep-rooted anger that pushed him that way, that was now suddenly gone.

He had his theories on why that was, probably because of losing most of the reserves of his Chaos Energy, but in the end, now it didn't matter. The city was in their hands. In the hands of teenagers. The thought was a daunting one, but maybe it would be better in their hands than his. Just look at the destruction he had wrought.

Xanor would ultimately never know. He saw the resolution in Jet's eyes. He had faith.

"Well, well, how the mighty have fallen," came a voice from outside his cell.

The voice was too poisonous to be a guard, Xanor realized. He turned his head to see Marath, leaning in on his cell with one arm pressed against it. In the darkness of night, Marath's green eyes gleamed.

"How...how did you get in here?" Xanor asked.

"Oh please," Marath responded. "We both know that wouldn't be challenging for me. But you, taken down by a few teenagers. So much for being the ultimate power in the city?"

"I kept you at bay for long enough, didn't I?" Xanor shot back.

Marath tilted his head in response.

"Fair. I don't know if you understand how you did so," Marath cryptically said. "And I'll keep it that way for now."

Xanor squinted at Marath. Even though most of his cruel intentions were gone, one question burned in his mind.

"Why...why didn't you kill the teens? Why kill Paladin instead?" Xanor asked.

Marath grinned, and it sent chills down Xanor's spine.

"Because I knew Paladin would never dethrone you. But the boy could. He just needed the right push. And I needed you out of the way for what comes next," Marath responded.

"You couldn't have possibly planned for all this..." Xanor said, the words getting stuck in his throat.

"Who do you think stole your Constructs? Who do you think lured the boy out of that bunker?" Marath teased.

"Why the boy? Why do you need him?" Xanor asked, almost gasping for air.

With this, Marath's grin disappeared for a brief flicker. The blink of an eyelash. Then it was back.

"Jet Thompson has a grand role to play in my plans. He is not aware of it yet-but he's the key I've long needed," Marath cryptically answered.

"No...no, he's just a boy. How could you know what he would become-all those years in the bunkers, and, and before-how?"

"Because. I plan for everything," Marath quickly responded. "Now, thanks to him that the gangs have no supervillain to answer to. Now that there is a power vacuum in the city, what comes next..."

Marath walked away as he spoke, his voice trailing. Xanor involuntarily jumped to his feet and ran to the bars. He almost slammed into them, looking for Marath.

Marath was nowhere to be seen, but Xanor could somehow still hear his voice, no louder than a whisper.

"...what comes next will be chaos."

AUTHOR'S NOTE

One of my earliest memories is when I was four years old and my Dad, my brother and I were all sitting down in our bungalow's basement to watch Batman Forever. We had rented it from Blockbuster, my mom was out for a night with her friends, so we popped some popcorn and we prepared to watch a superhero movie. Even then, even when I was that young, I knew there was something special about Batman, about superheroes. That their stories were something meant to inspire us, thrill us, and most of all entertain us. That fundamentally, superhero stories were *fun*.

As the years went by, I remember similar feelings of unbridled excitement every time a superhero movie was coming out. This excitement for superheroes reached a fever pitch crescendo of joy for me with the release of The Avengers in 2012. My love for these stories and characters extended well past these movies, however. Cartoons, television shows and video games starring my favourite caped crusaders naturally took priority over things like Pokemon in my childhood.

Then when I was in the sixth grade something magical

happened. Near our house a brand new library opened up that was within walking distance. On our first visit, my brother and I were ecstatic to see they had a dedicated teen zone-and we eagerly rushed over there. Lining several rows were more comic books than I had ever seen. Graphic novels, trade paperbacks, hardcovers, manga, this section had it all.

This really kickstarted my life long love of reading comics. My muse however, the creme de la crop, was Ultimate Spider-Man by Brian Michael Bendis and Mark Bagely. When I finally began making my own money as an adult, I sought out all of the trade paperbacks I had read in that library and purchased them all. That led down a journey of frequenting my comic book store more regularly and becoming embroiled in the monthly tales of all my characters, and really before I fully understood it I had become a comic book fan for life.

That's what brings us to The Sidekick. After experimenting with writing in High School, I saw the breadcrumbs of a grand, ambitious adventure I could weave and create. Like most stories, it has changed and morphed over time, the beginning and ending points of stories have been altered, and characters look and sound radically different than first imagined. But fundamentally, it has always continued to be the same thing. And that is a celebration of everything I love about comic books and superheroes. A celebration of how they can inspire us, thrill us and entertain us. Most of all, I want Vinton Chronicles to be *fun*.

That is my guiding star as I navigate the rest of the series. While I view the world very differently as an adult than I did as a four-year-old, there are far more shades of grey and complications than a child can really comprehend, I want this book series to hopefully remind you of your earliest memories of superheroes. That despite how complicated life can be, our superheroes are heroes. And above all, you have fun reading the series.

Thank you for taking these first steps with me. I can't wait to share with you all Jet's next adventure.

ACKNOWLEDGMENTS

The Sidekick exists in its current form to the thanks of many wonderful people who have made this adventure possible. I would be remiss if I didn't first thank all of my family for their amazing support throughout this process, asking how they can help promote the book and/or checking in on my progress, every little bit helped me keeping pen to paper as it were. My parents deserve a mention here for indulging me when I said I wanted to go into journalism instead of the sciences post high school. Your support in my teenage decision making skills were instrumental in getting me to this point.

I also want to thank my original 'beta' readers, people who have checked out my various different writings at different stages. I want to give a special shout out to my friends Ray and Alex, who have been reading my work since high school. If you hadn't read my original attempts at crafting a story-I can confidently say The Sidekick wouldn't exist. So thank you from the bottom of my heart.

A special thanks to my publishers and editors at Wicked Ink, Raymond Griffiths and Adam Bamford. Thank you for taking the chance on my story and the future adventures of Jet Thompson and his friends. Your editorial direction and pushing has helped enhance the story in ways I could never consider on my own, and The Sidekick is all the stronger in your very capable hands.

In addition, a special thanks to a few artists who have helped shape the characters and world of Vinton Chronicles. Agustin C. helped draft the initial character designs that can be found on my website jeffmedhurst.com and enabled me to secure the copyright for their designs. His work really helped set the tone. Adam Rebottaro did an amazing sketch of Jet during his climatic stand in the Hero Plaza. And Devon McKellar drew up an amazing landscape of what the city of Vinton would look like from a distance, further helping cement the world and tone of the series.

Last and certainly not least, I need to thank my amazing wife and my beautiful kids for your endless support. Linnea and Miles, you might be too young at the time of publishing to understand how much you have impacted the man your dad has grown into, but believe me you've made me an infinitely better person. And to Tiana, I wouldn't even know where to begin with how much you've helped this process, so I'll simply say thank you for believing in me. At every point in this journey, and in every journey to come, your belief in me will always be enough to carry me through and make my writing the best it can be.

ABOUT THE AUTHOR

© Jeff Medhurst

Jeff's love for storytelling began young, inspired by urban fantasy and comics. After honing his craft through a Bachelor of Communications in Journalism and a stint as a staff reporter, he earned a Bachelor of Education and has taught English for five years. His debut short story, *The Boy and the Fish*, was published in Northword magazine in fall 2023. Excited to share his Vinton Chronicles series through Wicked Ink Publishing, Jeff balances writing with family time and enjoying comics, video games, and movies.

https://jeffmedhurst.com/

instagram.com/jeffmedhurstwrites

tiktok.com/@jeffmedhurstwrites

x.com/JeffMedhurstW

9 781998 278299